Chapter One

Whiting swung closed the great oak double doors, cutting off the view of the funeral cortège as it began its stately progress down the long drive to the South-wood family chapel.

The late March sun had not yet reached the front of the Hall and the last sound Marissa heard as the door closed was the sharp crack of carriage wheels breaking the icy puddles on the gravel.

'Shall I bring tea to the small parlour, my lady?' the butler enquired, sympathy colouring his usually grave tones. He wondered if he should send for her maid, for the Countess looked so pale, a fragile fig-ure of black and white lost amongst the chequer-board of the great entrance hall, dwarfed by the tow-ering classical statuary.

The Dowager Lady Southwood raised wide hazel eyes to meet his anxious gaze and almost yielded to the temptation to retreat to the cosy sanctuary of her morning room, the little fire, her pile of books, the undemanding affection of Gyp, her King Charles spaniel.

'No, Whiting.' Her sense of duty, as always, reas-

serted itself. 'Please bring my tea to the Long Gallery: I must be there when they return from the...
chapel.'

Holding her prayer book in her clasped hands, Marissa moved slowly across the hall, up the curving stairs into the Red Salon, then through into the Long Gallery, which ran the entire length of the west front of the great house.

After two years of marriage she was too used to the chilly splendours of Southwood Hall to even notice the towering columns, the perfect geometry of every room and the exquisite correctness of each detail of decoration and drapery. Restoring his grandfather's Classical masterpiece to its original impeccable state had been an obsession of her late husband's, but try as she might she could admire the Hall, but she could never love the soulless integrity he had created.

To reach her chair in the Long Gallery Marissa had walked almost a hundred yards. She was nineteen years old, yet today she felt nearer ninety. Every step dragged as if she had a lead weight attached to her black kid slippers, and she sank gratefully down on a red satin chair.

Upright and graceful, she opened the prayer book at the Psalms and composed herself to read, but when the footman brought in her tea she realised with a start that she had taken in not one single word.

'Thank you, James.'

'Thank you, my lady. Will there be anything else?'

'Not for the moment. Go and see if Mrs Whiting needs any assistance with the refreshments.'

As he left James inadvertently let the heavy panelled door slam, startling Marissa out of her chair. How her lord would have hated that discord! She almost expected to hear his voice issuing a quiet, chilly rebuke. But she would never hear the third Earl of Radwinter speak again. She shivered: by now the vault door would have slammed shut with force and finality, leaving him to the silent keeping of his ancestors.

She moved restlessly to the window, which gave a sweeping view across the trees of the park to the salt marsh and the faint line of the grey sea beyond. The movement behind the bare trunks of the limes forming the Great Avenue marked the return of the cortège of carriages bearing the gentlemen mourners. They would be back soon: Marissa chided herself for her morbid, almost Gothic thoughts when she should have been bent on the consolation of prayer. As she watched, her hand resting on the fringed brocade of the draperies, another carriage approached from the east. No doubt this would be her husband's aunt Augusta, coming to pay her respects to a nephew to whom she had hardly spoken a word during the latter part of his forty-five years.

Although she hardly knew the formidable spinster, Marissa was grateful to have female support during the ordeal of the funeral meats and the inevitable reading of the will. The late Earl had disliked the idea of a female companion for his wife and the intrusion upon his privacy, and the spinster cousin she had invited to join her in her widowhood had not yet arrived from Cumbria.

Marissa stepped back from her vantage point: it was most incorrect to be gaping from the window, not behaviour becoming to the widow of the Earl of Radwinter. She paced slowly back to the head of the flight of semi-circular steps which led down to the hall and waited for her guests.

As she stood, smoothing her skirts of dull black silk, she was aware of the subdued bustle of the staff all around her. Footmen were carrying trays into the Long Gallery, Whiting was supervising the arrivals and the maidservants were whisking away heavy coats, hats and gloves from the chilled guests.

'My dear child!' It was Aunt Augusta, red-faced from the cold and long days in the hunting field, her clothes curiously old-fashioned. But she was so alive, thought Marissa with envy. Alive, vital, noisy and interfering, a woman who cared not a fig for anyone else's opinion or for convention, despite her fifty-seven years.

Marissa hardly knew the half-sister of her lord's father, but that did not stop her liking her, and she took her hand with a look of speaking gratitude as the redoubtable spinster stood beside her.

'Chin up, girl! You are doing splendidly.' And indeed, on the face of it, her niece by marriage was. A courageous child, this widow of her cold fish of a nephew. Far too young for him, of course; far too young, they had all said, to be mistress of this great mausoleum of a house. Yet she had coped with dignity and grace. Augusta glanced sideways at the composed profile as Marissa spoke to each of the guests in turn. Could she really have been happy?

Every line of the widow's gown as it skimmed her tall figure was perfect, every lock of what Augusta suspected was a veritable mane of black hair was disciplined into a smooth coiffure, and the pale oval of her face showed nothing but the solemn calm suitable to the occasion. Did she ever smile? the older woman wondered. Let alone break that composure with a spontaneous outburst of either laughter or tears?

Once all were assembled in the Long Gallery the footmen began to circulate with trays of sherry, Canary and Madeira. Marissa, looking at the pinched features of some of the older men, wished she had defied convention and ordered mulled wine to be served to warm their blood. But that would have presented far too festive an appearance, and that would never do.

The older Mr Hope, the senior partner of the solicitors who had served the family for generations, was at her elbow, clearing his throat in a meaningful way.

'I think we should progress to the reading of the will, my lady. If those concerned and the staff assemble in the library, ma'am, I will deal with the bequests to the servants first. They can then leave us to the greater matters in privacy.'

The solicitor turned to catch the eye of various people, and Whiting was already marshalling the staff to move into the book-lined room when James appeared and, hastening to the butler's side, bent to whisper in his ear.

This indecorous behaviour caught the attention of the assembly, and, following the butler's astonished gaze, thirty faces turned as one towards the closed double doors.

They swung open and a man stepped into the gallery, pausing on the threshold to survey those within it with calm interest. He was tall, long-legged, immaculate in black superfine and silk cravat. Dark blue eyes scanned the room from under brows slightly raised at the startled expressions which greeted his arrival, until his gaze met that of the Dowager Countess.

Marissa felt the blood leach from her face and a high-pitched singing start in her head. With an almost physical effort she dragged her eyes up from the man framed in the doorway to the portrait which hung above. Charles Wystan Henry Southwood, third Earl of Radwinter, stared haughtily down, blue eyes chilly in a white face below raven black hair. Beneath, come back from the vault, he watched her with those same eyes, hair bleached by death.

With a little gasp of horror Marissa let the darkness engulf her, falling heedless towards the hard parquet floor.

Her aunt seized Marissa in her strong, horsewoman's grip, but even as she did so the man was there, catching Marissa up in his arms. Augusta was not a woman to be scared of ghosts, but even she was severely shaken by the stranger's appearance as he stood there, showing no sign of effort as he held the tall girl against his chest.

'Where shall I take her, ma'am?' he enquired, his voice cultured, deep, yet with a slight exotic lilt.

Lady Augusta pulled herself together. 'Through here, in the library. There is a chaise longue. Whiting, send for her ladyship's maid!'

From the black depths of her swoon Marissa was faintly aware of being caught up in a strong embrace, of a feeling of warmth and safety and the hot scent of sandalwood. She murmured something indistinguishable and snuggled closer. The grasp tightened, then she was laid down and the blackness swirled over her again.

Lucian Southwood backed out of the room, his gaze lingering on the porcelain features of the woman who lay so still. His blood was stirred by the recollection of her body against his, of the trusting way she had clung to him, of those parted red lips, almost the only colour in her deathly white face.

'I assume I am speaking to a member of the Southwood family?' a dry voice enquired at his elbow.

'Yes, I beg your pardon, sir. I am Lucian Southwood, cousin of the late Earl, newly arrived from the West Indies.' There was no mistaking the other man's profession. 'Am I addressing the family's legal representative?'

'You are, sir. Gabriel Hope at your service. A letter from me is even now on its way to you in Jamaica; we had no idea you were in England.'

The two men were alone together, the rest of the party having tactfully withdrawn to the far end of the Long Gallery. Lucian was aware of the curious glances being cast his way and the low-voiced conversations, no doubt speculating on the identity of this stranger.

'I arrived in London three days ago with my sister. I had business to transact, but had no intention of bringing myself to the attention of the Earl. You may be aware, sir, that my father fell out with his family and the two lines have had no contact since he made his own fortune in Jamaica. Imagine my surprise when I opened *The Times* yesterday to see the announcement of my cousin's death and the notice of today's funeral. It was too late to send a message, but I felt it my duty to attend.'

He glanced over his shoulder to where a feminine bustle now surrounded the form of Lady Southwood on the chaise longue. 'However, Mr Hope, please believe I would have stayed away had I any idea of the effect my arrival has obviously had. Mr Hope, please can you enlighten me as to why the Countess reacted as she did?'

In reply the solicitor took his elbow and turned him to face the door through which he had newly entered, and the portrait that hung above it.

'My God!' Lucian stared up at the features that might have been his own. Only the colouring was different, one so dark, the other so fair, as though an artist had drawn an exercise in opposites. Lucian's hair was naturally a dark blond, but over the years the unrelenting Caribbean sun had bleached it to the white of coral sand. The long spring voyage had diminished his tan, but even so he made the man in the portrait appear ghostly pale.

'You have, if I may so observe, sir, the Southwood features, if not the colouring.' Mr Hope nodded towards the many oils which hung in the Gallery, depicting generations of Southwoods.

'I had no idea,' Lucian said slowly. 'My father always said I favoured my grandfather, while he himself took after his mother's family. It is astonishing, especially as my father and the late Earl's father were only half-brothers. But what an appalling shock for her ladyship, so newly widowed! If I had had the slightest notion I would never have come.'

Mr Hope was looking at him assessingly. 'It is

perhaps as well you have, sir. You cannot be un-aware that you are the heir presumptive.'

'But surely my late cousin had children?'

'No, he was not so blessed in his lifetime. How-ever—' Mr Hope became even drier '—we must make no assumptions until several months have passed.' He coughed in a meaningful and somewhat embarrassed manner.

Again Lucian looked at the woman on the chaise. He could not see clearly into the other room, but it appeared she was now sitting up. Despite that slen-der figure, could she be carrying her late husband's child?

Something was tickling the back of his hand. Lu-cian brushed his fingertips across the dark superfine cloth and pulled away a long, springing dark hair. As he pulled it it curled like something alive into the palm of his hand. Absently, still talking to the solicitor, he wound it around his little finger, trap-ping it under the band of his signet ring.

In the library Marissa pushed gently at the hands that were trying to keep her on the chaise longue. 'No, I must get up! My guests…I must go back… how foolish to faint! I cannot think what came over me!'

'Well, I can,' Augusta declared with her typical bluntness. 'I nearly fainted myself when I saw his face. He must be Richard's boy—he's the spitting image of your late father-in-law. No, sit still a min-ute, you foolish girl, and sip the water Simpson has brought for you.'

Meekly Marissa took the water and tried to make sense of the last few dizzying minutes. 'Who is Richard?'

'My late brother. I last saw him in '78; he was
only eighteen when he left for the West Indies. He
and my father never got on, but they had one final,
irrevocable row about money and Richard swore
never to set foot in Southwood Hall again. And he
did not,' she added reflectively. 'He was buried in
Jamaica, and by all accounts made himself a fine
fortune before he did so.'

Marissa rubbed her fingers across her aching forehead, as if it would clear her thoughts. 'So,' she
began slowly, 'the man out there is my lord's
cousin…'

'Indeed. I think he has a sister as well. I suppose
they are half-cousins, if there is such a term, because
Richard and I were the children of our father's second marriage.'

So that explained the almost supernatural likeness. Marissa made a supreme effort and stood up.
Her hands went up to her hair, tucking the few way-
ward strands which had escaped firmly back into the
tight chignon. The late Earl had hated to see her with
her hair out of place.

Her eyes met the stranger's direct gaze, and for a
long, long moment everyone else in the room ceased
to exist. He made a movement towards her, then
checked it, and Marissa realised he was afraid of
alarming her again. She found she was holding her
breath and released it with a soft sigh.

Mr Hope touched Lucian's arm with a murmured,
'Might as well get it over with now,' and led him
forward to be introduced.

'My lady, may I present the Honourable Lucian
Southwood, newly arrived from Jamaica. The late
Earl's cousin,' he added meaningfully. He only

hoped it would not be an unpleasant surprise to the Countess to meet the man who, if she were not carrying a male child, would inherit her late husband's title and estates.

Marissa found her small, cold hand engulfed in a strong, warm, tanned grip. The warmth seemed to spread through her chilled body, and the remembrance of being caught up and held in an enfolding embrace caused her heart to lurch for a moment. It must have been Mr Southwood who had carried her to the chaise.

The colour rose in her cheeks and Lucian thought it was like seeing a marble statue suddenly come to life. Even as he thought it the colour ebbed and she freed her hand. 'Sir, you are welcome to Southwood Hall. I am only sorry that it should be in such mournful circumstances.'

Lucian bowed, and found himself, along with several others, being ushered back into the library by Mr Hope. Lady Augusta sat firmly beside Marissa and the gentlemen ranged themselves around the desk at which the attorney seated himself.

Mr Hope produced a pair of eyeglasses which he set on his nose after fussily polishing them. He extracted a key from his waistcoat pocket, unlocked a brass-bound box which had been placed before him, and gazed impressively over the spectacles at the assembled company.

Lucian suppressed a smile, covering his mouth with long fingers. The old boy was milking the situation for all it was worth, no doubt to justify the large fee he would eventually charge the estate.

'As you know,' Mr Hope began gravely, 'we are gathered here to hear the testamentary dispositions of the late Charles Wystan Henry Southwood, third Earl of Radwinter, newly deceased.' His clerk emerged from the shadows, produced an impressive document tied up in red tape from the box, broke the seal, handed it to his principal and effaced himself again.

'Harrumph. I shall begin with the bequests to the staff.'

There followed several pages of gifts, small pensions and life interests in estate cottages. Lucian reflected that his cousin had made very correct, if not generous, provision for his faithful servants, but wondered at the total absence of any personal mentions or expressions of gratitude. He glanced across at the widow and saw she was sitting with absolute rectitude, her gaze fixed on the carved over-mantel of the fireplace. She looked composed, almost frozen, but as he watched he became aware that the jet drop earrings were trembling against her white neck. He wondered if she were normally so composed or whether her deep grief had frozen her heart.

He did some rapid mental calculations. As far as he could recall his cousin had been forty-five years old: this girl could scarcely be more than twenty.

Mr Hope had droned his way through the minor bequests and the servants had filed out of the room, leaving only the immediate relatives, Dr Robertson and the family chaplain, the Reverend Mr Field.

After another four more pages of interminable legal phrases Mr Hope regarded his stupefied audience over the top of the vellum and announced, 'In essence the position is straightforward. The title and the estate, both entailed and unentailed, with the exception of that in the Countess's marriage portion and the Dower House, descends to the male heir of the late Earl.'

Marissa transferred her gaze sharply to his face. 'But…'

Mr Hope swept on, a touch of colour staining his sallow cheeks. 'The matter is delicate, but none the less it is my duty to tell you that under these circumstances it is normal…' he paused '…and prudent, to wait a certain number of months before the succession can be…clarified.'

It suddenly dawned on Marissa that Mr Hope, that dry lawyer, meant that they all had to wait to see if she was pregnant. Without thinking, she blurted out, 'But there is no need to wait!'

Lady Augusta gasped, 'Hush, my dear! Not in front of the gentlemen!'

But Marissa was adamant. The thought of the whole household watching, waiting, studying her looks, her health, her mood, week after week, for signs she was with child, was insupportable. Better to get it over with now. 'I can assure you, Mr Hope, that there is no vestige of doubt that my lord is without a direct heir.'

Mr Hope snatched off his eyeglasses in agitation and looked wildly at the doctor and Lady Augusta. They stared blankly back at him. At length he managed to regain some composure and asked, 'Dr Robertson, Lady Augusta, perhaps if I may prevail upon you to retire to another place with the Countess and discuss this matter further…'

Scarlet to her eartips, Marissa swept out of the room towards her bedchamber, followed by a bemused and embarrassed Lady Augusta and a scandalised doctor. Her head high, she dared not look at anyone else, but she was acutely aware of Lucian Southwood as he rose when she passed him.

Then all thoughts of anyone else left her as she sat in her room, whispering answers to Dr Robertson's tactful questions. But her mind was only partly with him. It was in this very chamber only a week ago she had had to tell her lord that once again she had failed in her duty and that she was not carrying his heir.

He had never reproached her in words, but his disappointment had sent him out to ride furiously across the frozen parkland where small drifts of snow still lingered. It was one of these which had concealed the rabbit hole which had tripped his horse, pitching the Earl head-first onto the iron-hard ground to break his neck in an instant.

Marissa knew it was her failure as a wife, her lack of duty to her lord, which had killed him. Her eyes filled with tears at the thought and Lady Augusta, seeing this, held up her hand to stop the flow of questions from the doctor. 'Enough. Surely you are satisfied with what the Countess has told you?'

'Indeed, indeed.' The doctor leaned across and patted her clasped hands in an avuncular fashion. 'You have been very brave and very frank, my dear, and in doing so have been a great help to those administering the late Earl's estate. But it is a melancholy thought that the direct line must cease—' He broke off as Lady Augusta gave him a sharp kick on the ankle and one solitary tear rolled down the young widow's cheek.

Dry-eyed, and with her head held high, Marissa resumed her seat in the library and the gentlemen hastened back to their positions. The doctor had a rapid, whispered conversation with the lawyer, who nodded and took up his papers once more.

'I am in a position to tell you, ladies and gentlemen, that the title, honours and estates of the third Earl of Radwinter pass immediately to his heir, the fourth Earl, Lucian St Laurence Southwood of Jamaica, who by great good fortune is with us today. My lord.' He stood up and bowed to Lucian, who acknowledged the salute with equal gravity.

Marissa was conscious of a huge sense of relief, as if a great weight had been lifted from her shoulders. Now she could relinquish this great house, this mausoleum which so chilled her soul and deadened her spirits, and move to the Dower House. It would be someone else's responsibility to manage the impeccable running of the Palladian splendour which her husband had created. She wondered how swiftly such a move could be effected.

Lucian, watching the brief play of emotions over the pale countenance, was unable to interpret the expression. Surely it had not been—could not have been—relief? No, it must have simply been thankfulness that this ordeal of the will-reading was finally at an end. He was acutely aware that his own presence, his very appearance, must be a painful reminder to her of her loss. But he could not now take his leave, return to the West Indies, for he was responsible now for this huge estate and all its people, including her.

Whiting was announcing luncheon and Lucian held back to allow the Dowager Countess and her supporters to precede him to the dining room, where the great table was laid out with the funeral meats. But Marissa turned and waited for him. 'Mr... My lord…' and he realised she was expecting him to take her arm and lead her in. Once again he marvelled at the strength of will and composure in one so young. Her hand, resting on his sleeve, was taut with tension; he felt she was like a violin string, stretched almost to the point of breaking.

The place at the head of the table was laid, but the chair was draped in black, and Lucian led Marissa to her place at the foot of the long board, taking the place to her right.

The chaplain said grace and the party settled with a thankful collective sigh. Gradually the volume of conversation rose as everyone relaxed and tongues were loosed by the consumption of fine wine.

What the devil did one talk about under these circumstances? Lucian wondered, helping the widow to roast beef. Back home in Jamaica even a funeral meal was more relaxed, more informal and emotional. There was something about the heat and the sunshine, the vibrancy of colour, the closeness of nature—a dangerous nature—that would make this sort of rigid formality impossible.

And what a brutal way to treat a grieving young woman, to expect her to maintain a rigid composure surrounded by this sombre flock of dark-coated old men. He shivered slightly and instantly she was all attention, the perfect hostess.

'My lord, you are cold.' And yet he had seemed so warm when he touched her… 'Whiting, more logs on the fire. This country must seem very chill after the heat of the West Indies.'

'Indeed, yes, madam. My sister declares she will never feel warm again, but now I have been back in

England for almost a week I find I am becoming accustomed.'

Marissa cut a minuscule portion of beef and raised it to her lips. She wondered if she would ever feel warm—or hungry—again. 'You have a sister, my lord? I am afraid I know nothing of your family— are there others still in Jamaica?'

'No, madam, there is only Nicole and myself. I intended bringing her to London next year to do the Season, when she is seventeen, but she plagued me so much to bring her on this trip so she could see the sights and buy some London fashions that I could not resist her.'

Marissa saw the fond smile on his lips and envied the ready affection in his voice. How wonderful to have a loving brother like that, to have such a bond with another person. 'You are very fond of your sister, my lord, I can tell.'

Lucian, surprised by the longing in her tone, glanced at her quickly, but her face was closed and he answered lightly. 'She is the bane of my existence, madam. I have spoilt her to death and now I must pay the price. When you meet my sister you will be in no doubt that we had a French mother!'

'I hope to meet her very soon. You will be sending to London for her?'

'I must think what to do. All this has come as a great shock to me and I am entirely unprepared. I visit London every few years on business, and that was my purpose on this occasion. Now I will have to return to Jamaica to place my affairs there fully in the hands of my agent. I will have to meet with your—' he caught himself '—the estate manager here, and with Mr Hope, so that I can be confident that all will be well in my absence.'

There was a long pause. Lucian twisted the wine glass between long brown fingers. Marissa found she could not take her eyes off his hand, nor forget the warmth of his touch through the silk of her gown. What would it be like to be held in his arms again…? She caught her errant thoughts with an inward gasp of horror. How could she entertain such longings? It was wrong, wrong…and in any case it was a delusion that comfort lay in the arms of a man…

'Lady Southwood, when you feel able, I must speak with you about your wishes. Needless to say I would not want you to feel you must make any change in your arrangements. This is your home and you must stay in it as long as you wish.'

Marissa looked him straight in the eye and said with utter conviction, 'My lord, I have lived here for only two years. It is the Southwood family seat, but it has never been my home. My cousin Miss Venables will be joining me soon from Cumbria. When she arrives I will move to the Dower House.'

She realised she must have startled him with her frankness, but all he said was, 'It shall be as you wish, naturally. You must instruct the estate manager to move whatever you want from the Hall into the Dower House, and to have whatever resources you need for your comfort there.'

'Thank you, my lord. Would you wish me to continue to oversee the housekeeper in your absence?'

'That would be most kind, if it would not be an imposition. We will speak of this tomorrow, and of course you must decide which servants you wish to take with you.'

Marissa thanked him, and turned to her other neighbour. Throughout the rest of the meal they spoke of nothing but inconsequential matters, and with her mind relieved of the need to guard her every word she found her attention wandering to the man at her side.

His manners were correct and impeccable, as be-fitted a gentleman, but there was a foreignness too. Perhaps it was the slight French accent on certain words, the lilt that came into his voice when he spoke about the West Indies. He was a handsome man—all the Southwoods were, to judge by their portraits—but this man had a dangerous, vital energy that radiated even in this sombre company.

Under the pretext of dabbing her lips with her napkin, Marissa stole a sideways glance from under her lashes. His hair curled over-long on his collar, the blond hair shot through with the warmth of the tropical sun. His face was lean and tanned and there were white lines at the corners of his deep blue eyes, as though he often screwed them up against the sun-dazzle on the Caribbean sea. His nose was straight, his mouth was as firm as her husband's had been, but the new Earl's lips looked as though they more readily curved into a smile than tightened in dis-pleasure.

He was attractive, dangerously so. But he was also a man, and that meant that whatever face he showed in company there was another, darker side to his character, as there was with all men. Marissa reminded herself that was something she should never forget.

Chapter Two

Marissa gave up on the unequal struggle to sleep and threw back the heavy silk coverlet, wincing as her feet touched the polished boards by the bed. She padded across to the banked glow of the fire and held out her hands in an attempt to draw its warmth into her restless body.

In time she supposed the numbness would pass, but for the moment she was gripped by a strange sense of unreality. Only the routines and duties of the chatelaine of a great house made everyday existence possible: she had never been so grateful for the sense of duty which had been inculcated in her from childhood.

But in her chief duty she had failed, and failed repeatedly. Marissa gazed into the flickering red depths of the fire and remembered again her lord's cold disappointment that she had once again failed to conceive the heir to Southwood. Not that he had shown anger: the Earl had never allowed himself to show his emotions, least of all to his wife. And he had expected the same restraint from her.

At least that discipline had enabled her to bear the

embarrassing ordeal of the doctor's questioning yesterday, the knowing eyes of the men in the library as the will was read. Her cheeks burned hot and Marissa turned from the fire to cool them. As she did so her eyes fell on the door which led, via a suite of dressing rooms, to her lord's bedchamber, the Master Bedchamber. On an impulse she hurried into her dressing room and opened the connecting door. The key, as always, was on his side. With a swift twist of her wrist Marissa pulled it out, closed the door and locked it from her side.

It was a foolish, pointless gesture, barring the way into that empty suite beyond with its black-draped bed and mirrors veiled in mourning for the dead Earl. But it was her room now, hers at least until the man who occupied the Red Bedchamber, the best guest room, decided to take control of his inheritance. And by then she would have long gone to the Dower House.

The view from her windows showed an expanse of parkland glittering with frost under a chill moon. The windows were already rimed on the outside; by morning the frost-fingers would have crept up the panes inside too. Was the new Earl able to sleep in the big bedchamber, his warm Caribbean blood cooled by this unseasonable spring? Doubtless he would have been snugger in the Radwinter Arms at the park gates, where he had originally left his valise. But it was unthinkable that the fourth Earl should not sleep in the house of his ancestors.

A familiar restlessness filled her. Marissa felt the urge to run, to feel the blood sing in her veins, her heart beat wildly in her chest—to let go of all the rigidity and formality which had kept her confined these past few days. She slipped her long white silk peignoir on over her nightgown, pushed her feet into kid slippers and opened the door onto the corridor.

All was silent, then the sound of the hall clock striking one reverberated through the corridors. The night watchman would have done his rounds of the house by now, checking for open windows and guttering candles, and would be dozing quietly in his hooded porter's chair by the front door. Occasional lanterns illuminated the galleries and the moonlight flooded in through the long windows.

The patterned marble floor stretched enticingly long and clear before her. Marissa picked up her skirts and ran, ran as she had so often done in the freedom of the night. Her feet made only a slight pattering on the hard floor as she flew, hair loose, skirts billowing. She took the newel at the top of the stairs in both hands as she passed and swung round it, a bubble of laughter beginning at the back of her throat. Her eyes shone with exhilaration, with the freedom of the movement.

Marissa paused, panting slightly, between the doors of the Library and Long Gallery, trying to decide which way to go. She could dance in the Gallery under the disapproving eyes of the marble goddesses. But then she remembered the equally disapproving eyes of the ranked Southwood ancestors and her child-like enthusiasm waned, leaving her feeling guilty that she should be behaving so in a house of mourning. She was alive, vital, while they were all consigned to dust.

Her shoulders drooping, Marissa turned to retrace her steps in a more decorous manner. She never knew what stopped her: perhaps some sound, or the mysterious sense of another presence close to her. There was someone in the Gallery.

Tiptoeing in, she paused in the doorway. In the strong moonlight the figure by the south window was plain to see. He had his back to her, but there was no mistaking that burnished head, the width of the shoulders, the height of the man emphasised by the sweep of his heavy brocade dressing gown.

Lucian Southwood was standing braced with his hands on the mullions on either side of the long window. His head was bowed, as though the weight of the world was on his shoulders. Marissa had an impulse to run to him and throw her arms around his waist, to tell him that, whatever it was, she would make it all right. She took half a step, then checked herself. What was she thinking of? She did not know him, but she did know that one thing you never dared do was to show you had seen a sign of weakness in a man. She had only made that mistake once...

The stone mullions were chilling his hands to the bone, but Lucian scarcely noticed the additional discomfort. It was so damnably cold—yet he sensed that Southwood Hall would chill him even in the height of summer.

His life had been turned upside down in a matter of hours: his rambling home by the deep blue sea, his estates, the fleet of ships, his friends, the relaxed, unconventional society of Jamaica. All those were lost to him. He was responsible now for this great estate and all its people. He was the keystone that an entire economy rested on.

And his cousin's widow, so young, so beautiful, so vulnerable—and now his responsibility too. She appeared to have no family to support her, no friends to comfort her in a grief that must be devastating. And he, Lucian, was in the position her own child should have occupied. What a bitter reminder he must be to her, not only of her childlessness but, in his astonishing likeness, of the husband who had been taken from her so abruptly.

The die was cast; there was nothing to be gained by dwelling on it and he had never been a man to rail against the inevitable. His duty was clear. Lucian pushed himself away from the window, absently rubbing his chilled hands, and straightened his shoulders. Tomorrow he would send for the steward...

The skin on the back of his neck prickled: someone was in the room with him, watching him. He spun round, his sword hand reaching instinctively to where his rapier would have been, then froze in amazement.

For one mad moment he thought a ghost had appeared. The figure poised for flight in the doorway was almost elemental in its whiteness, save for the cloud of black hair framing the face and the dark-shadowed eyes. Then he recognised her.

'Lady Southwood! Please...do not go, I am sorry to have startled you.' He held out a hand to arrest her movement and saw the tension in her body relax slightly. 'I should not be wandering about the house at this hour, but I confess I could not sleep,' he added lightly, searching for a way to make this extraordinary encounter ordinary.

'Why should you not wander as you will? It is your house,' she replied matter-of-factly. Marissa found herself stepping into the room, drawn by some strange compulsion, when she knew propriety ruled that she should bid him goodnight and return to her chamber immediately.

Lucian came to meet her halfway, noting the tinge of colour in her cheeks, the rise and fall of her breast. Why, he must have scared her half to death, for she was breathing as though she had been running for her life.

'I hope your room is warm enough, my lord. I do appreciate how chilly you must find it after the warmth of the Caribbean. Let me ring for a servant to make up your fire.' She made as though to tug the bellpull.

'At this time of night? Surely no one is awake?'

'But of course. There is always a footman on duty throughout the night in case anything is required.'

Lucian laughed down into her face, imagining the staff at White Horse Cay if he demanded that they sat up all night just in case he wanted some small service performed. His father had freed his slaves, much to the scandal of the surrounding planters, but none of the staff had left him, regarding themselves, quite correctly, as just as much part of the family as they had ever been. Most of them had known Lucian since he was a child, and still tended to treat him, at the age of twenty-eight, as a faintly irresponsible boy.

Charmed by the infectious amusement in his face, although completely ignorant as to its cause, Marissa found herself smiling back.

Lucian caught his breath at the transformation. The hazel eyes sparked green, the serious little face was suddenly warm and full of life, the dark cloud of hair seemed to crackle with vitality. Without thinking he took her face between his palms, bent his head and kissed her full on her smiling mouth.

It was so unexpected, so startling, so pleasurable, that for a brief, shameless moment she kissed him back with soft, generous lips. It was as if his warmth was flooding her veins, touching the icy core of her with the heat of the sun and of him.

The realisation of what they were doing seemed to hit them both simultaneously. Even as she began to pull back she felt his hands release her. Lucian, his face sombre with shock, took two rapid steps back.

'Madam, I cannot begin to apologise for my out-rageous behaviour,' he began. Her eyes were enor-mous with shock, her lips—the lips that had quiv-ered against his—were parted in dismay. Without a word Marissa turned and ran.

Lucian strode to the wall and hit his fist hard into the unyielding wooden panel beside him. 'Damn, damn, damn…! You bloody insensitive fool!' How could he have succumbed to a moment of weakness like that?

She was his cousin's widow; only hours before she had buried her husband. He had already scared her into a faint by his unexpected appearance, had witnessed her humiliation at the reading of the will. He must be a constant reminder of the loss of her husband and the absence of an heir. And then, in-stead of offering her his brotherly support, he had taken her in his arms and kissed her!

And she, shocked, grieving, without affectionate friends at her side, had for a brief moment gone into his arms seeking consolation. Lucian stalked back along the corridor to his bedroom, ignoring the pain in his bruised fist, furious with himself. 'You bloody fool, what are you going to say to her in the morning?'

On the other side of the Inner Court, Marissa slammed her door behind her and leaned, panting, against the panels. She pressed her fist against her mouth as if to stem the tide of tears gathering at the back of her eyes. What had she done? She had *wanted* to kiss Lucian, to be held against that warm strong body, never to have those gentle lips leave hers. She ran to the mirror, turning her face anxiously, expecting to see the marks of his fingers branded on her skin. There was nothing to show, yet she could feel them as if they still cradled her face.

How *could* she feel like this? It was improper, humiliating, shameful. Not only had she let him kiss her, but she had kissed him back! Even if she had, however briefly, accepted his embrace, she should never have answered it. No lady should ever allow herself to show passion in any form. Two years of marriage had reinforced that lesson well. How could she have felt so safe in his arms? How could kisses as gentle as those lead, as she knew they did, to the reality of the marriage bed?

Marissa let herself fall into bed, dragging the covers tight around her ears as if to block out her own tumultuous thoughts. How could she face him tomorrow?

But face him she had to. With the house full of guests, Marissa made a special effort to be early at the breakfast table, but even so the new Earl was before her. Whiting removed a plate bearing the remnants of a large beefsteak and placed a basket of fresh rolls in front of his lordship.

'My lady! Good morning.' Whiting bowed and moved to pull out Marissa's chair. Lucian rose to his feet and waited courteously for her to take her place at the oval breakfast table.

He watched her as she sat, her hair haloed by the weak sunshine that streamed in through the breakfast parlour windows. She might have been carved in marble for all the animation in her figure, gowned in deepest unrelieved black.

'Good morning, my lord,' she remarked calmly. 'I am sure Whiting has been looking after you. No, Whiting, I will just take tea.'

'Chocolate will be more sustaining, my lady,' Whiting coaxed, conscious that Mrs Whiting had given him strict instructions to make sure his young mistress ate properly. 'And a sweet roll, my lady—it is a bitterly cold morning, ma'am.'

'Very well. I will take a roll. But no chocolate, Whiting.' The thought of the rich liquid made her stomach roil. She could crumble a roll without the butler noticing she was scarcely eating a morsel...

Lucian buttered a roll while keeping a covert eye on the widow. Neither of the things that were uppermost in his thoughts could be carried out. The first was to apologise unreservedly for his behaviour last night in the moonlight; the other was to do it all over again. Then he saw how she was crumbling the roll and hiding the pieces under her knife. If she had been his sister he would have taken her on his knee, put an arm round her shoulders and coaxed her to eat. But she was not his sister; she was his cousin's widow.

Marissa's words broke into his thoughts. 'My lord...'

'Will you not call me by my given name?' he asked abruptly, scandalising Whiting, who was standing immobile by the sideboard. 'After all we are related, if only by marriage, and I am not used to this formality.' He saw her dubious face and added, with a charming smile, 'Will you not take pity on a stranger in a foreign land?'

Marissa doubted if his lordship was ever out of countenance, but once again found herself yielding to the charm of that smile. 'Very well…Cousin Lucian.' The door opened at that moment and Whiting, storing away this almost revolutionary informality to recount to Mrs Whiting at the earliest opportunity, busied himself with seating Mr Hope and some of the less elderly second cousins, who had decided against taking breakfast in their bedchambers.

Lucian stood up and bowed. 'If you will excuse me, Cousin, gentlemen, I have an appointment with the steward.'

Marissa managed to maintain a flow of polite small-talk for a few minutes, before excusing herself to go and talk to the housekeeper. As she made her way towards the green baize door which separated the servants' quarters from the main house she reflected that she had never been so glad to see Mr Hope as when he had come into the breakfast parlour just then.

How assured Lucian had been! He seemed not to have the slightest self-recrimination for his behaviour last night. And as for asking her to call him by his given name! She should never have agreed so readily, yet how could she have snubbed him in front of Whiting?

Marissa's heels clicked on the stone floor as her

pace increased to match her growing irritation with both herself and Lucian. That smile, the glint of white teeth in his tanned face, the slight exotic accent… Oh, yes, he was charming all right, and he used that charm very easily, too easily. Doubtless young women fell into his arms with such facility that what had happened last night was nothing remarkable to him…

She had worked herself up into such a state of righteous indignation that when she rounded a corner and found herself face to face with the object of it she made no attempt to hide her frown.

'Cousin Marissa! As you can see, I have become lost looking for the estate office.' His smile was charmingly apologetic, inviting her to laugh at his inability to navigate the big house.

'If you retrace your steps to the first door into the courtyard, cross the courtyard itself, then it is the green door in front of you,' she directed in clipped tones. Finding herself alone with him again was embarrassing; she was aware of a tightening knot of anger in her chest, though whether at herself or him she could not analyse.

'Cousin, is something amiss?' Lucian moved closer, not hiding his surprise at the coolness of her mien.

'You can ask me that after last night?' she demanded, her colour rising.

'I had thought perhaps I had been forgiven after you agreed to call me cousin this morning,' he began, only to be interrupted by Marissa's sarcasm.

'Oh, forgive me, my lord, if I have misled you. I foolishly believed it would be better not to discuss our…encounter…in front of Whiting. I should, of course, have regaled him with the entire episode! As it is, you put me in a position where I have scandalised him by agreeing to a form of address which can only be regarded as quite inappropriately informal. But doubtless in the West Indies you do things differently, so we must all learn to make allowances for the new Earl.'

'Why, you little madam!' Lucian stood and stared at her, amazed irritation replacing his look of rueful apology. 'I thought you were in need of friendship and some brotherly support...'

'Brotherly!' Marissa stamped her foot. 'Sir, what you did last night was not brotherly!'

'*I did?* It was only your good manners, I suppose, that led you to kiss me back?'

Marissa drew herself up to her full, unfashionable, five feet six inches, eyes ablaze. 'Why, you... you...you may be the fourth Earl of Radwinter, but you are no gentleman!'

Lucian stared down at her through narrowed eyes. 'If you were my sister I would put you over my knee for that! I have no time for spoilt young women whose every whim has been indulged by doting middle-aged husbands. I am truly sorry for your loss, madam, but do not think you can twist me round your little finger as you did my cousin.'

For a long moment she stared at him, speechless, and in her eyes he caught a look of such desolation that he caught his breath. But before he could say anything there was the sound of footsteps in the corridor behind him. He turned to find Poole, the steward, hurrying towards him, and when he looked back Marissa had vanished.

Lucian cursed his fiery temper: he was easy to

rouse, but all his family, friends and servants knew his rages blew over as fast as they arose. He would have to try and explain to Marissa, but now was not the time.

'My lord, I do apologise. I was not in the hall to show you to the office.' The steward was obviously alarmed, and Lucian realised his face must still be thunderous.

'Not at all, Poole.' He clapped the man on the shoulder. 'I was irritated with myself for losing my bearings. I swear a man needs a compass to navigate this place! Come, let us get down to business, for we have much to talk about.'

Marissa meanwhile swept downstairs to the housekeeper's room on a tide of hurt anger. So, he thought her an indulged child, did he? A bitter laugh escaped her tight lips at the unfair irony of the accusation. One thing she had never been was indulged. Left motherless at an early age, she had been raised by a father whose irritation at being saddled with a daughter had been eclipsed only by his determination that she be brought up in a manner that would ensure she would marry well and as quickly as possible. Her own preferences, not that she had ever been asked to express them, had been entirely irrelevant to her father's plans for her.

But as she entered the cosy parlour where the housekeeper was scanning the linen lists she felt her bitterness ease in the face of the familiar warmth and comfort that she always found there.

'There you are, ma'am!' The housekeeper pulled up a chair by the fire. 'Now, you sit down there, my lamb, and warm your hands. I know you didn't eat your breakfast: even if you fool Whiting, you can't fool me. Just bide there and I'll cut you a slice of my fruit cake and pour you some of this tea.'

Absolutely scrupulous in maintaining her young mistress's dignity in front of the other servants, in private the housekeeper treated her like a granddaughter. His late lordship had been a great nobleman but not an easy gentleman to live with, with his exacting standards: not a speck of dust, not a vase out of place, not a servant out of line. And woe betide the mistress if it was. Mrs Whiting had made sure that everything within her purview was as near perfection as she could make it, because any shortcoming had been visited not on her head, but on Marissa's. And she loved this young girl as if she was her own.

Something had upset her now; that was for sure. The porcelain-pale skin was flushed above the cheekbones, and her breathing was slightly ragged.

'Now you eat that up, my lady, while I finish these lists.'

'Thank you, Mrs Whiting. But there is so much we must discuss— Mmm!' She broke off to take another appreciative bite of the cake. 'This is delicious!' And it was the first thing that had not turned to sawdust in her mouth over the past week.

The older woman eyed her, then began to work round to the subject that had been uppermost in her mind for days. 'It must have been such a shock, his lordship's accident...I don't suppose you'll have had a chance yet to think about what you want to do now. And his new lordship arriving like that out of the blue, and everyone thinking he's off in those foreign parts...'

'Oh, I know exactly what I am going to do,' Marissa said with surprising conviction. 'I have sent for my cousin, Miss Venables, and as soon as she arrives we will move into the Dower House. His lordship can then do as he pleases without needing to refer to me.'

Mrs Whiting pursed her lips at the hint of irritation in Marissa's voice. So, she didn't take to the fourth Earl! That surprised her, for she thought him a well-set-up, very pleasant gentleman, even if his ways were a bit foreign.

'Had you thought about staff for the Dower House?' The housekeeper tried to keep her voice neutral.

Marissa pulled herself together and gave the question her full attention: she had wanted to speak to the Whitings about this. She knew, however much she disliked formality, that as the Dowager Countess of Radwinter she had a duty to maintain a proper household.

'I will need a butler and a housekeeper, three footmen, kitchen staff, chambermaids...Mary, of course, will come with me. But it is the butler and housekeeper who are the most important to decide upon. What a pity that Matthews from the London house is not married: his lordship will not want to keep it fully staffed while he is out of the country...'

The two women discussed the possibilities halfheartedly; no one seemed appropriate, but Marissa knew that because of her youth she would need to select her senior servants carefully. Even with a respectable companion like Miss Venables she needed the dignity of experienced and mature upper servants.

Eventually the housekeeper cleared her throat and

ventured, 'I know Whiting was going to raise this with his lordship, but as we're talking about it, my lady... He and I feel we're getting on in years. This house is a big responsibility, and his lordship's bound to want to bring his own people in. Would you like it if Whiting and I were to come with you to the Dower House?'

It was the perfect solution. Marissa looked at the housekeeper with shining eyes, but then doubt crept in. 'But you have a position here. This is one of the great houses of East Anglia—surely you would not want to descend to looking after a mere manor house?'

'I'd like nothing better, my love,' said Mrs Whiting with transparent honesty, then added cunningly, 'And my poor old joints aren't what they used to be...'

'Then I will be delighted if you will come with me.' Marissa hugged the housekeeper, who was therefore unable to see her face as she added, 'I will speak to his lordship about it.'

And as soon as possible, she thought as she walked back to the small parlour which did duty as a morning room. As she opened the door Gyp, her Cavalier King Charles spaniel, jumped down from the window seat with a sharp bark of joy and danced around her feet, plumed tail waving. Marissa scooped up the little dog, laughing as he tried to lick her face, rubbing her fingers through his silky hair.

'There's a good boy! Has James taken you for your morning walk, then? We will have a run after luncheon, I promise. Now, sit down while I look at the accounts.'

Gyp, recognising that he was not going to be

taken out just yet, settled down in front of the fire with a sigh and promptly fell asleep. Marissa sat at her little French bureau in the bay of the window and opened her account book. But she made no attempt to total the columns of figures, or to puzzle out why the cost of wax candles had become so high.

As she had thought, she could see clearly across the frosty courtyard into the estate office window. If she kept an eye on it, she would be able to intercept Lucian when he left and speak to him before luncheon. After all, she reasoned, biting the end of her pencil, she could hardly speak about the Whitings moving to the Dower House in the presence of the butler himself. And one or two of the relatives who had come for the reading of the will had decided in view of the inclement weather to wait a few days for the harsh frost to thaw; they too would be at the table.

But the truth was that Marissa felt bad about her bitter words to Lucian in the corridor: this was no way to deal with the man who was now master of Radwinter and, apart from her father, her closest male relative. He would be returning to London and thence to Jamaica within a matter of weeks. And by the time they met again that awkward encounter in the Long Gallery would be long forgotten...

Lucian appeared to be pacing the small office; she could see him passing and repassing the window, occasionally gesticulating with both hands to drive home a point. It appeared to be a perfectly amicable conversation. When she caught a glimpse of Poole, the steward was nodding in agreement.

At eleven o'clock a footman crossed the courtyard, balancing a tray with some caution. The cobbles were rimed with frost in the shadows which still lay around the edges of the courtyard and Marissa suppressed a smile at the sight of the man mincing along in his leather-soled buckled shoes, while struggling to keep level the tray laden with two tankards and a platter of bread and cheese.

The arrival of the food did not appear to halt the discussion: Lucian continued to pace, despite the tankard in his hand. Almost an hour later the door swung open. With a clap on the steward's shoulder Lucian strode off, leaving Poole looking somewhat dazed in the doorway.

There was no doubt that Mr Poole was finding that dealing with the fourth Earl was a very different proposition from dealing with his predecessor. Charles had made his expectations crystal-clear and had then interfered only on the rare occasions when they had not been met.

Marissa dropped her pencil and whisked out of the door, running downstairs to waylay Lucian before he reached the Hall. 'My lord! Could you spare me a few moments?'

'Of course, Cousin.' He bowed politely and waited for her to precede him. Her earlier irritation appeared to have vanished, yet she seemed agitated, slightly out of breath. Her normally impeccable gown had a light sprinkling of golden hairs on the shoulder and one lock of her disciplined coiffure had come loose. Lucian curbed the urge to unpin the rest of it and set the whole cloud free around her shoulders.

'I realise it is unusual to receive you in my parlour,' Marissa began as she pushed open the door to her sanctum, 'but I have a particular reason for wishing to speak to you alone.'

At the sight of the answering glint in his eyes she sat down hastily by the fire and gathered Gyp onto her lap. The spaniel curled a lip at the intruder, but Lucian, sinking into the chair opposite, snapped his fingers and the little dog jumped down and trotted over to sniff at his feet. After a moment he curled up again, his chin comfortably on one of Lucian's boots, and went back to sleep.

'Well, I must say!' Marissa was indignant at her pet's perfidy. Gyp disliked men generally, although he tolerated the footmen who took him for walks, and he had particularly hated the late Earl.

'I do not know why you should object,' Lucian observed mildly. 'He is much more of a handicap to my improper behaviour lying on my feet than he ever was in your arms.'

Marissa could feel a flush rising to her cheeks. 'I think we should forget that incident, Cousin; put it behind us and pretend it never happened.'

'Feel free to pretend what you like,' he returned ambiguously.

'Er…yes, well, what I wanted to speak to you about was the Dower House.'

'I too wished to discuss that with you. Poole tells me it is in good condition and well furnished, if not in the latest style. That will be rectified. Of course you must stay here for as long as you wish. I will be gone for many months, perhaps a year, in Jamaica, and when my sister and I return there will still be no need to drive you from your home. You have only to say which suite of apartments you wish to retain and they are yours…'

'No!' The word burst from her before she could contain it, and Lucian looked at her in surprise. 'I mean, no, thank you, Cousin Lucian. The Dower House will do me very well, and I intend to move there as soon as my companion, Miss Venables, arrives from Cumbria and the funeral party disperses.'

Lucian steepled his fingers and regarded her gravely over the top of them. 'I do beg your pardon, Cousin. I should have realised that this house must hold unbearably painful memories for you now.'

Marissa dropped her gaze to her hands clasped tightly in her lap. 'Indeed, yes,' she said quietly. 'I will be glad to be gone from it.' After a moment she rallied slightly and added, 'But of course I will regard it as my duty to oversee the housekeeping here in your absence.'

Lucian noted her use of the word 'duty' yet again. She was so young to be so serious about her duty. He could imagine her over the coming year, clad in her unrelieved mourning black, forcing herself day after day to revisit Southwood Hall in pursuit of her duty.

'This is a charming room,' he remarked, in an attempt to ease the tension. The colours were soft: rose-pinks, delphinium-blue, touches of coral. There was an Aubusson rug on the polished boards, the furniture was in the country style, and the upholstery bore the marks of Gyp's scrabbling claws. It was warm, cosy, slightly untidy, with books overflowing the table, Gyp's drinking bowl in the hearth, a sewing basket with the lid askew and skeins of thread spilling out.

'It is a very untidy room.' She laughed suddenly. 'But then, my lord never came in here...' She stopped, aware she was in danger of saying too much, revealing too much about her marriage and herself.

Rather hastily she went on, 'But the reason I wished to speak to you alone is the question of the servants. Mrs Whiting has told me that she and her husband are finding this big house too much for them now. They would like to come with me to the Dower House, but we are all conscious that you must have reliable staff in place. Perhaps you would be bringing your own staff from Jamaica?'

'I have my own butler, Edward Jackson: I could not leave *him* behind if I tried! If the Whitings wish to go with you, then they do so with my blessing. Is there a reliable couple you could recommend to take their place here? It will, after all, be very quiet here for at least a year whilst I am away and you are in mourning.'

'The butler at Grosvenor Square—Matthews—is a good man and Whiting considers him ready for greater responsibility. And I imagine you will close the London house while you are away. However, Matthews is unmarried, so you will need to engage a housekeeper. Mind you,' Marissa added thoughtfully, 'Mrs Wood, our cook here, is quite capable of managing the housekeeping while there is no one in residence. And with the Whitings close at hand, if she and Matthews have any difficulties they will have ready advice.'

Satisfied with such a neat solution, Marissa sat back against the cushions with a sudden happy smile which illuminated her face and made her look absurdly young. Gyp started out of his doze, as though the foot he was resting against had moved, and Lucian said abruptly, 'An admirable solution. Shall we visit the Dower House after luncheon?'

Chapter Three

Marissa asked Mrs Whiting to accompany them on their expedition to the Dower House. It was, of course, entirely proper to take a chaperon, but, that aside, Marissa recognised in herself a growing susceptibility to Lucian's charm that made her wary of spending too much time alone with him. It would never do to become accustomed to his company, she chided herself.

The housekeeper was delighted at the opportunity to survey her future domain. 'The Dower House was the home of Miss Anne Southwood for many years, my lord,' she explained as the carriage made its cautious way along the frozen drive. The coachman was concerned about the horses' legs on the iron-hard ground, and the slow progress made the three occupants of the carriage glad of the footwarmers and thick fur rugs they were wrapped up in.

'She died just before you came here, my dear…my lady, if you recall. But the house has been well looked after, so we should not find much to concern us.' She chatted comfortably on about how she had instructed the elderly married couple who had stayed on after their mistress had died to light fires and to clean and air all the rooms. 'For once you let damp in—with us so close to the sea, my lord—you never get rid of it.'

'It seems strange that we are so close to the sea yet cannot see it,' Lucian remarked. 'I can smell it when the wind is onshore, but I can neither hear nor see it, and I am used to doing both at home in Jamaica.'

'Yes, the land rises so gently to the house, and there is over a mile of saltings and marsh before the beach, so that you must ride almost to the dunes before you see it,' Marissa explained. 'If it were not so cold I would suggest going down there, but the wind will cut like a knife without the protection of the trees.'

'I find it hard to believe it could be possible to be any colder,' Lucian said with a grimace as the avenue of holm oaks widened out to reveal the neat little Queen Anne Dower House, sitting like a doll's house in a hollow surrounded by its walled gardens.

The Bishops, the elderly couple who were caretaking, were on the look-out for them, and the chilly party found themselves whisked into a snug hall with a fire burning in the grate and cheerful brocade hangings shutting out the draughts.

Mrs Bishop soon took Mrs Whiting off to discuss the vexed question of the kitchen range and its persistently smoking chimney, leaving her husband to conduct his lordship and the young Dowager around the house.

'I had forgotten how charming this house is!' Marissa exclaimed in delight as they entered the drawing room. She walked across to look out of long windows which opened onto what would be a flourishing rose garden in the summer. 'And how nicely you and Mrs Bishop have kept everything!'

Bishop, much flattered by the attention, proudly conducted them round every one of the three reception rooms, the little library and the six bedrooms.

'This will do me very well,' Marissa declared as they climbed the back stairs to check that the servants' accommodation was in good order.

'I agree. It is a charming house, and very home-like and comfortable,' Lucian agreed. 'But, Lady Southwood, do you not feel it is perhaps a little old-fashioned, especially in contrast to the Hall? Shall I order a complete redecoration and refurnishing to be set in train?'

Privately he found the house delightful, and did not find the worn fabrics or faded paint objectionable. It was welcoming, a house that had been home to happy people. Southwood Hall, in all its Palladian magnificence, was a rich man's showpiece, an ice palace. How he was ever going to make it a home for himself and Nicole he could not imagine.

'No! Leave it as it is!' Marissa spoke vehemently, and then saw the quickly suppressed look of surprise on Lucian's face at her warmth. 'I mean…I would prefer to live here a while and get to know the house before I decide on any changes.' Seeing that his lordship was still regarding her quizzically, Marissa fell back upon a tactic she had always found mollified Charles. She dropped her eyes and murmured, 'I will be guided by you, my lord, but at the moment I feel too shaken to make any decisions…'

There was a pregnant pause. Marissa kept her eyes down, sensing that this man was not convinced by a show of feminine weakness from a woman who had only hours before been most decided in her plans to leave the Hall, engage a companion and arrange her own domestic staff. However, he merely replied blandly, 'It will be as you wish, Lady Southwood. You have only to command the steward when you have decided what you want to do.'

Mrs Bishop bustled in, dropping a curtsey before addressing her husband vigorously. 'Now then, Bishop! What are you about? Keeping my lady and his lordship up here in these attics! Come you down, ma'am—I've laid tea out in the little parlour.' She led them down, chattering as she negotiated the winding stairs, and pushed open the baize door into the main house. 'Not that the little parlour is the right room for afternoon tea, I knows that, but it is the cosiest on a day like today, there's no denying that…'

As the door closed behind her Lucian enquired with a laugh, 'Does that woman ever stop talking?'

'Probably not, but Mrs Whiting knows how to manage her. Tea, my lord?'

'Thank you.' He leaned across to take it, his fingertips just brushing hers on the rim of the saucer. 'I thought we had agreed that you would call me Lucian when we are alone?'

Marissa regarded him over the tea table with steady hazel eyes. 'And I thought I had consented to call you cousin.' She really could not afford to be sent into a fluster every time she found herself in his company. It was the informal manners of the West Indies, of course; that was why he seemed so warm, why his conversation seemed so intimate. But underneath it all he was a man, and they all had the same expectations, the same demands. On the surface Lucian Southwood simply had a different style.

They fell silent, sipping tea in the warmth of the parlour, and gradually Marissa relaxed, letting her mind fall to wool-gathering. Lucian could not tell what Marissa was thinking, but he thought he had never seen her look so…so… He groped for the word in his mind… So *real*. When he'd first seen her she had seemed another marble statue in the gallery, or one of the portraits come to life. Everything about her had been constrained and stiff; now, in this cosy little parlour, he felt he was with a real flesh and blood woman.

The fire had brought a glow to her cheeks, her shoulders were no longer set as she leaned back against the faded chintz, and one tendril of hair had worked loose and hung behind her left ear.

'Will you not be lonely?' he asked suddenly.

'Lonely? Living here?' Marissa was taken aback. Loneliness was a state to which she was accustomed; it was her normal condition. 'Why, no more than usual… I mean, I will have Miss Venables, and Mrs Whiting, of course. And Lady Augusta will visit, even though we are in mourning.'

'No, I mean… Forgive me, but do you not have any friends of your own age?'

'No, my lord,' she said simply. 'I came straight from my father's house in Hampshire: I met my lord at the start of my first Season, so I had no opportunity to make close friends amongst the other debutantes. And my lord, being older than myself, had his own circle of friends, which of course became mine.'

Lucian cursed himself for his tactlessness, for this

conversation had brought a tautness to her face and the old wariness back to her eyes. Her devotion to her late husband was unquestionable, and he was a fool to keep reminding her of a pain so newly inflicted.

To cover the awkward moment, he said bluntly, 'Would you advise me, Cousin? I have an idea in my mind concerning my sister Nicole which I would like to venture with you. She is very young—only sixteen—and she found the sea voyage very distressing. Despite being used to inshore boats all her life, she was sick from the moment we reached deep ocean, and I know she dreads the return journey.' He leaned over to put his cup down, a deep furrow between his eyes. 'Now I have to tell her that we must return almost at once, that she must say goodbye to her home and friends and face yet another onerous ocean journey.'

'Oh, poor child!' exclaimed Marissa with ready sympathy. 'What an awful prospect for her—and for you to see her suffer so!' It was obvious to Lucian that Marissa's idea of his sufferings—those of a caring and sensitive brother—were far removed from the reality of living with a wilful and tempestuous girl. Nicci had been allowed to run wild, and so far had never been asked to face anything unpleasant in her life. There would be endless rows, sulks and tears from the moment he broke the news until they arrived back in London—perhaps a year hence.

'I want—I would like—to leave her here in your care, and not to expose her to the rigours of both the journey and the pain of parting from her home again.' He leaned back in the chair and watched Marissa's face, gauging her reaction. 'I know it is asking a lot, to take on the care of a young, high-spirited girl under any circumstances, let alone these…' He watched the calm, thoughtful face before him and realised with a start that Marissa could only be three years older than Nicci, and had married scarcely older than his sister was now.

Had she always had this grave air of reflection, of inner constraint? Had she ever been a headstrong young girl, and, if so, what had it taken to effect the change in her?

'But of course she must come here to me!' Marissa exclaimed. 'I could not bear the thought of her suffering so!' In her unknown cousin's plight she felt again the terror of being plunged into an unknown world, of having to learn the rules and expectations of a new way of life, cut off from everything that was familiar. 'Poor little thing! She must be so homesick, and missing you. With whom is she staying?'

'A West India merchant by the name of Montfort and his wife. It is my habit to stay with them on my visits to London, and fortunately they have several children, including a girl of Nicci's age.'

'It must be a comfort to you to know she is in the care of friends. Mrs Montfort will be helping her to buy her mourning, I expect.'

Lucian reflected ruefully that if Mrs Montfort was succeeding in getting Nicci to concentrate on anything as dull as buying mourning, let alone wearing it and behaving in a manner befitting her new station in life as sister of an earl, then he would eat his hat.

'I cannot tell you what a comfort it will be to have her living quietly in the country. I just hope it is not an imposition on you in your present state of mourning.'

'Oh, no, it will be a pleasure to have her here.' It would be a novelty too, to have someone to look after. And sixteen was such a vulnerable age for a young girl trembling on the threshold of womanhood...

Marissa woke the next morning with an unfamiliar feeling of pleasurable anticipation. Not only would Miss Venables be arriving soon, and they would be able to make the move to the Dower House, but planning for Nicole Southwood's stay was a delightful novelty. It would be like having a little sister.

Gyp, delighted to be admitted to his mistress's bedchamber, snored at the end of the bed. He had always been banished to her little parlour at night, but now there was no one to object he was becoming a familiar shadow at her heels wherever she went in the house.

Mary was already pulling back the drapes to reveal a foggy morning. 'It's set in a thaw overnight, my lady. Much warmer, but there's this danged fog, and the mud is something dreadful.'

'Language, Mary!' Marissa reproved halfheartedly. 'You will never make a London lady's maid saying words like "danged".'

'Yes, my lady. Sorry, my lady. Here's your chocolate, ma'am. Mrs Whiting asked me to say, ma'am, that she would like a word this morning about what you wish done with his late lordship's suite.'

'Yes, please tell Mrs Whiting I will speak with her after breakfast.'

Half an hour later, fully dressed for breakfast, Marissa hesitated on the threshold and glanced back at her dressing room door. If she were to discuss her lord's chambers she had better take a look around them now. She could not face walking into that suite for the first time since his death with anyone else there.

Her hand shook slightly as she turned the key and opened the door into the formal sitting room which lay between the two dressing rooms. It was a characterless space, used by neither husband nor wife. She hurried through it without a glance; it held no memories, no threat to her equanimity.

His dressing room was immaculately tidy, just as his valet had left it. The door into the bedchamber beyond stood ajar, opening into the darkness of the shrouded room. Before she could change her mind Marissa strode across and wrenched back the heavy curtains from the windows. Foggy light poured across the floor behind her.

Marissa turned slowly on her heels to survey her lord's chamber, her heart thudding in her chest. To her heightened imagination it felt as though he was still there. She could sense the sharp tang of his cologne. Every item on the bedside table was perfectly aligned. Nothing had been removed or changed since his death; all was as he would have demanded it should be.

Then, as she turned, Marissa's heart gave a painful lurch. There on the side table lay his gloves, his riding crop, his hat, just as though he had walked in and put them down a moment before.

'My lord!' she whispered, but there was no answer in the high-ceilinged chamber. Her hand crept to her throat as she was gripped by a powerful sense that he was not dead. Dr Robertson had prevented her from seeing the body; she realised now he had feared she might miscarry if she was with child. And no lady ever attended the actual interment.

Marissa ran from the room and was halfway along the corridor to the main stairs before she could calm herself, control her breathing. By the time she reached the breakfast room she had outwardly regained her composure, but inwardly her fantasies battled with her common sense.

Like an automaton Marissa passed bread and butter, made conversation with the elderly relatives who were taking their departure that morning. By the end of the meal she had decided that she would walk down to the chapel and visit the family vault. Of course he was dead, she knew that, but perhaps if she saw the tomb with her own eyes she could lay to rest this spectre.

The dining room door opened and Lucian entered. He had been out already: there was colour in his cheeks from the raw cold and his hair curled damply from the fog. He took a cup of coffee from Whiting and wrapped his cold fingers round the porcelain, addressing the guests who were finishing their breakfast. 'I hope, gentlemen, that this fog will not impede your journeys. Will you not stay a few more days until the weather clears?'

'It will be better once we are away from the coast, sir,' Sir Thomas Cribb, a distant cousin, declared. 'The sea fret lies heavy here, always does. Too damp, this spot; I've always said so,' he added under his breath.

'Should I not ring for your valet, my lord?' Marissa enquired. 'This cold fog seeps through damp to one's very bones.' And, she reflected, was enough to produce pneumonia in someone used to tropical climes. Not that the Earl was looking unwell; far from it. Used to her husband's pale skin and immaculate hair, to her, Lucian's tan and unruly crop seemed vibrantly alive and healthy. Try as she might, she could not become used to the physical similarity between the two men which underlay these differences.

'Thank you, no. I intend going down to see the Home Farm once our guests have departed—if we cannot persuade them to stay. I must confess I had not appreciated the scale of the estate here: there is much to put in hand before I leave.'

Marissa, enfolded in a thick wool cloak with a bonnet and muff, waved goodbye to the last of the guests from the front steps of the Hall and waited while Lucian mounted and cantered off in their wake towards the Home Farm.

Whiting was hovering, waiting for her to re-enter the house. 'Thank you, Whiting. I shall take a turn round the pleasure grounds for some air.'

As the front door closed Marissa walked briskly down the gravel path that wound into the shrubbery. The evergreens dripped with fog moisture and the snow lay in depressingly grubby patches against their trunks. She increased her pace and emerged onto the open greensward that fronted the little stone family chapel.

As she laid one black-gloved hand on the latch of the gate the cold struck through the fine kid, yet she hardly noticed it. She stopped, in the very act of opening the gate. What was she about? she chided herself. Why was she suddenly prey to this ridiculous compulsion? Of course Charles was dead, his neck broken in his fall. And it was her fault: once again she had disappointed him; once again he had ridden out in cold fury at her failure as a wife... Why had he ridden over the Common when only the other day she had heard the gamekeeper remarking on the extent of the rabbit holes and the damage they were causing? It could only have been because he had been distracted by yet another disappointment; yet again there was no sign of an heir to displace the estranged cousins in Jamaica.

Marissa turned to leave, then hesitated. If she went in now, saw the vault, it would make an ending to her life at the Hall. She could start again, afresh...

The door creaked open on reluctant hinges and the cold, damp air rolled out to meet her. Shuddering, Marissa huddled deeper into her cloak and stepped inside. The chill pressed up through the soles of her sturdy walking shoes as she walked slowly towards the great vault, hung with wreaths of laurel.

The family always worshipped in the parish church which lay on the boundary of the estate: the chapel was used only for family interments. All around were the slabs and monuments denoting the resting places of many generations of Southwoods, back to Sir Ralph, lying in his armour, his dog at his feet.

Her lord's grandfather had constructed this new vault with its great iron-bound door. The space for a new plaque was empty, awaiting the carved tribute to her lord, but a hatchment with his coat of arms hung above, and a painted board stated simply:

Charles Wystan Henry Southwood, Third Earl of Radwinter, 1770-1815.

How well the marble mausoleum suited him in its cold, classical perfection. Yes. He was dead. For the first time Marissa truly believed it. She was free of him. A tiny glow of warmth burned inside her as she tried the word under her breath. 'Free…'

For two years she had longed to be free, longed to wake up and find, not that he was dead—never *that*—but that he had gone, vanished from her life by some miracle. For two years he had dominated her by his will, controlled her every act, wrung out every drop of spontaneity and warmth from her, given her only wealth and status, demanded only perfection—and an heir.

She had married him determined to be a loving and dutiful wife, but she had found that only duty was expected of her. And, however hard she'd tried, she had never been able to please his exacting standards—by day or by night.

The vault seemed to be full of his personality as Marissa stood there, relief and a dreadful guilt that she should feel like this flooding through her. Then there was a step behind her and the door, which she had left ajar, swung open with a thud.

Marissa whirled round, and for one hideous moment believed she saw him standing in the doorway.

'My lord!'

Then she saw it was Lucian, his breath curling warm on the cold air, a look of concern on his face as he took in the expression on hers.

Marissa drew in one difficult breath and then burst into tears of shock, guilt, relief. After one horrified moment Lucian strode across and gathered her in his arms, holding her tight while she sobbed, cursing himself under his breath. He had done it again, scared the poor child by coming on her unawares, reminding her at the worst possible moment of what she had lost.

Riding back from the Home Farm, he had seen the chapel door standing ajar and had come to secure it. He should have realised it might be Marissa, visiting her husband's grave to mourn in peace. He had broken in on her grief and by doing so had broken her composure and the control that had been helping her to cope with her loss.

Trying to explain and apologise would only make things worse. Gently Lucian urged her towards the door and out into the open, where the sun was at last penetrating the fog in fitful rays. He closed the door firmly behind them and found a handkerchief.

She spoke, her voice muffled against his great-coat. 'He has really gone, has he not? He will not be coming back?'

Later it was to strike Lucian as an odd choice of words, but then he hardly noticed it as he patted Marissa gently on the back until the sobs subsided and she took his handkerchief with a watery smile.

He offered her his arm. 'Come, Cousin, let us walk back slowly past the lake. The sun is finally beginning to warm that west-facing bank.' And it would give her time to regain her composure before facing the servants.

They walked on in silence, Marissa's hand tucked warmly into the crook of his right arm, his horse ambling quietly behind them. The fog was curling up off the surface of the lake like smoke, and the fringing reeds stood brittle and dead in the still water. Flocks of duck were dotted across the lake and rose in panic at the sight of the people.

Marissa blew her nose and struggled to find a suitable topic of conversation. She ought to feel awkward, yet she did not, and the Earl seemed quite unperturbed by her sudden tears. Perhaps having a sister had made him adept at soothing agitated females and more tolerant of emotional outbursts than fathers or husbands would be. Charles would never have tolerated tears, whatever the cause, and her father would simply turn and walk away if any emotion was shown.

A pheasant suddenly flew out of the tussocks around the lake with a strident alarm call, and across the meadow came the plaintive bleat of sheep carried clearly on the still air.

Agriculture seemed an unexceptionable topic. 'Did you see all you wished at the Home Farm, Cousin?'

'Thank you, yes. Everything appears to be in excellent order. My late cousin was obviously a good landlord.' If not a well-liked one, he added to himself. Everyone he'd spoken to had been as one in agreeing that this was a well-managed estate, run to the highest standards. No one had spoken to him of a sense of loss, or with any warmth of the late Earl. Yet every one of the estate workers he had encountered had enquired anxiously and with obvious respect after the welfare of the Countess.

Lucian glanced down, but the rim of the bonnet hid her face from him. Her hand rested trustingly on his arm, the kid-gloved fingers surprisingly firm. It seemed as though she was the only person who had found something in his cousin to mourn: there was no mistaking the genuineness of that flood of tears or the cold hurt in her eyes. This was no rich young widow weeping for form's sake.

They discussed the estate and its workers as the great house loomed into view. Lucian was impressed again by Marissa's depth of knowledge of the families at Radwinter: who was related to whom, who had a daughter in service in London, which of the pensioners suffered from arthritis and needed help in his garden…

'If you want to know more about sheep husbandry, then Reuben Childs is your man; he knows all about it. I imagine that sheep are not common in the West Indies? He is Mary's grandfather; she is my maid… Oh, look, another carriage. Perhaps it is Miss Venables arrived at last! Poor thing, what a cold and long journey she must have endured.'

It was indeed her spinster cousin Jane, daughter of her father's elder sister, who had made a most regrettable marriage to an impoverished curate. She had compounded the offence this had given her brother by living happily in their rambling Cumbrian vicarage and producing a bevy of equally happy and unambitious children.

Despite Sir George Kempe refusing to acknowledge the existence of his sister or her family, Miss Jane, the eldest of five girls, had written to congratulate her young cousin on her marriage and they had fallen into the habit of exchanging greetings on birthdays and at Christmas. Miss Venables, in her early forties, had been earning her own modest living as a governess, but had confessed to Marissa that she did not find it a congenial existence and was hoping to find a position as a companion.

Marissa's first action, once the immediate shock of the Earl's accident had died away, had been to write to Miss Venables urging her to join her and enclosing a bank draft to hire a post chaise and postilions.

Miss Venables was standing in the front hall as Marissa and Lucian arrived. Her modest pelisse and bonnet were matched by the few items of luggage which stood beside her, yet she did not appear overawed by the splendour of her surroundings, which she was regarding quizzically, nor by the host of superior servants who were bustling around her.

Marissa hurried forward, her hand outstretched in welcome. 'Cousin Jane! How very glad I am to meet you. I do hope you have not had too fatiguing a journey! Please, let me make you known to my husband's cousin. My lord, Miss Venables, who has so kindly hurried to support me. Cousin Jane, the Earl of Radwinter.'

Miss Jane's thin eyebrows rose a further fraction as she returned his lordship's bow with a demure curtsey. She might be a spinster of forty-two summers, but that did not dull her discernment of good looks or breeding, and the Earl had both in abundance.

'Shall we go up to your rooms, Cousin?' Marissa enquired as the footmen carried the luggage out of the hall. 'Luncheon will be in about an hour, but I am sure you would like a cup of tea to warm you.'

As soon as they were alone in Miss Venables's rooms, Marissa turned a look of glowing gratitude upon the other woman. 'I cannot express how much I am obliged to you for coming to support me in such haste! I do hope it did not cause any inconvenience to your employers.'

'I had already given them notice,' Jane replied, removing her pelisse. 'For, although I loved their children, I could scarcely tolerate the parents. Your letter could not have come at a more apposite moment, my dear Lady Southwood...'

Marissa crossed and impulsively took her hands. 'You must call me Marissa, for I hope and believe we shall be good friends.' She found her fingers gripped warmly in response.

'I do believe it too, Marissa.' Miss Venables, a shrewd judge of character, had liked her young cousin on sight. But there was something very wrong. Something that transcended the shock of recent bereavement. She could sense it, but now was not the time to probe.

Mary came in and dropped a curtsey. 'Shall I unpack now, ma'am? James has put the tea tray in your parlour, my lady.'

'Thank you, Mary.' Marissa turned to her cousin. 'Mary will see to your needs until we can find a suitable girl of your own. Now, let us go down to my sitting room—the fire should be well alight by now.'

Seated either side of the hearth, with Gyp curled up on Miss Venables's feet, they found themselves slipping into an easy conversation as though they had known each other for years.

'You are honoured indeed by Gyp's attentions as footwarmer! He is normally most wary of strangers. Although perhaps he is mellowing, for he likes his lordship too.'

'One can quite see why,' responded Miss Venables. 'From the little I saw of him just now he seems to be a gentleman whose manners and appearance are such as to be universally appealing.'

She sipped her tea, then, looking up, caught Marissa's eye and was intrigued to see the young woman blush. That was interesting: Marissa did not strike her as a person who could shrug off the loss of a husband, even one so much older, in order to flirt with an attractive man.

'Why, I declare this fire is almost too warm,' Marissa murmured, pushing her chair back and fanning her warm cheeks.

'It must be disconcerting to have a stranger, however amiable, in the place of your husband,' Miss Venables observed. 'And presumably his lordship will be bringing his wife here as soon as possible. Has she remained in Jamaica?'

'Lord Southwood is not married, but he does have a young sister who has travelled to London with him. He has asked if I will be willing to have her live with us while he returns to the West Indies to settle his affairs, for he expects to be away for quite some time.' Marissa realised that her original letter to Miss Venables had been of the briefest, and added, 'I did not explain when I wrote, but I am moving to the Dower House in the grounds as soon as possible.'

Miss Venables placed her cup on the table before replying calmly, 'It will be most pleasant to have a young person with us, I am sure. But will you not regret leaving your home? It is truly...er... magnificent.'

'How tactfully you put it, dear Jane!' Marissa laughed. 'Since you ask me, I will answer you candidly: I hate this mausoleum. It is cold, impersonal, and has never felt like my home. I do hope you will like the Dower House as I do. His lordship has said I may redecorate it as I wish, but it is like this room: comfortable and a touch faded, warm and just big enough.'

'I like it already, my dear.'

There was a tap at the door and Whiting entered. 'Luncheon is served, my lady.'

Lucian got to his feet as the ladies entered. The conversation was general as soup was served and replaced by a platter of cheese and cold meats. Then he turned to Marissa. 'I trust it will not be inconvenient, Lady Southwood, but with the weather turning milder I thought it would be as well to leave for London after this meal. I should reach Downham Market before it is too dark. I will put up at the King's Head there, rest the horses and push on first thing.'

'Your sister will be so pleased to see you, my lord,' Miss Venables remarked. 'I collect that she is rather a young lady? To be in a strange city, even with friends, can be unsettling.'

'Indeed, ma'am,' Lucian rejoined blandly, although the person to be unsettled was most likely to be Mrs Montfort, charged with keeping control of an impetuous young lady who was all agog to explore Town when she should have been choosing mourning gowns.

Marissa listened to the conversation with something approaching dismay. Why had Lucian not mentioned his intention to leave today? Had her outburst of emotion repelled him? He had behaved with great tact and kindness at the time, but, like all men, would find such displays distasteful. Of course she had known he was going up to Town to fetch Nicole, but somehow she had not expected it to be so sudden. And she had not expected to feel so bereft.

Doubtless it was because she was so used to having a man in charge of affairs: she would soon become accustomed to his absence when he left for Jamaica. Her little household of ladies would by then be well ensconced in the Dower House and she would be so busy she would not notice.

After luncheon Miss Jane declared her intention to rest a little in her room, and bade farewell to his lordship. They exchanged a few words about the route and Marissa drifted across to the windows, gazing out over the grey, dripping parkland which echoed her mood so well. She did not want Lucian to go! It was so strange to feel like this: always before she had been happy to be left alone, left to her own thoughts and devices.

As the door closed behind Miss Venables Marissa turned, a bright smile on her lips, her hand outstretched. 'Well, I trust you have a safe journey, my lord. Please do everything in your power to assure your sister of the warm welcome that awaits her here.'

'You are very formal, Marissa,' he said with a twinkle in his eyes. 'But I will give Nicci your message.' He took her hand in his firm, warm grasp and bent to give her a cousinly salute on the cheek.

The soft, satiny skin seemed to quiver at the touch of his lips; the scent of her filled his nostrils and he heard her sharp intake of breath. Neither knew which of them moved, but suddenly she was in his arms and his lips had fastened on her mouth in a deep kiss that held a wordless question. Marissa responded, her hands grasping his lapels to draw him deeper in, her senses drowning in the realisation of his strength, his warmth, his power.

And then he broke away, his face darkened with anger, his fist slamming hard down onto the dining table sending the china jumping and a fork bouncing onto the floor.

'Damn it! I must have lost my senses!' And he was gone, the heavy door slamming behind him, cutting off the sound of his booted feet on the boards.

Chapter Four

'I do think we could begin to move into half-mourning now, my dear,' Miss Venables remarked as she buttered her breakfast roll. 'It has been thirteen months, after all, since the third Earl's sad demise. This lovely weather makes one think of summer and light gowns—'

'And here we sit like three moulting crows in our sad blacks!' Nicci interrupted her, springing to her feet and pulling back the drapes at the breakfast room window even farther, to let the sunshine stream in.

'Nicci, dear,' Miss Venables protested, although more out of habit than any real expectation of being heeded. Thirteen months in the company of Miss Southwood had left both Marissa and Jane inordinately fond of the young woman, but still struggling to tame the natural high spirits which her unconventional upbringing had fostered.

Nicci was charming, polite and warmly affectionate, but also headstrong, outspoken and still struggling with the social *mores* of English country society. Fresh, pretty, blonde and spirited, she was a favourite with the daughters of the surrounding gentry and had a coterie of friends, all, like her, seventeen and on the verge of their come-out.

Constrained as they were by the rules of mourning, the ladies had spent a quiet year, only attending the most private gatherings. But time had still flown. The Dower House had been refurbished to their liking, and if pretty dress silks had been missing from their lives there had still been the excitement of choosing furnishing fabrics and arguing amiably over colour schemes.

'Is it this morning that you are joining the Vicar's daughters for your dancing class?' Marissa enquired, sipping her breakfast chocolate. Nicci was learning dance and deportment with the two Misses Woodruffe, the Vicar's daughters, and Miss Catherine Ollard, the Squire's youngest. Miss Venables had taken the rest of her education in hand, declaring Nicci to be woefully ignorant of most of the knowledge required of a fashionable young lady.

'Yes, but when I get back please may we write to the silk warehouse in Norwich for some samples of dress fabrics?'

Miss Venables watched Marissa as she laughingly agreed to write that very morning. What a difference a year had made to her dear cousin! In company Marissa was still grave, poised and reserved, but when they were alone the young widow allowed her warm, funny, caring nature to blossom and the house was often full of laughter. She never referred to her late husband unless she had to, and then only in the most formal terms. Miss Venables felt she understood that marriage no more now than she had at the beginning.

Occasionally she found Marissa deep in thought, a little smile playing wistfully round her lips, but as to the object of her musings, she could only guess.

'I think we could go as far as fawn, pearl-grey, violet...all with black edging, of course,' Marissa was saying as the door opened and Whiting entered with a salver.

'This morning's postal delivery, my lady.' He proffered the letters to Marissa, who began to sort through them.

'Aunt Augusta...yet another account...the oddest handwriting on this one...two for you, Jane dear. Nicci, here is one for you, a little battered from its travels.'

Nicci reached for the package eagerly. 'It is from Luc!' she cried joyfully, slitting the seals with her butter knife and tearing open the wrapper. 'He is coming home! Oh, Marissa, Jane—Luc is coming home at last!'

'Where was it posted my dear?' Jane enquired calmly. 'Do take care, you are getting butter on your cuffs.'

'When?' demanded Marissa abruptly. 'I mean... when was it posted?' For some reason her heart was beating erratically and she felt breathless. She pressed one hand to her bodice, briefly, as if the gesture would still the sudden turbulence in her breast.

'It was posted in Kingston, and he says he expects to be in London...' Nicci was scanning rapidly '...why, by this week!'

'My goodness!' Miss Venables sprang up, her napkin dropping unheeded at her feet. 'There will be so much to do at the Hall! All the rooms under

Holland covers and nothing aired! Matthews must
be apprised of this immediately... Marissa, my dear,
are you quite well?'

'Er...what?' Marissa pulled her scattered wits together and focused her attention on her cousin. 'Yes,
everything you say is eminently sensible, Jane. Perhaps we should ask the Whitings to lend a hand.
Matthews has managed admirably, but there is all
the difference in the world between Southwood Hall
without the family at home and what his lordship
will require.'

She got up gracefully, leaving her unopened letters unheeded on the table. 'Nicci, we will travel in
the gig with you and drop you at the Vicarage before
we call at the Hall. Pull the bell for Whiting, would
you, please, and then we must fetch our bonnets and
wraps and be off.'

Nicole, as usual, took up the reins of the gig, but
was soon relieved of them by Miss Venables. 'Really, my dear Nicci, you will have us in a ditch, and
that poor pony does not know whether it is coming
or going!'

'Oh, but I am so excited!' Nicci surrendered the
reins without demur, but sat jigging on the seat.
'Must I go to my class? How can I concentrate on
dancing and deportment when Luc may even now
be within sight of shore!'

'Even if he is landing in Bristol as we speak,'
replied Miss Venables repressively, 'it will still take
him at least three days to accomplish his journey.
And surely he will want to spend at least one day
in London on his way.'

'He would not!' Nicci wailed. 'He could not be
so cruel as not to come to me at once!'

Marissa sat silently listening to the interchange,
her feelings alternating between dread and excitement. She had spent the last year imagining the moment when Lucian would return, yet thirteen months
from their parting she was still no clearer as to what
she felt for him.

At night her lips burned with the guilty remembrance of his kisses.

But by day she remembered all too clearly the
anger in his voice and the sound of his fist crashing
onto the breakfast table when they parted. She had
behaved shamelessly, no better than a hussy, and she
had disgusted him.

It was in their nature that men had carnal desires,
but it was unthinkable that a woman of breeding
should exhibit the slightest passion, incite caresses,
offer warmth and passion in return. Her lord had
made it perfectly plain early in their marital relations
exactly what was required of her, and she had
learned quickly that any attempt on her part to
change that would be met with swift retribution.

Perhaps the passage of time had erased the memory of her behaviour from Lucian's mind. None the
less, she must guard against ever letting him see the
warm, passionate woman inside her well-modulated
exterior.

Still distracted by her thoughts, she was scarcely
aware that they were bowling briskly up the Vicarage drive. Miss Venables, who had an unexpectedly
dashing driving style, was thoroughly enjoying herself, her sallow cheeks tinged with pink and her eyes
shining.

A tall figure was walking slowly towards them,
and Jane drew up as they came abreast of him. 'Mr

Ashforde, good day to you! A lovely morning, is it not?'

The Honourable Reverend Crispin Ashforde was probably one of the most beautiful young men any of the ladies had ever seen. The second son of Viscount Bassingbourn had scandalised his noble papa by choosing the church over the army or government office, and was currently setting every susceptible heart in the surrounding parishes aflutter.

Black-haired, white-skinned, with a perfect classical profile, he looked as though he had stepped from a plinth in Southwood Hall. Yet Mr Ashforde's disposition was such that the patent adoration of young ladies was lost on him. Serious, studious— and, in Miss Venables's opinion, thoroughly boring—he was regarded by all the matchmaking mothers as a perfect catch. Nicole, however, possibly the least eligible female for an earnest cleric that could be imagined, had caught his attention. And she, dazzled by his looks and piqued by his serious nature, had fallen head over heels in love.

Miss Venables knew puppy love when she saw it and was tolerantly inclined to ignore it.

'My lady, Miss Venables, Miss Southwood.' Mr Ashforde raised his hat and bowed. 'A very clement morning, is it not? One is put in mind of the words of Horace in the *Odes,* is one not?'

'Frequently,' Miss Venables responded drily. 'But you must excuse us. Miss Southwood is already late for her class.'

'But wait!' Nicci was blushing prettily. 'We must tell Mr Ashforde our news!' She turned her radiant face to him and blurted out, 'My brother is expected home from the West Indies at any day.'

'What marvellous news! I shall look forward to calling upon him at the earliest opportunity,' Mr Ashforde assured her earnestly. 'Good morning, ladies.'

As Marissa and Jane regained the coast road the older woman sighed heavily. 'Oh, dear, I do believe the young idiot will be asking his lordship for Nicci's hand as soon as he sets foot over the threshold of the Hall. I fear the Earl cannot but be displeased with us for allowing such an attachment to develop.'

Marissa was startled at the thought that his lordship might think them at fault. 'But Mr Ashforde is not ineligible, Jane. After all, his father is Lord Bassingbourn, and although he is the second son I believe he has a not inconsiderable fortune from his late great-aunt. And he is such a nice young man, so gentle and serious.'

'My dear Marissa, you sound as if you approve! I had not felt any anxiety, assuming that it was a mere youthful flirtation. But I am made uneasy by the speed with which Mr Ashforde announced his intention to call. Nicci is far too young to think of marriage, and her upbringing has left her immature and sheltered from Society. You cannot wish her away on an earnest young curate, however well connected. She has her whole life before her. And,' she added tartly, 'you cannot wish her on him! What a dance she would lead him, poor boy.'

Marissa did not argue, but whatever Miss Venables said, she could not but feel that Mr Ashforde was a safe choice for Nicci. Her young cousin must never know what marriage to a sophisticated, demanding older man could bring. She would never allow Nicci to experience the heartache and the loneliness that such a disparity in ages and temperament would mean. She knew the girl must marry, but Marissa's heart was full of fear for her and she was determined to favour the curate's suit.

Miss Venables, noticing with concern her silence, and the ebb and flow of colour in her cousin's cheeks, reined in at the gates of the Hall. 'There is no necessity for you to be cooped up talking to Matthews about setting the house to rights. Why not walk down to the beach? It is a lovely morning and the sea air will do you good.' She expected Marissa to protest that it was her duty to see to the arrangements, but to her surprise her cousin nodded.

'Thank you, Jane. I will make my own way back to the Dower House in time for luncheon.'

Thinking about marriage had recalled all the early memories of her lord's courtship, if it could be described thus. The Earl had asked her to dance twice at Almack's, and at first she had been flattered that the eligible, wealthy and handsome Earl of Radwinter should show her such attention. But formal observance had been all he ever showed, and after two months of impersonal conversations when they met she had been stunned when her father informed her that he had accepted on her behalf an offer of marriage from the Earl. Marissa, as a dutiful daughter, had had no say in the matter, and in a matter of weeks had found herself the Countess of Radwinter.

An unseasonably warm breeze blew over the salt grazings on either side of the track. Marissa flicked back the fronts of her wool pelisse and strode out, the fresh air filling her lungs. Fortunately she had put on stout walking shoes, and after a few minutes the megrims had left her and she was filled with the promise of spring and the excitement of Lucian's return.

He would have forgotten that disgraceful encounter the day that he had left, she assured herself. He would settle at the Hall with Nicci and the estate would come to life once more. From his letters to Nicci she had a vivid picture of his life in Jamaica, of the warmth and the vibrancy, of his energy... And she and Jane would continue their comfortable life in the Dower House, gradually mixing more in Society as the mourning period came to an end.

The saltings were cut off from the sea by a ridge of old sand dunes, now covered in tufty grass and gorse bushes and crowned by a ridge of Corsican pines, bent and gnarled by the wind.

Marissa scrambled up the steep landward side, the sand slipping and shifting under her boots. She was panting by the time she gained the summit and stood there, one hand on the rough red bark of a tree, the other shading her eyes as she gazed out across the wide beach to the glitter of the sea beyond.

The dunes swept down in a low shallow slope to the beach, an almost irresistible invitation to run, to swoop down like a bird, free in the spring sunshine. Marissa cast a swift glance around, but there was no one in sight, not even a fishing boat. She untied her bonnet strings, unbuttoned her pelisse and set both under a gorse bush, and then, gathering up her skirts, she began to run down the long slope.

Almost immediately her foot caught in a twisting root, half covered by the shifting sands. She fell, rolling on the slippery turf. After one startled moment Marissa let her body go with the movement, eyes shut, rolling down the dune as she had seen small boys do many a time in this very spot.

Her eyes were tight shut, her hair shedding its pins, and sand was getting everywhere, but she did not care, laughing aloud with the sheer exhilaration of the sensation.

At last, with a gentle bump, she landed at the bottom, resting against a tree trunk. She lay panting on her back, her eyes still tightly shut, the vanilla scent of the gorse blossom filling her nostrils.

Her breathing steadied and she relaxed, the sunlight red through her closed lids. The picture of the broad, empty stretch of beach and sea filled her mind. Gradually a small incongruity dawned on her: there were no trees below the point where she had started to run…

Cautiously she opened her eyes and found herself looking at a pair of travel-stained leather boots. Her gaze moved upwards to take in buckskin breeches covering long, strong legs. Horrified, Marissa snapped her eyes shut, then, hardly daring to do so, she opened them again and looked up into the man's face.

It was Lucian. His eyes were vivid against a deep tan, his teeth showed in a wide, white grin of amusement. With perfect formality, as though he were meeting her in the drawing room, he bowed and said, 'Good morning, Lady Southwood. I trust I find you in good health.'

The lilting accent of the West Indies was back in his voice. Marissa's bones felt as though they were melting; she could not move, speak, could hardly breathe, so overwhelmed was she by his unexpected appearance. Somehow, in thirteen months, she had forgotten the sheer physical impact of his presence, the force of his personality.

Lucian's amused gaze was travelling down the length of her dark brown walking dress. Marissa could feel it was twisted tightly around her body, and from the feel of the breeze she realised with horror that her legs were exposed to the knee. She dared not look, but she had a horrible fear that her garters were showing.

She struggled to sit upright, knowing that the very action was causing her bosom to heave and the dress to cling more tightly.

'Allow me.' Warm hands grasped both of hers and Marissa was pulled to her feet in one easy motion.

'My lord…' She found her voice with an effort. 'Thank you. I lost my footing at the top of the dune. I could not stop…'

He smiled without speaking and Marissa's voice trailed away as she stood looking up at him. His hair was overlong again, shot through by the sun with gilt. Around his eyes the tiny laughter lines were paler against the tanned skin, and she noticed for the first time how his dark lashes were tipped with gold.

He must have set out that morning early, and in a hurry, for he had not shaved. She had to fight down the urge to trace the stubble above his upper lip with her forefinger to discover whether it was rough or soft to the touch.

Marissa felt as though she was enmeshed in a feverish dream. Even her feet felt trapped by the soft sand. With an effort she took a step away from him and stumbled.

'Are you hurt? Have you twisted your ankle?' He

was at her side again, one hand burning even through the twilled cotton of her sleeve.

'No…no… It is just this soft sand. My goodness,' she laughed shakily, 'I must look a regular fright. Whatever must you think of me?'

'I think you look utterly—' He broke off, the laughter gone from his eyes, his expression strangely intent.

Unable to cope with the silence, Marissa blurted out, 'What are you looking at?'

'You…' Then he laughed. 'And the twigs in your hair.'

'Oh, no!' All her awkwardness was forgotten as Marissa hastily ran her fingers through her dishevelled curls, realising that all the pins had fallen out in her headlong tumble. Twigs showered out and fine sand ran down her neck. With an impatient 'tut' Marissa brushed at her skirts, shaking what seemed to be a pound of sand out of her petticoats.

Tactfully Lucian turned his back, striding up the slope to rescue her bonnet and pelisse from the bush where she had left them. Flushed, but feeling more in command of herself, Marissa buttoned the pelisse and pulled on her bonnet, doing the best she could to bundle up her loose hair inside it.

Her fingers were on the bonnet strings when Lucian said, 'Stop.' She froze in obedience, not even asking why. He was close again, his eyes fixed on her face. 'You have sand on your cheekbone,' he murmured. 'Here, let me…'

Before she could raise her hand his fingertips were stroking the fine grains from her skin, gently brushing them away from her eyes. The warm, gentle touch hypnotised her into closing her eyes, and for a long moment she stood there, his fingers tracing the curves of her face.

Marissa turned her face into his hand, and in response his palm cupped her cheek. His breath whispered warmly on her mouth and she waited...

There was the thud of hooves on the turf and a rattle of carriage wheels. Marissa opened her eyes to find Lucian standing a good three strides away from her and a groom hastening around the edge of the dune where the track petered out onto the beach.

'My lady! Miss Venables sent me to tell you that— Oh, your lordship, I did not know you were here. Begging your pardon, my lord, Miss Venables was wishful of letting her ladyship know you had arrived, sir.'

'Yes, I saw her ladyship on the dunes and rode down to greet her.' Lucian turned to hand Marissa up into the gig and swung up onto his patiently waiting horse. 'I will ride with you,' he informed the groom as the gig moved off along the sandy track.

Marissa pulled herself together with a supreme effort and remarked, 'I am sorry we were so ill-prepared for you, my lord. Nicole received your letter this morning and we had not looked to see you for at least the next three days. Miss Venables is even now at the Hall putting in hand preparations for your arrival. Your sister, I am afraid, is at the Vicarage—at her dancing class.'

She felt she was prattling mindlessly, and was acutely conscious of the presence of the groom beside her. The man cleared his throat, 'Pardon me, my lady, but James has gone in the carriage to collect Miss Southwood: Miss Venables sent him off as soon as his lordship's baggage coach and carriage arrived.'

Miss Venables was once again rising to the occasion, Marissa thought with relief. She could be relied on to know exactly what to do under any set of circumstances, which, considering that she herself could hardly string two words together sensibly just at the moment, was a very good thing.

'Your journey was smooth I trust, my lord,' she enquired, finding her eyes fixed on his hands, strong and brown on the reins. Unaccountably she could not meet his eyes, the embarrassment of being caught out in her hoydenish behaviour almost paralysing her. She had intended meeting him graciously, assured in her new role as the Dowager, and instead had been discovered romping in a way which would have been inexcusable even for Nicci.

'I was fortunate with the winds and landed in Bristol a week ago. I can only assume that the ship bearing my letter was delayed.'

Marissa was all too well aware that men rarely considered the problems of domestic arrangements and all that was involved in making a great house ready for its master and could well believe it had not occurred to Lucian to write from Bristol. 'What a delightful surprise for Miss Southwood,' she said weakly.

Luc turned in the saddle, blue eyes creased in amusement. 'That is a very polite way of telling me I should have sent word from Bristol, and that I have caused the household a great deal of work,' he remarked. 'I have no doubt that I will be due a severe scold from Miss Venables! Tell me, how should I best make my apologies?' His smile was broad and white and quite shameless.

Marissa, very conscious of the groom beside her, was constrained in her reply. 'Southwood Hall stands ready for your lordship whenever you choose to arrive. But I can only apologise that the London house was so unprepared. As you will recall, Matthews is here at the Hall, and there is only a skeleton staff left in Town.'

'No matter. I had no intention of setting everyone in a bustle for one night: I stayed at Fenton's Hotel and was perfectly comfortable.'

Marissa was taken aback by such consideration for the servants. Her late husband would have expected to be able to walk into any of his establishments at any hour of the day and night and find all in perfect readiness and order.

'And how is my sister? Has she led you a merry dance this past year? From her letters I have lived in daily expectation of a communication from you desiring me to remove her from your household immediately.'

The groom repressed a snort with great difficulty, bending over the reins to hide his broad grin. Miss Southwood was a rare handful, not but that she wasn't a nice young lady it was a pleasure to serve. Always a smile and 'please' and 'thank you'. But she was full of mischief and he was just glad she wasn't *his* sister!

'It has been a pleasure to have her with us,' Marissa said repressively. What had Nicci been writing? 'We have been living very quietly, of course: I can only hope dear Nicole has not been intolerably bored.'

Luc did not reply, merely smiled, reflecting that Nicci's letters had indeed shown all the frustration to be expected from a lively young woman suddenly placed with strangers in a cold, new world of formality. But his sister had soon stopped bemoaning her life, and gradually a picture of a happy trio of ladies had emerged. It had intrigued him to see Marissa through his sister's innocent eyes. Nicci had written a few months ago:

> *I love her very much. She is kind and funny, but there is a great sadness at the heart of her which I do not understand. She never speaks of his late lordship, but it cannot be that, surely, for he was very old...*

Luc had smiled wryly at the thought that a man of forty-five could be considered 'very old' and could only assume his sister saw him, seventeen years younger than the earl, as middle-aged.

'There's Miss Southwood now, ma'am,' the groom observed, pointing to the coast road where a small carriage had just turned out of the Vicarage drive.

'My lord, please ride to meet your sister; I will join you at the Hall.'

Lucian needed no further prompting. He urged the horse into a brisk canter and had soon intercepted the carriage. Even at that distance Marissa could hear Nicci's shrieks of delight as the girl came tumbling out of the carriage in a flurry of petticoats and flung herself at her brother's horse.

Luc had dismounted by the time Marissa's gig came up with them, and was laughingly attempting to disentangle Nicci's arms from around his neck before she throttled him. The narrow road was completely blocked by horse, carriage and gig, but the arrival of a carter with a timber wagon soon dispersed the reunion.

They formed quite a procession on the way back to the Hall, Nicci hanging out of the carriage window animatedly bombarding her brother, who rode alongside, with questions. Marissa shuddered with despair at the girl's unrestrained behaviour but knew that there was no hope of curbing it in her present high state of excitement.

The baggage coach and the travelling carriage were pulling away from the front of the Hall as they drew up, but the great doors stood open and the scene glimpsed through them resembled nothing so much as a disturbed anthill.

Miss Venables, flanked by Matthews, stood in the centre of activity, directing footmen and maidservants as they scurried to disperse the piles of baggage which stood heaped around. Marissa, following Lucian and Nicci up the steps, became aware also of Whiting, who was regarding two male strangers with as near to horror on his well-schooled countenance as she had ever seen.

A dapper individual guarding a dressing case was doubtless his lordship's valet, but it was his companion who was causing Whiting's discomfiture.

Marissa was not surprised. The man was evidently, from his immaculate clothing, an upper servant, but the correctness of his dress was totally belied by his features. Built like a prizefighter, he was standing with folded arms, the upper muscles straining the cloth. His face, tanned like leather, was crossed by a wicked scar which bisected his eyebrow from temple to cheekbone leaving a slash as white as his cropped hair. Standing in the hallway surrounded by classical perfection and the scurrying English servants he appeared foreign, dangerous and utterly out of place. In fact the only place where Marissa could envisage him looking at home was on the deck of a pirate ship.

Nicci, spotting him, dropped her brother's arm and with a shriek of 'Jackson!' threw herself into his arms to be enveloped in a bear-like hug. Miss Venables's eyebrows rose almost to her hairline at this unseemly and inexplicable behaviour, but before she could protest Nicci was set firmly back on her feet and the man was admonishing her in a surprisingly cultured voice. 'Lady Nicci, please conduct yourself with decorum. What will Miss Venables be thinking of you?'

To almost universal amazement Nicci lowered her eyes and said meekly, 'Yes, Jackson, but I am so very pleased to see you, you know.'

'Well, you can best show that by helping Miss Venables,' the man replied repressively, but with a twinkle in his grey eyes.

Jane Venables crossed the chequerboard tiles to greet the Earl. 'My lord, welcome home to Southwood. It is a great pleasure to have you back amongst us.'

'Thank you, Miss Venables.' He smiled down at her over their clasped hands. 'I must apologise for my lack of forethought in advising you of my arrival, but I see that the usual high standards here have not slipped.' He nodded pleasantly at Matthews and Mr and Mrs Whiting. 'Matthews, I would like a word with you this evening after dinner about the future domestic arrangements, meanwhile Jackson and Laurent will accompany me to my suite.'

'Very good, my lord.' Matthews bowed. 'A cold collation is set out in the small dining room if you and the ladies would care to partake.'

'Lady Southwood, if you would excuse me for half an hour to remove the dust of the road from my clothing, I will join you shortly.' Lucian bowed and was gone, his two servants at his heels.

Alone in the dining room, with the hubbub of the hall shut out, Nicci burst out, 'Oh, I am so pleased that Luc brought Jackson with him. I was so afraid he would leave him to look after the Jamaica estates.'

Miss Venables fixed her with a gimlet stare from her position in one of the window seats. 'And just who is this Jackson, if I may enquire?'

'Why, our butler, of course!' Nicci exclaimed in surprise. 'But he is much more than that! He has been with us for years, originally as captain of one of my father's schooners. But no one is quite sure where he came from—he will never speak of it. And then when Luc was seventeen he saved his life when the schooner was attacked by privateers. Jackson was terribly injured, almost given up for dead, but Luc brought him back home and he has been our butler ever since old Peters had his heart attack. Why,' she added disingenuously, 'Jackson has almost brought me up. He is terribly strict, you know.'

Miss Venables shuddered. 'I am not reassured. No doubt this Jackson is a good man, in his rough way, but he is hardly suitable as butler in a great house.'

'Wait and see! You will get used to him,' Nicci promised airily. 'Oh, where is Luc? I am starving!'

'Nicole, dear, ladies do not speak of their appetite; it is most improper.' Jane appeared to become aware of Marissa's appearance for the first time. 'Why do you not remove your bonnet and pelisse, Marissa?'

Reluctantly Marissa did so, sending her hair tumbling onto her shoulders and releasing a small shower of fine sand onto the polished boards.

'Marissa! What have you been doing?'

'Rolling in the sand by the look of it,' Nicci said gleefully. 'Luc did not see you, did he, Marissa?'

'I tripped,' she replied with uncharacteristic shortness. 'I must go and tidy myself before luncheon.'

She was very conscious of two pairs of eyes— one censorious, one gleeful, and both speculative— as she left the room, and was still feeling flustered when she returned, her hair brushed and pinned and her face washed.

Luc arrived at the door as she did. He was freshly shaven and dressed in clean riding clothes. Marissa kept her eyes down as he opened the door for her and ushered her to her place at table.

They all ate hungrily, helping themselves from the cold meats spread out before them. The meal was punctuated by the tale of Luc's journey and the many people he had brought messages from for his sister. Marissa watched him from under her lashes, her heart unaccountably beating faster in his presence. He seemed to bring warmth and energy with him and to infect everyone around him with his vitality. It was as though the warm Caribbean sea and the hot sands were just outside this chilly mausoleum of a house.

'You must have a dance, to celebrate your return,' Nicci was suggesting as Marissa came back to herself with a start.

Miss Venables coughed warningly, and with a swift look at Marissa Lucian turned to his sister. 'I do not think that would be appropriate Nicci: we are still in mourning.'

Nicci bit her lip in mortification, instantly catching his suggestion that she might be upsetting the widow. 'Oh, I am sorry, Marissa. That was very thoughtless of me. I did not mean...'

Marissa leaned across the table and touched her hand. 'Do not worry, Nicci, I know what you meant. But it would be a pity indeed if our neighbours did not have the opportunity to meet the Earl as soon as possible. I do not think a small dinner party would be out of place, if his lordship consents.'

'A capital idea,' Luc agreed, sitting back and smiling at all three ladies. 'How long would it take to arrange such a dinner, and—' he grinned at Nicci '—order your new gowns?'

Chapter Five

Laurent smoothed an imaginary wrinkle from the dark blue superfine cloth across his master's shoulders, then stood back and viewed the finished effect critically.

'For heaven's sake, man,' Luc protested as the valet made another dart forward with the clothes brush. 'We have been at this long enough; the guests will be here shortly.' He grimaced down at his legs. 'Knee breeches! Anyone would think we were in London instead of the depths of Norfolk.'

'It is *à la mode,* my lord,' Laurent demurred. 'It is expected, and, after all, it will be a social event spoken of for months afterwards in the neighbourhood.' He gave a final, unnecessary polish to his lordship's shoe buckles and added gloomily, 'After all, what else is there to talk of in this place which *le bon Dieu* has undoubtedly forsaken?'

Lucian fixed him with a stern eye. 'If I have to learn to be a respectable earl, then you must learn to be a respectable valet, Laurent.'

'Pah!' The man picked up his lordship's discarded linen and stalked towards the door. 'I will be respectable, my lord, but do not demand that I like this place. I will die of the pneumonia, *sans doute,* if I do not first expire from the food.'

Luc grinned at his own reflection in the glass. The man had been with him for years: he had tried to encourage him to stay in Jamaica, knowing he would hate England, but the valet had insisted that his place was at his master's side, although it would be the death of him.

Not that Luc couldn't see his point: he too yearned for the warmth, not just of the weather, but of the people. The social *mores* of English society came hard when one had lived a life characterised by informality, driven by the climate and the dictates of nature. And he missed the Caribbean sea: the cold, grey waves washing against the coast here bore no resemblance to the inviting blue depths of Jamaican waters, filled with fish as bright as jewels.

There was little point in dwelling on all that: it was past, and his new life as the fourth Earl of Radwinter was waiting for him. Tonight's soirée was his first foray into county Society, and for the sake of Nicci's future—and his own—he had to make it a success.

Lucian strolled over to the window, resisting the urge to run one finger under his collar, resenting the control that the formal evening suit imposed. But Marissa would be expecting to entertain in this style and he could not let her down. He had not failed to notice the air of rigidly suppressed excitement under her perfect poise. Like a cat's fur in a thunderstorm, her mass of hair seemed to crackle with energy under the restraint of its pins. It reminded him of the night she had found him in the Long Gallery: the one long hair that had curled itself around his finger like a living thing was still where he had placed it, between the pages of his pocketbook.

A mile away across the park Marissa too was completing her toilette. Seated in front of her dressing table mirror, she watched Mary's deft fingers capture, twist and pin up her hair. On an impulse Marissa reached up and teased out the short curls around her hairline.

'Oh, that *is* pretty, my lady!' Mary exclaimed in astonishment. Never had she known the Dowager permit the slightest curl to escape from its tight chignon, but it well became her, emphasising her cheekbones and softening the curve of her brow.

'Yes…that will do,' Marissa decided, rather surprised at her own reflection. 'Now, the diamond set, I think, Mary.' The maid fastened the diamond necklace around her mistress's neck, then began to secure the coiled hair on her crown with matching combs. Marissa adjusted the cold stones on her throat, then lifted the drop earrings and fastened them to her lobes. She had never particularly cared for the set, although her husband had insisted she wear it often. Now, against the severity of black silk, the stones sparked with a hot fire she had never seen before.

Mary helped her button her shoulder-length white kid gloves, then clasped a diamond bracelet around her wrist. As she stood Mary bent to tweak out the heavy flounce around the hem, then puffed up the little sleeves before draping a white silk stole with a long fringe over Marissa's elbows.

There was a knock on the door and Miss Venables entered, resplendent in deep plum satin, two spots of colour staining her cheeks. 'My dear, you look lovely! The carriage is here, and we must be off, for it is six o'clock and we promised his lordship that we would be there to help him receive.'

The shadows were lengthening in the park as the barouche pulled up at the front door. Marissa was suddenly seized by the odd sensation of arriving as a guest at what, until so recently, had been her own house. She was looking forward to this dinner party, for it would be the first where she would not have to sit in constant fear that some detail would be found wanting, a shortcoming that would be visited upon her later by her lord. It was not the only reason for her anticipation, but it was the only one that she was prepared to acknowledge to herself.

The door was opened by Jackson, dignified in evening black, but still managing to look dangerously out of place. He bowed the ladies in, handed their cloaks to a footman, and conducted them past a small string ensemble who were tuning up on the landing and into the Salon.

'Lady Southwood, Miss Venables, my lord.'

Lucian felt his jaw drop and pulled himself together rapidly. For a moment he had not recognised the dazzling young woman in the doorway. He had seen Marissa virtually every day for the last fortnight, but she had always been the Marissa he had come to know: poised, rigidly groomed, controlled, friendly yet distant.

But this was a different woman. Her hair sparkled in the candlelight, her skin, always so white, seemed creamy against the diamonds, and with a shock he realised that she was not much older than his sister.

Marissa saw Lucian's admiration in his face and

her eyes sparked green with pure pleasure. For the first time she felt the sensation of being admired without any obligation to anyone else. She was not in the marriage mart, obedient to her father; she was not presenting herself as an adornment of her husband. She was herself, and she was revelling in it.

Nicole, who was wearing a pretty gown of midnight-blue appropriate to a young lady who was not yet out, gasped audibly. 'Oh, Marissa, how pretty you look!' She dashed over, caught Marissa's hands in hers and turned to implore of her brother, 'Do you not think Marissa looks pretty, Luc?'

'No, I do not,' he drawled, his eyes on Marissa. His sister gasped indignantly, but before she could protest he took the wind out of her sails. 'I think she looks beautiful.' Marissa blushed rosily, her heart suddenly beating more quickly, and she could only be relieved when he turned to her friend. 'Miss Venables, may I be so bold as to compliment you on the elegance of your gown?'

Miss Venables was responding with a gracious inclination of the head as Jackson entered and announced, 'There is a carriage approaching, my lord.'

Hastily the party assembled themselves to receive their guests and before long the Salon was alive with the sound of chattering voices and the swish of silk.

When they had constructed the guest list Marissa had been apologetic about the lack of distinguished company. 'With the start of the Season so close our more fashionable neighbours are up in Town,' she had explained. 'The Blackwoods, the Exeters... I wonder if the Scotts have left yet...'

In the end the guest list had included the local squirearchy and professional people, with a touch of aristocratic eccentricity in the form of Lady Augusta, who now had Sir Henry Ollard trapped against the mantelpiece and was berating him over the state of his coverts.

'How you expect to enjoy a decent run if you cannot provide the cover for the foxes I do not know!' Sir Henry, a mild man, was protesting faintly that his keepers were doing their best, but was making no headway.

Lady Ollard, making polite conversation with Mr and Mrs French, raised her eyebrows but passed no comment, being well used to Lady Augusta. The Frenches, more recent arrivals on the local scene, tended to start nervously when Lady Augusta approached them. Mrs French, having moved from the bustling heart of the City, where her husband had made a substantial fortune, was finding it difficult to adjust to an entirely new social scene.

Her sons Stephen and James, however, found the country perfectly palatable: still at the age where country sports held more appeal than the company of young ladies, they spent their days with their new friends and were dragged reluctantly to parties.

Miss Catherine Ollard was attempting, not very successfully, to engage Stephen in conversation, but as both he and his brother were more interested in Mr Ashforde's description of a recent shooting trip her efforts were wasted. The Misses Woodruffe, probably the only young ladies in the neighbourhood who remained uncaptivated by Mr Ashforde's startling good looks, were chattering to Nicci about clothes, but she was only half listening, her shining eyes fixed on the perfect classical profile of the young curate.

Lucian, politely extracting himself from a discussion of a local political scandal which was engrossing Dr Robertson, Mr Hope and Miss Venables, strolled across to where Marissa was standing by herself, watching the group of young people.

'And what is my little sister up to now?' he enquired softly.

'Oh, nothing.' Marissa smiled tolerantly, her focus still on Mr Ashforde. 'She is enjoying the party, which is only natural. I am afraid it has been so very dull for her at the Dower House this past year, and she really has been very good.'

The child deserves a diversion, she thought, and Mr Ashforde, so kind, so gentle, might prove to be more than that in time. Her lips curved in a soft smile and Luc, following the direction of her gaze, frowned suddenly. He said abruptly, 'Is that the curate? What's his name…Ashton?'

'Ashforde,' Marissa corrected. 'He is very much a favourite hereabouts, quite an embellishment to local Society. He is the second son of Viscount Bassingbourn, but so unlike his elder brother. Mr Ashforde is dedicated to his calling, and so erudite.'

'Popinjay!'

'Oh, no, never that! I admit his quite extraordinary good looks draw more attention to him than he would wish.'

'You think him good-looking, then?' Luc eyed the white skin, classical features and elegant figure of the curate with distaste and an uneasy feeling that with his black hair and cultured manners Mr Ashforde must offer a reflection of the late Earl to a woman who was still mourning her husband.

Marissa turned to Luc in surprise. 'Good-looking?

Why, certainly, he is perhaps the most handsome man I have ever seen: he could take his place on a pedestal here in the sculpture gallery and rival Adonis.' Luc's expression mystified her. What had Mr Ashforde done to displease him so? It was so much accepted that Mr Ashforde combined excellent manners with physical perfection that it seemed quite natural to discuss him as one would any other beautiful phenomenon. Not finding herself attracted to the curate, it did not occur to Marissa to be self-conscious in the way in which she discussed him with Luc.

Luc still seemed strangely out of humour to Marissa's acute eye when Jackson announced that dinner was served. Luc offered Lady Augusta his arm and Marissa found Sir Henry, who would sit at her right hand. Gradually the party sorted themselves out and processed past the string quartet into the Small Dining Chamber, a cavernous room only slightly less imposing than the Grand Dining Chamber. Luc, having viewed the larger room, had announced flatly that he would not use it, and had instructed Jackson to move the best silver to the Small Chamber.

Huge fires blazed at either end of the room, despite the mild weather outside, and a myriad of candles reflected off the polished mahogany and massed silver. Marissa took her place at the foot of the table, facing the new Earl. She had protested when he had asked her to act as hostess, but Nicci was not yet out and Luc had flatly vetoed her suggestion that he ask Lady Augusta to preside.

Luc's eyes were on Marissa as he listened to a lecture from Lady Augusta on the probable shortcomings of his cook. Judging by the array of dishes that the servants were even now bearing in, Mrs Wood could stand up to the worst criticisms from her ladyship.

Marissa could not help herself worrying about the arrangements, but relaxed as the dishes were laid out. Stuffed soles, a fricassee of veal, chickens, curry of rabbits, a vegetable pudding, sweetbreads, buttered lobster and a fat goose created a cornucopia of local fare which Marissa hoped would show Luc the best that his estate could offer.

She met Jackson's eye and saw a glimmer of satisfaction in their dark depths. The footmen were removing covers and pouring wine. The volume of conversation began to rise and with a sigh of relief she smiled down the length of the table at Luc. At that distance the likeness to her late husband disappeared; all she was aware of was Luc's mane of blond hair, caught by the late evening sun, the relaxed grace of his body, the broad set of his shoulders. Despite the formal evening clothes he still managed to radiate a dangerous sense of exoticism.

And yet she felt safe with him. If it had been Charles in that seat she would have been picking at her food, her stomach churning with nervous anticipation of an error, a slip by the servants which would mar his expectations of perfection.

Luc caught the smile, read the pure, uncomplicated pleasure in it and his irrational jealousy and bad humour vanished. Of course she was not hankering after that young puppy of a curate! Nor, for the first time since he had known her, did she seem trapped in some sad memory.

His attention was distracted momentarily by the

giggles of the Vicar's daughters and Miss Ollard. They, and Nicci, seemed so much younger than Marissa. He had resigned himself to the thought that sooner or later he was going to have to go up to London, brave the Marriage Mart and find some suitable young lady to be mistress of Southwood, mother to his heir.

He looked again at Marissa, almost luminous at the other end of the table, her skin glowing in the candlelight, the diamonds glinting at her throat and in her dark hair. Why had he not thought of her before? There was no bar to marriage with a cousin's widow. She was beautiful, intelligent, mature beyond her years, well used to running a large establishment. Nicci loved her, that much was plain. And she was not averse to him—when he had kissed her it had been as though a fire had kindled into life.

Yes…why not indeed? Why not broach it this evening after the guests had departed?

Marissa was too far away to read his expression, but she noticed his sudden stillness, the intensity with which he was gazing at her, then he seemed to recollect himself and began to talk to Lady Ollard on his left-hand side.

It was time she stopped daydreaming and paid attention to her guests, Marissa chided herself. She listened intently to Mr Woodruffe's knowledgeable suggestions for plants for her refurbished gardens at the Dower House, charming him with the graceful deference she showed to his experience.

'Now roses are always safe on these heavy soils, and of course you are sheltered from the worst of the winds in that dip. Lavender, now, might suffer, although if you get your gardener to dig in plenty of gravel that will stop any root-rot…'

He was well away, needing only occasional nods and murmurs of encouragement. Marissa glanced down the table and frowned slightly to see Nicci's heightened colour. Her laugh was becoming rather shrill and she had been talking to Crispin Ashforde almost exclusively. It would never do for her to be setting her cap at him too obviously, especially when Lucian seemed disinclined to like the young man. She would have to do something to change that opinion, for she was still convinced that the curate would be the ideal husband for Nicci.

The servants were removing dishes, re-laying the table with an array of sweetmeats and desserts. Syllabubs, jellies, a confection reproducing the frankly hideous fountain in the West Court in sugar, baskets of pastries and custards were set before them. One of the footmen lifted the heavy epergne loaded with fruit from the sideboard to place in the centre of the table. It was off balance, and another man hurried to help him, but before he could do so the top layer of fruit spilt over, thudding onto the table and scattering between the chair-legs.

Footmen scrambled for the fruit, Jackson seized the epergne and set it firmly on the table and Luc laughed out loud. The guests, cheerfully fielding fruit as it rolled in their direction, joined in.

Still laughing, Luc looked down the table and saw Marissa, white as a ghost, hands gripped onto the arms of her chair, her expression one of stricken horror. He had seen that look before, on the face of a servant expecting to be whipped by a neighbour of his who was notorious for his brutality. Even as that impossible comparison came into his head she had collected herself and was apologising graciously to the guests on either side of her.

The old Marissa was back, the shield of social propriety was in place, and the spontaneity and joy he had seen on her face had utterly vanished. The meal seemed to drag on, and throughout the dessert course he noticed she toyed with three grapes on her plate and never lifted a mouthful to her lips.

Luc rubbed his temples as he cudgelled his brain for an explanation of the dramatic change in Marissa's mood. He was still puzzled as she rose, catching the eye of Lady Augusta, and led the ladies out, leaving the gentlemen to their port.

Marissa struggled to regain her composure as they entered the Salon. Mechanically she encouraged Lady Augusta in her efforts to set up a four for whist, and found music for the young ladies to play later.

Was she never to be free of Charles? Would her husband always haunt her, dominating her in death as he had in life? She shivered as she remembered what had always followed any domestic transgression for which he held her responsible. The late Earl had believed that physical punishment was necessary to discipline servants, hounds and his wife. He would never show the slightest sign of displeasure in public: chastisement belonged in the bedchamber...

Half an hour later, when Luc led the gentlemen back in to join the ladies, the whist table was already established and Miss Catherine Ollard was turning over the pile of music sheets on the piano, rather too obviously hoping that she would be asked to perform.

'Will you not play for us, Miss Ollard?' Marissa asked, seeing the young girl's eagerness.

'Oh, well, that is, I do not know if my playing is... Oh, well, if you insist, Lady Southwood.' She sat at the piano, settling her skirts and opening a volume of ballads on the music rest before her.

The younger Mr French came forward with alacrity. 'May I turn for you, Miss Ollard?'

The Woodruffe sisters raised their eyebrows at each other, but sat politely to listen, and the other gentlemen disposed themselves about the room.

Luc came and sat next to Marissa on one of the pair of sofas flanking the fireplace. He stretched out his long legs, folded his arms and whispered out of the corner of his mouth, 'Did you *have* to do that?'

He was rather too close for convention, the sleeve of his coat almost touching her gloved arm. Marissa felt the warmth of him, smelled the sandalwood cologne he wore and felt her heart begin to thump. Somehow she managed to give him a reproving stare and whisper, 'Shh!'

Under cover of the opening bars he leaned closer and whispered in return, 'You look even more magnificent when you frown at me!'

'Do not be ridiculous!' She could feel the colour rising up her throat and turned her head away. Why he should be flirting with her she could not imagine, but that was undoubtedly what he was doing. She might never have been involved in flirtation before, but she could recognise it when it was happening!

'There is nothing ridiculous about it; you must

know how beautiful you look this evening.' His eyes rested appreciatively on her averted profile.

'I know no such thing!'

'Fishing for compliments, my lady?'

The sheer audacity of it brought her head round, her eyes sparking with indignation. 'My lord!'

'But no young lady appears at a social occasion with a new hairstyle unless she is well aware of how well it becomes her.'

She could hear the laughter in his whispered teasing and it only served to add to her indignation. 'Sir, I am not a *young lady.* I am a Dowager.'

'Surely the youngest and most beautiful in the land.' He broke off to applaud the end of the ballad. 'Well done, Miss Ollard, a very pretty air indeed! Will you not favour us with another?'

Miss Ollard flushed and began to rise from the pianoforte. 'You are very kind, my lord, but I believe it is time to make way for someone else. Or…Miss Woodruffe, if I were to play, will you not sing?'

Having restored peace with her friend, whose meaningful looks she had been only too well aware of, Miss Catherine struck up an Elizabethan love song. Miss Woodruffe warbled prettily, causing Luc to moan softly in anguish.

'Luc, you are impossible,' Marissa hissed, while maintaining an appreciative social smile. 'You will have to get used to this sort of thing.'

'Remind me to have the pianoforte chopped up for firewood,' he retorted, low-voiced.

Marissa could not help but smile. 'Miss Sophie Woodruffe plays the harp, and she often brings it with her.'

'Oh, my God!' He dropped his head into his hands in mock despair. 'Then I shall invest in a pair of earplugs at the earliest opportunity.' The air came to an end and before they could embark on another Luc was on his feet, leading the applause. 'Ladies, thank you, that was delightful; it almost moved me to tears.'

Neither young lady could work out why, but somehow it did not seem appropriate to continue playing, and at that moment Jackson forestalled any further entertainment by ushering in the footmen with the tea tray.

Marissa was dutifully circulating around the room, exchanging pleasantries with the guests, admiring Lady Augusta's winnings at the whist table, where they were playing for penny points, and congratulating the young ladies on their musical performance.

Seeing that the Earl was within earshot, she added wickedly, 'And I do hope you will bring your harp to the next soirée here, Miss Sophie. His lordship has just confided in me that it is quite his favourite instrument.' She looked him square in the eye, her face alight with laughter.

As he passed her he bent his head and whispered, '*Touché*, Marissa.' His eyes followed her slender, elegant form as she moved around the room, gracefully putting everyone at their ease, taking the opportunity to thank Jackson for the success of the arrangements as she passed him.

No, it would be no hardship being married to Marissa, and the contrast with the immature young girls only pointed up her obvious advantages. He would ask her to marry him tonight, find an opportunity to speak to her alone.

He found Sir Henry at his side, the older man also watching the Dowager Countess. 'Good to see her enjoying herself again,' the baronet observed. 'I've missed seeing her out riding, you know: damned fine seat on a horse. Of course your cousin would never permit her to ride with the hounds. Great stickler for decorum, the late Earl.'

Luc looked thoughtful. 'Tell me, Sir Henry, I am not familiar with the fine details of English social niceties yet, but would it be considered inappropriate for Lady Southwood to be seen riding at this stage in her mourning?'

'Good grief, no! It's been well over a year, has it not? Perfectly acceptable, and it seems a shame to deprive her of something she enjoys after all she has been through.'

Luc clapped his guest on the shoulder. 'Sound advice, Sir Henry. I am obliged to you.'

Marissa accepted a cup of tea from Jackson and went back to her place on the sofa. Luc, waving aside the offer of refreshment, joined her. 'Tell me, Marissa, do you miss riding?'

Taken aback, she exclaimed, 'Oh, yes, very much! I used to ride every day when the weather permitted.'

'Surely it would be acceptable for you to ride again now?'

'I suppose so…yes. I must think about buying a horse.'

'You must have had a horse. Is it not still in the stables here?'

'My lord preferred me to ride a variety of mounts,

depending on the occasion and the season.' With some constraint she added, 'My lord viewed a rider in the landscape as being part of the composition of the parkland.' Seeing his puzzlement, she expanded, 'In autumn, for example, against the backdrop of the newly ploughed fields and reddening foliage, I rode the red roan in a chestnut-brown habit. In winter, he wished me to ride in garnet-red on the grey.'

Her face was serious as she explained his lordship's detailed rules for creating a landscape almost Palladian in its perfection, in order to set off the house like a jewel in its box. Luc would have laughed out loud if he had not been so fearful of offending her. He had heard wherever he went murmurings of his late cousin's eccentricities, but had put them down to the whims of a dilettante rich enough to indulge his every desire. Now he was beginning to wonder if the third Earl had not been... unbalanced.

'That being so, I will send instructions to the stables that any mount you choose should be at your disposal.'

'Why, thank you, my lord! That would be wonderful. I shall so much look forward to that. I have missed my rides out about the estate. Oh, I see Lady Augusta waving; I believe she wishes to converse with me. Will you excuse me, please?'

Luc watched as Marissa crossed to where the older woman was now rising from the card table, ready, it seemed, to take her leave.

'I'll be leaving now, my dear. I can't get used to the French fashion of late dining; it plays havoc with my digestion. But I've had a splendid time, particularly when the footman dropped the fruit, eh?

Didn't get that sort of entertainment with stuffy old Charles!'

It was as though a bank of freezing fog had swept into the room. Marissa had forgotten that incident, and the memories it had evoked, the fear of her lord's cold, studied, anger. Yet here she was, surrounded by friends, admiration, laughter. It was madness to be afraid of Charles now; she was beyond his reach, and his retribution. She was free now, free to rebuild her own life, and she never need be in the power of another man again as long as she lived.

The guests had begun to leave. Marissa detached Nicci from a rather too intimate conversation with Mr Ashforde and the two of them joined Luc at the head of the staircase to see the guests off to their waiting carriages.

Marissa was still mulling over the words she had heard pass between the young couple as she had approached them. It had sounded suspiciously like the arrangement for a tryst, but when the curate had shaken hands with Nicci Marissa had been able to detect no trace of anything other than normal courtesy.

Miss Venables put a hand on Marissa's arm. 'Will you wait for me for a few minutes, my dear? I have just remembered that Mrs Wood promised to give me a chicken pie for Widow Smith down at the woodcutter's cottage, and if I take it now it will save me the extra journey tomorrow.'

Marissa smiled back at her. 'Of course, my dear Jane. Now, Nicci, you should be off to your bed.'

'Indeed, my lady,' Jackson concurred, coming up

behind them. 'You will get black circles under your eyes, Miss Nicci.'

Nicci sighed theatrically, but did as she was told, kissing Marissa affectionately before skipping off to recount the highlights of the evening to her patiently waiting maid.

Luc had descended the stairs for a last word with Sir Henry and was still below, talking to one of the footmen. Marissa took a deep breath and made a resolution: she would lay the ghost of her lord once and for all. She would stare that portrait in the face, exorcise her fear. She only had to convince herself: he was not coming back and had no power over her life any more.

In the Long Gallery all was still, quiet, dark. She set down the branch of candles she had snatched up from the corridor and for a long moment stared at the painted likeness over the door. There: it was nothing but pigment on canvas; that was all that remained of his cruelty and control.

'I am free of you, Charles,' she said out loud. 'There is nothing you can do to me…'

As she spoke the candle flames flickered in some draught, and the painted eyes glinted as if alive. Shadows chased across the thin mouth as though the lips were forming words: cold, unemotional words calculated to wound and crush her spirit.

All her defiance dissolved. Marissa felt the tears of despair welling up in her eyes before they broke in a storm, coursing down her cheeks to drop onto his cold diamonds which encircled her throat. She was not free, she would never be free, the fear and the guilt would live on in her heart for ever.

In the doorway behind her Luc stood stock-still,

his hand still on the doorknob, the slight draught he had caused in opening it still eddying around him.

He checked his instinctive desire to gather her in his arms, kiss away her pain. But he had no right, and she would not welcome his intrusion into her grief. How could he have been such a fool as to think that the mere passage of time had healed the loss of her husband? And how could he ask a woman who was so obviously in love with her dead husband to marry him?

He backed quietly away, cursing himself for a fool. He could not offer her anything to make up for the love she had lost, and it seemed cold-blooded in the extreme to suggest to Marissa that a marriage between them might be mutually convenient.

A few moments later, unaware that she had been observed, Marissa resolutely dried her tears and pushed back the damp tendrils of hair from her temples. She turned her back on the portrait and walked steadily from the Gallery. Behind her the painted eyes seemed to follow her exit.

Chapter Six

Sunshine flooding through the muslin drapes at her bedchamber window roused Marissa from a deep, but surprisingly dreamless sleep. Sitting up against the pillows, she gazed out at the burgeoning fresh green of the Home Wood and chided herself for the state she had got herself into the night before in the Long Gallery.

Why, it was perfectly Gothic, worthy of a sensational novel! She could not spend the rest of her life dwelling on what had gone before. Marriage to Charles had had…dark moments, but it was spring, and time for a new beginning. And on a beautiful day like today the best remedy for the megrims was fresh air and exercise.

'Mary!' Marissa called, swinging her legs out of bed and stretching like a cat. 'Put out my green riding habit. I shall walk up to the stables after breakfast.'

Marissa arrived in the stableyard, flushed from her walk and quite unconscious of the attractive picture she made as she picked her way across the stone-flagged yard.

Peters, the head groom, alerted by a stableboy to her ladyship's presence, emerged from the tack room wiping his hands on a rag as he strode across to meet her. His weather-beaten face was alight with pleasure.

'My lady! This is a welcome visit after so many months!'

'Not a visit, Peters—I have come to ride. His lordship has kindly put a horse at my disposal.'

'Well, my lady, you know them all, none better. Do you have a fancy for a particular one, or shall I have some led out for you?'

'Oh, lead them out, please, Peters! I have missed them so.'

Minutes later she was taking chunks of carrot from the groom and feeding the roan, feeling its soft muzzle nibbling gently at her gloved hand. She ran her hand over the arched neck, enjoying the strength and vitality beneath the warm hide. The grey mare, jealous of the attention its stablemate was being paid, nudged Marissa none too gently and she laughed.

'Yes, you may have some too, Tempest! I remember you well! Is she still such a handful, Peters?'

'Indeed she is, my lady! Had young Ned off three times yesterday, just because she took agin that herd of cattle in the Long Meadow. Very wilful she is, ma'am, but as I recollect you never had any trouble handling her.'

Marissa ran her thumb down the centre of the grey's nose, managing to tickle the most sensitive spots and reducing the animal to a state of docility that belied the flash in its eye.

'She tried to unseat me once or twice in the be-

ginning, before we came to an understanding—
didn't you, my pet? I'll take her, Peters. After all, I
do not think it would be wise for Miss Southwood
to ride her, and she is not up to his lordship's
weight. There is no reason why the Dower House
stables cannot house her, is there? Allen can take
care of her along with my carriage horses. I will take
her out now and perhaps you would be so good as
to have the rest of her tack and so on moved down
this morning.'

'Certainly, my lady. Ned! Sim! Come and saddle
up Tempest, and Ned, get the rest of her tack shifted
down to the Dower House stables as soon as may
be and tell Allen to make up a loose box.'

Marissa touched his arm and said quietly, '*Both*
saddles, please, John.'

The head groom's grizzled eyebrows drew together in a worried frown. 'Is that sensible, my lady?
His new lordship's not going to like that.'

'His new lordship is not going to know, any more
than my lord did.'

'Yes, but, ma'am, his late lordship was away as
often as not, and this one isn't! What's he going to
say if he finds out you are riding at night, by yourself and…' he hesitated and dropped his voice still
further '…astride.'

'Do not worry, John. I will take care.'

'I'll see to the saddle myself, ma'am. And I'll
have a word with Allen; he's a good lad—he'll keep
his mouth shut and not go gossiping.'

Marissa let Peters toss her up into the saddle and
held Tempest with a firm hand while she arranged
the long skirts of her habit to her satisfaction and
the groom adjusted the girth and stirrup leather.

The mare was skittish, and determined to see what she could get away with. She took exception to the muck barrow which Sim was wheeling across the yard, behaved as though the stable cat was a dangerous tiger and tossed her head impatiently at being made to stand.

Deliberately Marissa forced her to walk out of the yard and across the spread of gravel before the house. She was concentrating so hard on the horse, on ensuring that her seat on the side saddle was perfectly balanced after long months when she had not ridden, that she failed to see Nicci waving from the drawing room window.

'Oh, look, Luc, does not Marissa look fine? I wish I had a habit like that!'

'I wish you had a seat on a horse like that!' her brother retorted drily, but his eyes followed the slender figure in the fir-green habit. 'I hope Peters knows what he is about, letting her out on that mare, and without even a groom.'

'Is that the one you said I must not ride because it was so wild? It seems very docile this morning.'

Even as she spoke a pheasant erupted with a panic-stricken cry right in front of Tempest. The mare threw up her head and backed rapidly in a crab-like movement. Marissa sat tight and calmly brought the mare under control, urging her into a trot and disappearing from sight round the curve of the drive.

'That is why, my dear Nicci, I said you were not to ride Tempest!' Even though Marissa was out of sight Luc remained standing at the long window, his eyes fixed on the spot where he had last seen her. The sight of the slender figure in green, controlling the animal with such ease and grace, had stirred something deep within him. Instead of going down to the estate office to spend an hour reviewing leases, what he really wanted to do was send to the stables for his stallion and follow Marissa into the park.

'What are you doing this morning, Nicci? I have to see Poole for a while, but I can take you driving later.'

His sister gave him a brilliant smile, 'Oh, thank you, Luc, but there is no need. It is such a lovely morning, I thought I should take a walk.'

She was up to something, Luc thought as he crossed the courtyard to the steward's office, although what the devil it could be, he knew not. The sooner they were in London and that little madam had some of her hoydenish ways curbed the better. Although for the life of him he could not think who he could get to chaperon her.

One of the footmen was setting out a tray with sherry in the steward's room. 'Please send to the stables and tell Peters to send round my horse for eleven, James.' He would have his ride after all, and combine it with a visit to look at that drainage ditch Poole had been worrying about…

An hour later, after a long gallop through the park, Marissa reined in on a rise which gave her a view across the back of the house and the formal gardens. The golden stone shone in the spring sunlight, the gardens lapped green at the foot of the terraces and the garden boys were out raking the gravel walks into a perfection that would be entirely lost on their new master.

How her lord would have disliked her riding with-

out an escort. How he would have disapproved of
her habit, just the wrong shade of green against the
new foliage. And how wonderful it was not to have
to care what anyone thought! Tempest snorted and
shook her head, but Marissa kept her standing, enjoying the warmth of the sun through her jacket,
uncaring that her hair was coming down at the back
and that her cheeks were flushed with the exhilaration of the ride.

As she surveyed the distant gardens she became
aware of a black-clad figure, small in the landscape,
making its way through the rose garden. As the man
came within sight of the house the doors from the
small salon opened and Nicci ran down the steps
and joined him.

It was Mr Ashforde, Marissa realised, screwing
up her eyes against the light. The two began to walk
up and down the rose terrace between the still-brown
beds of pruned bushes.

How very odd that he should have come to the
back of the house, Marissa mused. And it was almost as though Nicci had been waiting for him. Oh,
dear, she did hope this was not a clandestine meeting—it would be fatal to the young couple's hopes
if Luc discovered such a tryst had taken place. She
was more than ever convinced that the kind and noble Crispin Ashforde would be the ideal husband for
Nicci, but this was not the way to go about it.

She collected up the reins and urged the mare into
a trot, following the track worn by the sheep and
the deer until she reached the fence around the pleasure grounds. The young couple were now easily
discernible, and she was close enough to see the

distress on Nicci's face as she broke away and ran into the house.

Marissa threw her leg over the pommel, slipped to the ground and tied Tempest's reins to the fence. Mr Ashforde was standing gazing into an ornamental pond, a dispirited sag to his shoulders.

'Mr Ashforde! Good morning!'

The curate was so startled that he nearly dropped his hat into the water. 'Lady Southwood! Good morning to you. A fine day, is it not?'

'Yes, it is. But never mind that.' Marissa was in no mood for social chit-chat. 'What is the matter with Miss Southwood? She seemed distressed.'

Mr Ashforde smoothed back his hair from his brow, his handsome face creased with worry. 'May I be frank with you, Lady Southwood?'

'Of course! You must know I regard Nicole in the light of a sister, having none of my own.' She smiled encouragingly at him.

He fingered his hat-band, much of his normal air of quiet confidence dissipated. 'I must confess to having formed an…attachment to Miss Southwood, and I have the honour to believe that my feelings are reciprocated.'

Marissa felt a momentary impatience with his formality. 'You are in love with each other?' she demanded.

'So I believe.' He blushed rosily. 'I must confess that I have never before felt an attachment of this nature…so I can only assume it to be the tender passion which animates me.' He added earnestly, 'You must believe that I only wish the best for Miss Southwood.'

'I do believe that, Mr Ashforde, although I must

warn you that his lordship is likely to take a less charitable view than I of your meeting Nicole unchaperoned like this.'

The young man's blush deepened. 'I too am deeply conscious that such a meeting could be construed as improper, but Miss Southwood was in such distress last night that I felt I should meet and talk with her where we could be private.'

Marissa was puzzled: she had no recollection of Nicci being in anything but great high spirits at the dinner party, but perhaps the eye of love had seen a deeper emotion... 'But why is she upset now?'

'Because I told her that I did not feel we should declare our feelings for each other until she had come out into Society. She is very young,' he added, somewhat ponderously.

'Oh, no,' Marissa cried. 'I am sure you are mistaken! I am certain that the Earl would look kindly upon your suit, for you are so well connected and suitable in every way. And, young though Miss Southwood is, surely a settled attachment with a long engagement would not be unacceptable to his lordship?'

The young man looked startled. 'If you are certain, then I will be guided by you—I had resigned myself to a longer wait, but in view of your counsel....' They had been walking as they talked, and were strolling around the corner of the house. 'Oh—there is the Earl now.'

Luc was cantering across the greensward from the direction of the Home Farm. Marissa gave the curate a little push. 'Strike while the iron is hot! Speak to him now! I will go in to Nicci.'

Nicci was pacing up and down in the Salon, traces

of tears on her cheeks. 'Marissa, darling, I am in such despair!' She ran over and grasped Marissa's hands. 'Crispin is so noble, so good, but he is ready to sacrifice our love for convention…for prudence!'

'For heaven's sake, Nicci!' Marissa was aware of an unsympathetic feeling of irritation with the young lovers. 'Do try for a little moderation! You are not going to win your brother round by histrionics; it will serve only to vex him. Men hate such displays of sensibility.'

'But you do not understand! It is hopeless. I cannot convince Crispin that he must speak to Luc, declare for me. He says we must wait until I am older.'

'Do not worry, Nicci, even now Mr Ashforde is speaking to your brother, asking to pay his addresses. I am sure all will be well if you will only—'

She was cut short by the sound of the front door crashing like a thunderclap. 'Nicole!' Luc roared.

The two young women instinctively clutched each other, and were gazing at the door, a picture of guilt, when Luc strode in.

Nicci gave her brother a weak smile. 'Why, Luc, whatever is the matter?'

He had tossed off his hat, his riding coat was open and he stood tapping the riding crop against his booted leg. The steady noise, as regular as a heartbeat, unnerved Marissa.

'You little minx! You know perfectly well what the matter is! You have cajoled that poor boy of a curate into believing himself in love with you, and what must the poor wretch do but ask me for permission to pay court to you. Hah! If it were not so absurd it would be laughable.' Luc strode irritably across the room.

'But we love each other!' Nicci cried dramatically, one hand pressed to her bosom.

'Oh, do not come the Sarah Siddons with me—I have no liking for high theatricals. Are you as much in love with him as you were with your drawing master? Or that young ninny Westlake you mooned over for months?'

'You are so unkind! This is the real thing!' Nicci promptly burst into tears and buried her hot face in Marissa's shoulder. Marissa responded by placing a comforting arm around the young woman.

'Sir, do not be angry with her. Mr Ashforde was only doing what he felt to be right. Why, he told me—'

'So you knew about this?' Luc ceased his pacing and swung round to face her, his eyes narrowed. 'And you encouraged it?'

'But he is such an eligible young man, so intelligent, so kind...'

'Such a milksop! One of these days that young man is going to be a bishop—can you imagine a more unsuitable wife for a bishop than this silly goose?' He pointed the riding crop at his sister.

Nicci wailed in protest and recoiled dramatically. Tightening her arms around the sobbing girl, Marissa raised her chin and protested, 'Sir, you are cruel and unfeeling!'

'Unfeeling, am I, madam? Allow me to know my sister better than you. Am I to assume you have been instrumental in promoting this touching romance?'

Marissa noted with alarm that he had gone pale with anger under his tan. His relaxed manner had deserted him: now he was a big man in a towering rage. Physically the resemblance to Charles Southwood had never been greater, but with Charles she had never seen hot anger, only cold, calculated displeasure.

The tattoo of crop against leather increased, menacing in the sudden silence. Marissa's heart beat, choking her. She tried to speak, found her voice trembling and steadied herself. Only the instinct to protect Nicci kept her from running pell mell from the room.

'I…yes, I did advise Mr Ashforde to seek your permission to see Nicci. No more than that. They are deeply attached. I had not expected you to be so brutal to the poor child.'

Luc grinned, but without humour. 'Which poor child? My silly little minx of a sister or poor young Crispin Ashforde? And I will thank you, madam, to mind your own affairs and not meddle in mine. Nicole, go to your room.'

Nicci broke free from Marissa's arms and dashed for the door. 'You are a beast, Luc, and I hate you!' she threw at him from the safety of the threshold.

'And you are a spoilt little hoyden who needs discipline, and I am determined you shall have it.'

He took one step towards her and Nicci fled. Marissa, calling up all her courage, stepped between him and the door, her slender figure rigid. 'No! I shall not permit it!' In her mind the sight of the riding crop in his hand could mean only one thing— she knew only too well what 'discipline' meant.

Luc's face flushed with anger. For a moment she believed he was going to lay hands on her, thrust her bodily from the doorway. Then he turned on his heel and brought the riding crop down in a furious arc to crack across the top of the occasional table which held Nicci's sewing box. The sound in the room echoed like a pistol-shot: the rosewood box fell with a splintering crash to the boards and Marissa fled down the corridor, up the stairs and into Nicci's room.

Marissa swept in without knocking and turned the key in the lock. At the sound Nicci, who had cast herself across the bed, looked up. 'Marissa! Why on earth have you locked the door?'

Ignoring the question, Marissa hurried across and gathered the girl in her arms. 'There, there, do not worry. I will not let him hurt you.'

'It is too late. He has already hurt me! My heart is in pieces!'

Despite the dramatic words, Nicci was already looking more composed. Marissa sat back and regarded her with some puzzlement. 'No, Nicci, I did not mean that... Luc is very angry, but you must not be frightened.'

'Frightened?' Nicci scrubbed her eyes and sat up, staring at Marissa in astonishment. 'Why should I be frightened of my own brother?'

'But he is so angry! His language so immoderate. And he hit the table with his riding crop...' Her voice faltered.

'Oh, so that was what the crash was.' Nicci got off the bed, all tears forgotten. 'He hasn't broken my sewing box, has he? He really is the limit!'

Marissa's puzzlement grew. Nicci was certainly not frightened, and now, looking back, her tears seemed little more than a temper tantrum.

'He does not often lose his temper,' Nicci explained. 'But when he does, we all hide! He once threw the soup tureen at Jackson when they were arguing about one of the ships. It was empty,' she added naively. 'Jackson caught it and threw it back and they both ended up laughing.'

Marissa got up and walked to the window, her back turned to Nicole. 'But he seems so violent…'

'Well, he *is* hard on the china, but he's as soft as butter, really. I've never known him strike anyone! You did not really fear that he would beat me, did you, Marissa?' Nicci came and put an arm around Marissa's tense shoulders. 'Marissa, I am sorry if we upset you—I'm sure you are not used to this sort of thing!'

Marissa kept her face averted, fearful that Nicci would see how shaken she was.

'Did your husband never lose his temper? I thought we Southwoods would all be the same.'

'He never…shouted.' Three little words that concealed so much pain. Marissa put a determined smile on her face and turned back to Nicci. 'I am so sorry if my advice has served you badly, but do not despair. I am sure Mr Ashforde will wait for you for as long as it takes.'

Nicci looked doubtful, but before she could speak there was a tap at the door, and when it was unlocked Jackson entered with a tea tray, an expression of dour disapproval on his weather-beaten face. 'He's gone out again,' he said without ceremony or preamble. 'You shouldn't have done it, Miss Nicci—he wants to know what I was about, letting you run around on the terrace with the curate and no chaperon! Huh!' He put the tea tray down with a thump and departed.

Marissa gazed after him in bemusement. 'He is very…unusual, is he not?'

'He is just Jackson,' Nicci said, as if that explained everything. 'Tea, Marissa? You know,' she added after a couple of meditative sips, 'I do not feel any longer as though my heart is breaking. Perhaps I am not in love with Mr Ashforde after all. It is a very lowering thought that Luc might be right and that I am indeed a flirt.'

Marissa's brow creased in consternation. 'But, Nicci! I thought you wanted to marry him!'

'I think I shall wait until I am out. It would be a pity to be engaged and not to enjoy Society—I should not be able to flirt at all!'

Marissa sighed, acknowledging to herself that she had learned a lesson that morning. Obviously not all young women were as dutiful as she had been, first to her father, then to her husband.

'I should not think there is much likelihood that your brother will take you up to London for the Season after this upset,' she said sympathetically.

'*Au contraire,* I think it might make him do it sooner. I heard him talking to Jackson yesterday about opening the Town house. And,' she added disarmingly, 'he needs a wife! That is what he means about discipline for me. He thinks his wife would look after me and bring me out.'

Marissa's heart thudded unaccountably. 'Wife? Is he thinking of getting married, then?'

'Well, Diane says he should get married. And he listens to her advice.'

'Who is Diane?'

'Oh, his mistress. Madame de Rostan, you know. She lives on the next estate to us in Jamaica. Her husband died ten years ago—he was much older than she was.'

Marissa set down her cup with a rattle, her colour high. 'Mistr... Nicci, you should not know about such things, let alone talk about them! I am sure Madame de Rostan is simply a close friend.'

She felt very flustered indeed, far more than Nicci's improper behaviour warranted. Luc had a mistress! Well, of course he had; he was a man and men seemed to need such...diversions. At least this woman was in Jamaica. The thought was comforting, but she did not like to dwell too much on why she should care.

Nicci looked at Marissa from under her lashes. 'I am sorry if I offended you, Marissa, but things are more openly known in the West Indies. And Diane is perfectly respectable and received everywhere. I do miss her; it will be delightful when she arrives.'

'Arrives? Here?'

'Oh, no, in London. She has a house over here and comes every two or three years for the Season and to buy clothes.'

Marissa's mind was in a whirl, her emotions in turmoil. Without thinking, she blurted out, 'Why does he not marry her if she is so respectable?'

'Why, Diane says they would fight like cat and dog if they were under the same roof. And besides...' Nicci wandered over to the clothes press and began to finger a pile of lace '...she is *years* older than he is.'

It was some comfort, but not much. No doubt in Miss Southwood's eyes anyone over twenty-five was quite in their dotage. Marissa stood up, suddenly exasperated with the whole Southwood family.

'I must go home, and I have left Tempest tethered to the fence. Will you be all right now, Nicci dear?'

Nicci crossed and kissed her on the cheek. 'Quite all right, and thank you for trying to help. I am sorry Luc was so cross.'

Luc was standing in the hall when she descended the staircase. Marissa faltered slightly at the sight of him, then she walked steadily down, giving him a cool nod as she passed him. He put out a hand, touching her arm, and was shocked to feel her flinch away from his touch.

'I must apologise for losing my temper, Marissa.'

'Please do not concern yourself, my lord. Nicci tells me it is a not infrequent occurrence.' Her tone was glacial.

Luc regarded her ruefully. 'I had hoped you would have forgiven me, for I was going to ask you a favour.' He led her into the study, closing the door behind them. Under his fingers he felt her stiffen; the tension was vibrating from her like a note from a bowstring. Damn it, he thought, she is still overwrought from last night, and now I have taken her into her husband's study. It must be full of memories for Luc had changed nothing, preferring not to use the unwelcoming room.

Marissa stepped away from him, holding herself erect. 'Forgive you, my lord? It is not my place to do so. I made a severe error of judgement in interfering between you and your sister, and it is I who should beg your forgiveness.'

To Luc her tone belied the sentiment: she could not have been colder had she been carved from ice.

He knew her bereavement ran deep, but there was something else; he was sure of it. If only she would open up and tell him—but he could hardly ask her to confide in him.

Luc retreated into formality. 'Then we have agreed; we shall speak of it no more.'

A short, uncomfortable silence ensued, until Marissa observed, 'You said you had a favour to ask me, my lord.'

'I have decided that I must take Nicci up to London; she is too restless for the quiet of the country and will get into one scrape after another. The Season has hardly begun; it will do her no harm to come out quietly this year.'

'Indeed? And I understand from Nicole that you yourself will be seeking an eligible alliance.'

It was a palpable hit: Luc coloured and looked away. Damn that little chit, prattling on to Marissa so improperly. And Marissa was making it obvious that she felt not the slightest regard for him if she could speak so dispassionately of his quest for a wife.

'Possibly,' he responded shortly. 'I had intended to ask you if you would consider accompanying us, helping me to launch Nicole into Society.'

'Me?' Marissa's eyebrows rose haughtily.

'And Miss Venables, naturally. But if you feel disinclined, madam, we need say no more. Nicole must wait another year for her come-out.' It seemed to Luc that Marissa must be considerably irked by him still to sound so unwilling.

'Surely you have other female acquaintances who could oblige you?' Marissa enquired, watching his face.

For a moment Luc thought that his wretch of a sister had said something about Diane, then he recovered himself. Even Nicci would not be so indiscreet. 'Unfortunately, no. No one suitable.'

'I will think about it, and also speak to Miss Venables: it may not suit her convenience,' Marissa responded coolly. 'For myself, it makes little difference where I spend my time.'

Luc regarded her, lips tight. She was deliberately provoking him, paying him back with her control for his intemperance earlier. He wanted to take her in his arms, kiss her until the ice melted, make love to her there and then on that wide mahogany writing desk…

Something in the warmth of his gaze made Marissa swallow hard. She gathered up the long skirts of her habit and turned to the door, her slender figure moulded in the tightly tailored costume. 'If there is nothing else, I will take my leave, my lord. Please do not trouble to show me out.'

Luc stood looking at the door which she had closed gently behind her. He raked his hand through his hair, then with a muttered oath poured himself a glass of claret from the decanter on a side table.

Tempest was thoroughly bored with being tied up to the fence, and made her displeasure known in no uncertain terms. Marissa had no intention of leading her round to the front of the house in search of a mounting block so she used a tree stump. The mare sidled and backed every time Marissa attempted to mount, and it took ten minutes before she was in the saddle.

Fighting a bad-tempered horse all the way back across the park to the Dower House, combined with the morning's upsets, did nothing for Marissa's own mood. She stalked into the house and up to her room, calling for her maid as she went.

In her chamber she pulled off her jacket without waiting for Mary. When the girl arrived, breathless from running upstairs, she asked, 'Has Miss Venables waited luncheon for me?'

'Yes, my lady. Let me help you with that, ma'am. What would you like to change into, ma'am?'

'Oh, anything you like, Mary. Just a simple gown. Look at my hair!'

Miss Venables was placidly reading in the dining room when Marissa joined her. 'Your colour is very good, dear,' she observed. 'Did you have a good ride?'

'My *ride* was very enjoyable. I have moved my favourite mare, Tempest, to the stables here. Would you care for some cold meat, Jane?'

'Thank you, yes. If your ride was enjoyable, it sounds as though something else was not,' Miss Venables observed shrewdly.

'I became embroiled in a dispute between the Earl and Nicci over Mr Ashforde, who has asked if he may court her.'

Miss Venables snorted. 'Has he indeed? Silly young puppy! He is no more in love with that girl than she is with him. No doubt his lordship put him right about that!' She buttered some bread and asked innocently, 'Embroiled, you say, my dear? How so?'

Marissa gave her an edited version of the morning's events.

'And his lordship was angry?'

'He was certainly extremely annoyed, and said so,' Marissa supplied. She had made no mention of his flaring anger, of the riding crop and the effect it had had on her.

'Oh, dear, so we are out of favour with the Earl.'

'Far from it, Jane dear. He has asked that we accompany Nicole and himself to London to do the Season and bring her out. I was so taken aback by his effrontery after all that had passed between us that I did not trust myself to give him an immediate answer.'

'Oh!' Miss Venables said, trying to conceal her dismay. 'But it seems an excellent plan to me—just think how much we would enjoy it after this past year. There can be no objection now to you coming out of mourning. We would have a splendid time: balls and parties and riding in the park. And entertainment of a higher kind, naturally. There will be the galleries and exhibitions... And the shopping, dear, think of the shopping.'

Marissa laughed out loud and leaned across the table to take her companion's hand. 'You are so good for me, Jane! We will like it exceedingly, in spite of his lordship. I shall tell him that we will oblige him.'

'At whatever cost to ourselves,' Miss Venables added, tongue firmly in cheek.

Chapter Seven

Marissa, Lady Southwood, thanks the Earl for his kind invitation to join his London establishment for the Season. Miss Venables joins her ladyship in accepting the Earl's amiable offer. Doubtless his lordship will favour them with full details of his plans at his convenience.

Luc screwed the letter up and tossed it onto the desk in front of him, anger welling within him. He had thought he was making progress in breaking down Marissa's reserve. And he had thought he was offering her and Miss Venables an opportunity for pleasure and diversion after long months of mourning. The cold formality of the note demonstrated just how wrong he had been.

He reached for the crumpled note and smoothed it out, letting his palm rest on it. Marissa was an enigma to him, and her parting words earlier that day echoed uneasily in his mind. She had said she did not care where she spent her time; he recalled her distress in the Gallery before the portrait of her husband. Despite her calm exterior Marissa must still be deep in grief... Was he being cruel in asking her to spend more time with him when his appearance must be a constant reminder of her loss?

Nicci bounced into the Salon without troubling to knock, shattering his reverie. 'Luc, you have quite destroyed my rosewood box! I shall have to send to Norwich for a new one—and if you expect me to pay for it out of my allowance, then I call that mean of you!'

'I am sorry for your box, you provoking brat! You may choose yourself a new box in Bond Street— and pay for it out of the ridiculously extravagant allowance I intend making you in London.'

Nicci whirled across to sit on his lap, wrapping her arms round his neck and planting a big kiss on his cheek. 'You are the most wonderful brother in the world! We can truly go to London? And I will have a truly magnificent allowance?'

'Far more magnificent than you deserve. You have soon recovered from your broken heart, have you not, you minx?' Luc asked, giving her a wry smile.

'You were quite right, brother dear. Mr Ashforde and I would not suit; I see it now. What is that?' She pointed at the letter underneath his hand.

'A note from Marissa accepting my invitation for her and Miss Venables to accompany us to London.'

Nicci jumped up, clapping her hands with excitement. 'I am so glad Marissa is coming, and dear Jane of course.' She regarded her brother from under her lashes and added innocently, 'What a good thing

Diane is setting up her own establishment and not staying with us.'

Her brother waved a warning finger at her. 'Have you said anything to Marissa about Madame de Rostan?'

Nicci coloured betrayingly. 'Well…I might have mentioned her in passing. As being one of our dear friends, you know.'

'Nicci!' Luc growled. 'How much have you told her? Have you said that Diane has been…very close to me?'

'Marissa says I should not talk about such things,' Nicci retorted betrayingly.

Luc dropped his head in his hands. 'Oh, Nicci. I really would prefer it if you would strive not to create the impression that my life is littered with mistresses! Or betray that you even know the meaning of the word!' No wonder Marissa was so frosty. After a happy marriage she was doubtless shocked to the core to hear that he had had an irregular liaison.

The next day was unseasonably hot for May: the clouds seemed trapped in the sticky heat, and nothing moved in the still air other than an army of small insects which buzzed irritatingly whenever one opened a window.

Up at the Hall Luc and Nicci, accustomed to the heat of the Tropics, thought nothing of it, but at the Dower House both ladies retreated to the shaded cool of the garden room and drew the blinds, Gyp panting in the corner, too hot to even chase birds in the garden.

They spent a desultory day making lists of things to be done, things to be packed and, much more enjoyably, things to be purchased as soon as they arrived in London.

'Oh, for some lightweight cottons and muslins,' said Miss Venables, fanning herself. 'I shall be so thankful to see the last of these dark colours and heavy fabrics!'

'And pretty straw bonnets, and parasols and little kid slippers,' Marissa said dreamily. She felt so restless, so full of energy despite the heat. She wanted to run, to gallop, but it was too hot to walk and it would not be fair to take Tempest out in the heat and flies. And beyond the parkland and the dunes the cool sea beckoned…

Marissa ordered a late dinner, and it was after ten when they sat sipping their tea. Miss Venables looked at the curtain, just stirring at the open windows, and remarked, 'Thank heavens! The breeze is getting up at last; perhaps we shall not have too unpleasant a night.'

Marissa got up and pulled back the curtains. The cloud had lifted at last, leaving a clear sky, and the full moon bathed the garden with light. The cool stirrings of the air lifted the fine hair at her temples, serving to rekindle her restlessness.

'I am going to retire now, Marissa, the heat of the day has quite sapped my energy. Don't be too long yourself, my dear. We have much to arrange tomorrow.'

'Goodnight, Jane. I shall follow you up soon.'

Marissa stood looking at the moon-bathed landscape for some time, breathing in the scents of the night stocks and roses, enjoying the peace and the cool. Despite her words to her cousin she felt disinclined to retire to bed.

Many times before, when her lord had been away from home, she had taken a horse out at night and ridden until she had exorcised the restless demons which possessed her and she could trot home, calm and collected and ready to resume the mantle of Countess once again.

Peters, the head groom, had been her loyal if unwilling accomplice in these escapades. At her orders he had sent the man's saddle down to the Dower House stables. Allen worked for her and her alone: if she told him to make Tempest ready he would do so unquestioningly.

Before she knew it she was pulling her breeches and jacket from the bottom of the chest of drawers. Mary had obtained them for her and had loyally guarded her mistress's secret. She buttoned up the linen shirt, tugged on her boots and shook her hair free of its confining pins.

In the light cast by the moon through the long windows she was quite transformed into an exotic creature no one would associate with the elegant Lady Southwood. As an afterthought she tossed a lightweight cloak over her shoulders and scooped up some linen towels from the washstand.

The candle was flickering in the window of the groom's room above the carriage house. Marissa banged on the door and when Allen came stumbling down the steps ordered him briskly to saddle up her mare. 'The man's saddle, please, Allen.'

Briefed by Peters, the undergroom complied immediately, only his unusually wooden expression betraying his surprise at seeing his mistress thus attired at this hour of the night. 'Shall I saddle up the hack and accompany you, my lady?'

'That will not be necessary, thank you. And there is no need to wait up for my return—I am quite capable of unsaddling Tempest and I would not keep you from your bed.'

'Yes, ma'am, thank you, ma'am.' The young man climbed back up to his room reflecting that it was nice of her ladyship to care about his rest, but Peters would have his guts for garters if he went to bed without checking that his mistress was safely returned.

Marissa walked the mare quietly across the cobbles and past the front of the Dower House: it would never do to rouse the household! Once they were through the wood she let the mare have her head and Tempest, with a toss of her head, settled gladly into a canter that sent the wind through her long mane. The cloak flew out behind Marissa and she shook her hair free to catch the wind too, so that mistress and horse seemed as one, flying over the moonlit turf of the parkland, cutting diagonally across the front of Southwood Hall. The big house lay silent and still, lit only by the dim lights of the watchman's lanterns.

In the master bedroom Luc lay, hands behind his head, gazing at the plaster moulding of the ceiling overhead as he had been for the last half-hour. Sleep was unaccountably eluding him and he found his mind turning again to the thought of Marissa, cold and angry, yet curiously vibrant in the clinging riding habit.

He grinned ruefully to himself, reflecting that enforced celibacy was doing nothing for his equilibrium. He and Diane had amicably ended their liaison over two years ago, and since then there had been a number of charming entanglements of which, thankfully, his sister knew nothing. But those too had ended when he had left Jamaica, and the provocative presence of Marissa only served to highlight his lack of intimate female companionship.

It was no good, he had to get up and do some work. There were some suitably soporific estate accounts he had promised his agent he would peruse. As he crossed he room he heard, faintly, the sound of hoofbeats on turf.

Luc threw back the curtains and looked out on the park, so bathed in silver light that it seemed almost as bright as day. A grey horse was cantering across his view, its mane flying. On its back was a slim figure, its cloak streaming behind it, a mass of hair swept back by the breeze.

It was Marissa. There was no mistaking the rider, despite, he realised with a shock, the fact that she was riding astride and clad in breeches.

'What the devil!' he exclaimed, staring at the wild creature who had Marissa's form yet who could not, surely, be that controlled, proper young widow who had so coldly conversed with him that day. As he watched she turned the horse's head towards the coast road and dropped her hands: the mare responded immediately, breaking into a gallop which swept them out of his sight in less than a minute.

His astonishment swiftly turned to fear for Marissa. What had prompted this wild ride? Had her despair finally overmastered her control? He remembered again her torrent of tears in the Long Gallery, the almost too casual way she had said she did not care where she spent her time. It obviously made no

difference to the depths of her misery whether she
was in Norfolk or in London; she was still in hell.

The image of that cold expanse of sea beyond the
dunes was suddenly very vivid in his mind. Luc
tried to tell himself he was overreacting, but even
as he struggled with his imaginings he was tugging
on breeches and boots, shrugging into a shirt.

He ran down the stairs, across the hall and out
through the front door, startling the dozing watchman as he snored in his hooded chair. Luc pounded
into the stableyard and flung open the door of the
stable housing his hunter. He threw the saddle over
the startled animal, tightened the girths and was
reaching for the bridle when Peters emerged, hair
tousled, eyes heavy with sleep.

'My lord?'

'Nothing! Go back to bed. I have a fancy to ride.'

Peters wisely refrained from commenting on his
lordship's dishevelled appearance and hastily effaced himself.

Luc swung up into the saddle without putting his
foot in the stirrup and was urging the big chestnut
hunter into a canter before it had even cleared the
stableyard arch. The park was empty when he
reached it, but he knew where she was headed and
he urged the horse into a flat gallop, headlong down
the driveway to the sea.

On the beach Marissa sat for a moment, breathing
in the cool sea air and watching the moonlight laying a path of silver across the waves. The light
breeze stirred her hair but it was not cold. The sea
would be, she knew, but it was irresistible, and so
shallow, even on the rising tide, that it would be
safe to swim.

She dismounted, tied Tempest to a branch and pulled off her clothes, leaving them in a heap on the cloak. The breeze caressed her naked body and she stretched like a cat, then walked slowly down the beach, kicking the fine sand, letting it run between her bare toes.

The water struck cold but she did not hesitate, wading out, relishing the chill kiss on her heated skin. The beach shelved so gradually that even after wading several hundred yards the water did not quite reach her waist. The moon was so big, so beautiful that she held her face up to its light and just stood relishing the tranquillity, the freedom, the aloneness.

The chestnut hunter breasted the dunes at the gallop, plunging as it scrambled down the far slope. Luc reined in hard, making it rear, unsettling Tempest who had fallen into a half-doze.

Luc swung down, dropped the reins and scanned the expanse of sea. There she was, standing like a naiad in the moonlight. Her hair cascaded down her bare back, white as alabaster in the cold light. As he watched, transfixed, she raised her hands and lifted the mass of dark curls off her neck, exposing the whole of her naked form before letting it drop once more.

She was beautiful, lovely beyond the imaginings he had striven so hard to control. Her slender waist, the curve of her hip rising from the lapping waves, took his breath away. Then she moved swiftly, disappearing into the water with barely a ripple.

Urgently Luc ripped off his shirt, tore off his boots and breeches and plunged into the water. The shallowness forced him to run, not swim, and he felt as though he were being dragged back with every stride. The cold water splashed up his back and chest as he ran, conscious of nothing but the need to reach her before she sank from sight below the grey water.

Marissa, unaware that she was not alone, floated tranquilly on her back, her fingers gently fanning the water to keep her in position. Vaguely she thought that the wind must be getting up, for she could hear splashing, although her ears were under water and she could hear little.

Frustrated by the impeding water, Luc plunged into a running dive, striking out strongly to where he had last glimpsed Marissa, praying through clenched teeth that she had not already sunk below the grey waters. Half blinded by the salt in his eyes, he surged forward, cutting through the water with powerful overarm strokes. His search succeeded better than he could have hoped as with startling suddenness he collided with a body.

Marissa had perhaps two seconds' warning as she floated serenely, her face to the moon. The surface of the sea rocked in a sudden swell, sending little waves across her face. Before she could react, before she could feel fear, a hard body crashed into hers. The breath knocked from her lungs, she was pushed under the surface of the sea. Water flooded her nostrils, stung her eyes, filled her ears: her bare behind grazed the rippled sand of the sea bottom and as she felt it her panic abated as she recalled just how shallow the water was. Curling her legs underneath her, she found her footing and stood up, coughing and spluttering as she took in air. Wildly she looked round for whatever it was that had rammed her, suddenly very afraid. The local people had tales of

sharks in these waters which she had always dismissed as fantasy—now she was not so sure.

But it was not a shark who seized her from behind. Strong arms clamped themselves around her
waist and she was lifted bodily from the water.
Pressed against hard, cold flesh Marissa kicked,
screamed and dug in her elbows. With a muffled
curse her assailant dropped her. Marissa's feet hit
the bottom and she dug in her toes and spun round
to face him.

'Luc!' She was so taken aback that she fell back
into the water with a splash. The realisation of her
nakedness kept her submerged, crouched so that
only her head and shoulders emerged. No such con-
siderations of modesty appeared to afflict Luc, who
stood there, hands on hips and chest heaving, regarding her.

'You must be mad! Whatever has possessed you!
This is no solution…' He caught a ragged breath
and looked at her with a strange mixture of anger
and concern.

'*I must be mad?*' Marissa was so taken aback that
she half rose, then rapidly remembered her nakedness and fell to her knees. 'What do you think you
are about, crashing into me like that? You could
have drowned me!' Her hair hung in sodden strands
across her face, dripping stinging salt water into her
eyes. She pushed it back with both hands, then
dropped her arms hastily to cover her breasts.

'Why should you worry about me drowning you
when you were hell-bent on self-destruction?' he demanded furiously.

'Self-destruction? Luc, have you completely
taken leave of your senses?' Her sense of bewilder-

ment was growing by the second. 'I came for a swim
because it has been so hot all day. I am a very good
swimmer, I would have you know, and I do this
frequently and quite safely.' She looked up at the
water-drenched figure. His hair was dark and sleek,
pushed back to reveal the strong planes of his face.
His powerfully muscled shoulders, moving slightly
with his breathing, gleamed as the moonlight struck
the water droplets. She did not dare let her eyes stray
lower...

He spoke slowly and deliberately, his relief firing
his anger as he realised just how badly he had mis-
read the situation. '*Swimming!* You are here in the
middle of the night, all alone and you tell me you
do this *often?* If you do not care for the risk you
put yourself to, do you not have some concern for
the impropriety of it?' He could hear how pompous
he was sounding, but he could not bring himself to
tell her his true fears. 'You have a position to uphold. You are the Dowager Countess of Radwinter.
What if someone were to see you? What do the servants think of you riding around in men's clothes?'

'My servants are loyal to me and do what I tell
them,' Marissa retorted coldly.

'Well, I shall speak to Peters in the morning and
have your horse brought back to the stables at the
Hall. We will have no more unsupervised riding.'

'How dare you seek to control my life?' Marissa
suddenly, and very satisfyingly, lost her temper. 'I
am neither your sister nor, thank heavens, your wife!
You cannot command me, my lord. Take Tempest
back, if you wish to be so petty-minded; I shall buy
my own horse. And Allen—who, if you need to be

reminded, is *my* groom—will look after it for me. I ride when and how and where I please.'

It was as if two years of subservience, of fearful obedience to her lord, had dissolved in a flash of anger. All her life men had controlled her. Well, now she was free, independent, able to do what she liked. She was so exhilarated by the thought that she stood up, forgetting her nakedness, intending to regain the shore and leave Luc standing there.

The expression on his face recalled her to her situation. His eyes widened as his gaze travelled down the lines of her form and he became, suddenly, very still. Marissa gasped, her hands springing to cover as much of her chilled body as she could, unwittingly striking the classic pose of a startled sea nymph. She found her eyes locked with Luc's, noticing with surprising clarity how the salt water had spiked his eyelashes.

Shakily she managed to say, 'I have had quite enough of this nonsense. Please turn your back; I want to go back to the shore.'

Luc did as he was bid, turning slowly to present her with a view of broad shoulders, a long, supple back tapering to narrow hips and taut buttocks. Marissa swallowed hard and turned abruptly herself. Too abruptly: her foot caught one of the rare stones on that sandy shore and she stumbled, falling with a loud splash and a cry back into the cold water.

Instantly he was beside her, lifting her up in his arms and holding her tight against his chest. 'You are frozen! You little fool, are you trying to catch pneumonia?'

Marissa could only shiver in response. Now she was out of the water, her wet skin fully exposed to the breeze, she was colder than ever. But it was not only the cold that was making her shiver; it was the nearness of this man, the strength of him, his obvious concern for her that she recognised as the source of his anger at her behaviour.

And something else, something that was dangerous insanity: she was falling in love with him. So this was what it was like, she mused as he made his way through the water, slowly, hampered by his burden and the dragging shallows. She had heard about love, but had never felt it, and now she recognised the months of thinking, dreaming about Luc for what they were.

Instinctively Marissa snuggled closer into Luc's arms, and was rewarded by a tightening of his grip. But as they neared the beach she began to think more clearly. This was a fatally stupid thing to do, to fall in love with this man. He was her husband's cousin, so like him to look at that they could be twins, one dark, the other blond. And, however different his behaviour appeared to be on the surface, all men were driven by the same urges; she had no doubt of that.

Luc had made it quite plain that he was going to look for a wife in London. And men did not expect love in marriage; she knew that. They sought duty, a good alliance, obedience and subservience. If he even guessed she was falling in love with him he would be embarrassed at best, appalled at worst.

As soon as his bare feet touched dry sand Marissa wrenched from his arms and was running to where she had left her clothes and towels piled under a bush at the foot of the dunes. She snatched the largest rectangle of linen and swathed it round her shivering body, keeping her back turned to him. Between chattering teeth, she said, 'Will you please go away?'

'I will, but I would appreciate it if you could spare me a towel, otherwise it will take me rather a long time to get dressed, wet as I am.' The anger had left his voice, leaving only a trace of faint amusement.

Without turning Marissa held out the smaller towel, conscious of just how close behind her he must be as he took it.

Seconds later, right behind her, he said, 'Will you not get dressed? You are shivering.'

'Go away, then!' she implored, her back still averted. 'How can I get dressed with you here?'

'For heaven's sake, Marissa, stop acting the prude! You have been a married woman, when all's said and done!'

'But not to you,' she snapped back.

Suddenly, incredibly, she felt the weight of her sodden hair lifted and strong hands were gently wringing the water out of it. Then Luc began to rub the damp mass with the towel he held, working down from the scalp to the finest tendrils lying on her shoulderblades.

'Stop it!' she demanded shakily, realising only too clearly that if Luc were drying her hair with the towel he was not wearing it himself.

'Stand still,' he admonished gently, carrying on the rhythmic stroking. 'If you will not dry yourself, I will do it for you.'

His hands touched her shoulders and Marissa whipped round, her hands coming up to push him away. They flattened onto the planes of his chest, but she did not push, only stood there feeling the cold skin against her palms, the beat of his heart under her fingers. Luc looked down at her for a long moment, then pulled her tight against him. She felt the heat of him under the cold skin, the hard strength of him, the frightening, arousing, maleness against her. His mouth came down slowly on hers and he kissed her softly, as if asking a question. Her response seemed to give him the answer he was looking for, for he deepened the kiss, his mouth moving sensuously against hers, his tongue probing gently the softness of her mouth.

Shocked, for her lord had never kissed her, except formally on the cheek, Marissa tentatively let her own tongue-tip taste his. The sensation made her knees feel weak, but she was rewarded by the soft groan in the back of his throat as Luc moved his hand in a sweeping caress down her spine. The towel, swept away by his impatient fingers, fell unheeded to the sand as his hands, cupping her buttocks, moulded her to him.

The heat of him was a shock, then a thrill as she caught fire too. Speechlessly she clung to him as he dipped his head to graze a long kiss from her earlobe down her neck to the swell of her breast.

Marissa gasped out loud as his sharp teeth found one peaking nipple and fastened gently on the aroused tip. His tongue teased and tasted her salty skin and Marissa whimpered as it circled and licked the tight bud.

Through her shock and sensuous delight Marissa struggled to understand what was happening to her. Her lord had performed his marital duties on her shrinking body with a haste—and distaste—which had shown only too clearly how she had displeased and disappointed him. Never had she expected that a man could give her so much pleasure—this must be what they did with their mistresses...

But underneath this tide of unfamiliar pleasure there was something else, a building yearning, a feeling of expectation that there was more to come, a goal to be reached, to be striven for.

Luc pulled her down gently onto the fallen towel, his hands never leaving her body, his mouth returning to hers for a long kiss that sapped her will and sent a frisson of delight pulsating through her being. It was there again, this sense of building pleasure, of expectation. Her body arched under his hands and she whispered, 'What are you doing to me?'

'Making love to you, I had rather hoped,' Luc answered huskily, his voice sounding slightly amused. His breath was warm on her chin, then his tongue was trailing insidiously down the curve of her breast to the other nipple where it recommenced its teasing.

Marissa drew in a shuddering breath, hardly able to wait for whatever it was that was coming to sweep her away. Luc's fingers strayed downwards over the swell of her hip to the softness of her inner thighs, gently parting and exploring with stroking caresses her secret core.

The wave of sensation swept over Marissa, shaking her in every part of her body. She cried out, arching into Luc's embrace, then fell back, lights exploding against her closed lids. As the pleasure ebbed, leaving her quivering in his arms, shudders shook her.

After an age she opened her eyes to meet his, smiling down at her. Marissa smiled tremulously back, reaching up her hand to stroke his cheek. Luc closed his eyes at the caress, then groaned. 'I really do not think sweetheart, that I can wait any longer…'

His mouth fastened on hers, hard and demanding, then his weight was on her, pressing her down into the yielding sand, his long legs twining with hers, separating them, easing them apart.

Marissa's eyes flew open. The man above, the familiar weight on her flinching body, the water-darkened hair and the Southwood features lit coldly by the moonlight—all this was horribly familiar. Automatically Marissa did what she had always done to allow her body to be used. She lay still and passive, not preventing, not welcoming the invasion, her eyes open and unfocused.

Luc froze, as he realised the change in her response to him, then rolled off her body and onto his feet in one swift movement. Never in his life had he taken an unwilling woman, and he was not about to start with this one. He ran down the short beach and plunged beneath the cold water, feeling its cold kiss dousing his heated arousal. He swam hard for two minutes, killing the fire in his veins, before turning back to the shore. As he swam he did not allow himself to think, to feel. As he strode ashore he saw Marissa had pulled on her clothes and was standing with her back to him beside her horse.

'The towels are by your clothes,' she said, her voice expressionless, as she heard him splash ashore.

'Thank you,' Marissa heard him say, his voice neutral. She walked away, leading Tempest to where a tree stump protruded from the sand at a convenient height for a mounting block. Her skin was still damp and her breeches clung uncomfortably as she bent her knee to mount, but she managed it and gathered up the reins to turn the horse homeward.

Luc, now dressed, ran to put a restraining hand on the bridle. 'Wait, please. Marissa, you must believe that I intend to marry you…'

'Indeed, my lord? It is doubtless very honourable of you to make the offer after your actions tonight. However, I have no more desire to marry you than you have shown up to now to marry me.' She gazed down at him with an expression he could not read.

'Desire?' He laughed without humour. 'If we are to talk about desire, madam, might I remind you that yours appeared to at least match mine. And certainly, unless you are a very good actress, you have obtained more pleasure from this night's encounter than I.'

The words were out before he could stop them. She jerked at the reins, sending Tempest plunging away into the dunes, but not before the moonlight caught her face and Luc glimpsed the hurt twist of her mouth, the pain in her eyes.

But she was gone, and after one hasty step towards his hunter he checked himself. There was nothing he could do tonight to make things any better. After a night's reflection Marissa would realise that she had to marry him. For himself, he reflected as he swung up into the saddle, the night's escapade had made up his mind: his cousin's widow would make an admirable wife.

Chapter Eight

The rhythm of Tempest's hoofbeats changed abruptly as she plunged down the bank from the saltings and onto the hard-packed surface of the coast road. It was enough to shake Marissa out of her mindless, headlong flight from the beach, from Luc. She reined the mare in and trotted more gently up the carriage drive until a path led off towards the Dower House through the trees fringing the park.

The moon had disappeared behind a bank of high cloud and Marissa slowed Tempest to a walk to allow the horse to pick its way across the tussocky grass of the park. Now that her instinctive flight had ended she found she was acutely aware of every sensation, every sound. Her wet hair clung to her jacket, soaking through the cloth between her shoulderblades, sand gritted between her toes inside the leather boots and her eyelashes felt salt-sticky. Yet despite these discomforts she felt alive, tingling with the awareness of her body. For the first time she felt truly aware of herself, of her skin, of her lips, of her breasts, of the caress of the night air on her cheeks.

She held her hot face up to the breeze as it sighed through the beeches and allowed her mind, at last, to be free, to think about what had just happened, what Luc had done to her.

Through the stillness hoofbeats sounded, almost preternaturally loud in the night. Marissa drew Tempest back farther into the shadows as Luc's hunter galloped by, his master low on its neck. Marissa let Tempest move forward slightly to the edge of the copse and watched as the big horse vanished under the arch of the stable block.

He was angry with her. She had rejected him, not once, but twice. He could never guess—and she could never tell him—why in the end she had rejected his lovemaking when he must have realised that she wanted him. *Wanted him*… Marissa rubbed her forehead in perplexity. It had never occurred to her before that a woman could want—could welcome—a man in that way. With Charles she had feared it, forced herself to do her duty, endured what had passed, prayed for it to be over swiftly.

But Luc…Luc had said he wanted to make *love* to her. He had intended that she should feel pleasure, had done everything to ensure it, been patient with her.

Tempest, sensing her mistress's distraction, began to walk slowly across the park, retracing her earlier route past the front of the big house.

Marissa was unconscious of the movement; her mind was replaying Luc's lovemaking. She shivered as she remembered the sensations that had awakened her body—and her mind. It had never occurred to her that a man would care for a woman's pleasure, would actively incite it, revel in it, enjoy it as much as she.

The realisation, when it came, hit her with the force of a blow. *This* was how it should be. It had been Charles whose warped view of the world had dominated her mind and body in the two years of their marriage. What she had accepted as normal was anything but. Suddenly the pattern of his behaviour was revealed to her as a whole: his demand for perfection in everything, his coldness, his cruelty. There, she had thought the word, for Charles *had* been cruel to her; she could see it now.

He had been unfeeling, self-centred, critical, frozen at the core, incapable of love, or even of caring for another person. He had made much of her childlessness, yet if she had produced an heir for him Marissa sensed that he would have found something else to blame her for.

Well, now he had gone, but he had left a legacy of fear. Tonight Luc had unlocked the door to the prison of her mind and emotions, shown her the daylight, the freedom beyond. But she was afraid of stepping out into the air. When Luc had sought to consummate their lovemaking she had panicked, frozen, rejected him. And just as the sight of Charles's portrait could reduce her to trembling fear, so his shadow would always fall across her bed.

Candlelight shone from a window in the front of the house; a figure moved across the uncurtained casement. It was Luc, returned to his chamber. Marissa gathered up the reins and turned Tempest towards the house, drawn by the light and the thought of Luc.

A figure loomed at the window, staring out

blindly from the lit room across the darkened landscape outside. She drew closer, so close that she had
to tip up her head to watch him as he slowly unbuttoned his shirt and shrugged it from his broad
shoulders. The candlelight glanced off his unruly
blond hair, and the recollection of the feel of it beneath her fingers sent a frisson down her salt-sticky
spine. She wanted to be there with him, her palms
flattened against the strong, satiny planes of his
chest, drawing in his warmth, his vitality.

But when he led her to the big bed it would happen all over again; she knew it, the fear would over-
whelm her desire for him. And she realised now,
loving him as she did, she could not risk that. A
man who loved her would be cruelly hurt by the
rejection; a man who wanted her would not tolerate
her rejection of him. And, after all, Luc had not
spoken of love, only of his *intention* to marry her,
to make things right after their scandalous behaviour
together on the beach.

Marissa turned her horse's head, dug her heels
gently into the soft flanks and rode steadily away.
No, loving Luc, being with him, was a fantasy. She
was irretrievably marked by the past and there was
no future for her with him.

A light burned in the stable loft as she wearily
slipped off the mare's back. Despite her orders, Allen had waited up for her. Even as she put her hand
on the door latch it opened and the lad emerged,
tousled and sleepy, hay sticking to his jacket.

'There you are, my lady. It's getting cold out. Let
me take her now.'

Marissa handed him the reins with a smile.
'Thank you, Allen, but I did say not to wait up.'

'I've been asleep, right and tight, my lady, in the
hay. Mr Peters would have my guts for garters if I
had gone back to bed with you out. 'Night, my
lady.'

Back in her chamber Marissa peeled off her damp
clothes and dropped them wearily on the floor, too
tired and drained to do more than get into her bed
and fall into a deep, dreamless sleep.

Jackson placed a dish of eggs on the buffet and
eyed his lordship cautiously. Normally breakfast
was a good time to discuss the household's domestic
affairs as Nicci never stirred from her room before
ten and peace could be guaranteed. This morning,
however, the Earl was looking heavy-eyed and preoccupied. The butler decided this was not the time
to raise the matter of the under-footman, who had
been found last night asleep on the pantry floor and
clutching an empty bottle of his lordship's best port.

He lowered the lids of the chafing dishes silently
and was about to take up position by the buffet when
one of the double doors opened and James peered
round. Jackson raised his eyebrows in silent reproof
but the footman ignored the look and beckoned urgently.

'Excuse me, my lord,' Jackson murmured, and
left the room. 'What are you about, James? You
know his lordship doesn't like being disturbed at
breakfast and he is not in the best of moods today.
Can't it wait?'

'I'm afraid not, Mr Jackson. It's her ladyship, you
see…'

'You mean, Miss Nicole?'

'No, her ladyship, the Countess. She's here, pacing up and down the hall—and *she's* in an odd mood too, I can tell you.'

'I'll come—and don't go gossiping about your betters, lad. Doubtless her ladyship is experiencing some problem with the travel arrangements up to Town.'

As he neared the head of the stairs Jackson could hear the swish of long skirts on the marble floor of the hall. Marissa was dressed for riding, her long green skirts trailing behind her as she paced. She was veiled, but even so, as she stopped and looked up at his approach, he could see the glitter of her eyes behind the fine mesh.

'Good morning, your ladyship. I hope you have had a pleasant ride. Miss Southwood is in her room: would you like me to send up a cup of chocolate for you?'

'Good morning, Jackson.' Marissa allowed none of her feelings to colour her tone. Now that she was standing still she was conscious of just how her agitated pacing must have appeared to the footman: she must pull herself together; this was no way to behave in front of the servants. She lifted her veil and handed him her gloves and whip. 'Thank you, no. I have come to see his lordship, not Miss Southwood.'

'His lordship is at breakfast, my lady. Will you wait in the Blue Salon, and I will let him know you are here?'

'Is he breakfasting in his chamber?'

Jackson was taken aback. 'Why, no, my lady, he is in the morning room…'

'Then I shall go up.' She was in no mood to be

kept waiting. 'There is no need to announce me, Jackson.'

'Not at all, my lady…' Jackson hastened up the stairs to precede her. Something was up and his lord-ship was not going to appreciate being surprised at his breakfast table, whatever it was about.

Luc looked up as the doors opened and the butler, looking uncharacteristically flustered, announced, 'The Countess of Radwinter, my lord.'

'I am not at home, Jackson…'

But it was too late. Marissa swept past the butler and said firmly, 'Thank you, Jackson. I can pour myself some chocolate.'

Without risking a glance at his employer Jackson effaced himself, closing the doors behind him. If it was not for the dignity of his position he would drop to one knee and apply his ear to the keyhole. As it was, he withdrew to a discreet distance and waited for the sound of breaking crockery.

'Good morning, Marissa,' Luc said coolly, resuming his seat as she sat, cup of chocolate before her, at the other end of the table. He raised one eyebrow and waited.

For her part Marissa was beginning to regret the impulse which had brought her here. A night's sleep had not changed either her feelings for Luc or her belief that they had no future together. Whenever she closed her eyes it was Charles's face she saw, Charles's weight she had felt as Luc's body moved over hers. And then the fear had come, as it always had before. And in the shifting shadows of the moonlight Luc had looked so much like his cousin.

The overwhelming, wonderful, unfamiliar sensa-tions she had experienced in Luc's arms, and her own instinctive responses to him had shaken her to the core and made it difficult to face him. Luc was watching her now, his deep blue eyes steady on her face. Under his scrutiny Marissa could feel a hectic blush start rising up the column of her throat, up her cheeks, until it reached the curls on her forehead.

'Why have you come, Marissa?' he asked calmly, leaning back in his chair. 'Not that is not always a pleasure to see you.'

Marissa realised she did not know. She had left the Dower House because she could not bear to stay still any longer. She was confused, almost angry, but she did not rightly know with whom. She wanted to be near him, yet his very closeness frightened her. She needed to be in his arms, yet was terrified of what that might lead to…

'Marissa?' Luc prompted gently.

'I cannot come to London,' she blurted out at last.

'Why ever not?'

'Um…' It had only just occurred to her how impossible it would be. How could she live under Luc's roof for months, seeing him every day, watching him as he set about the task of finding a wife when she had fallen in love with him herself? Still fiery red, she muttered, 'After last night…it is impossible. You must see that.'

'I do not see that it is impossible: far from it. You are naturally agitated that I allowed my passions to run away with me last night. We will be married, of course: it is an eminently suitable solution for both of us. You are the perfect mistress for Southwood Hall and, for my part, I can offer you the style of living to which you have been accustomed. If you wish a longer period to elapse before we announce our betrothal, then I accept that, naturally.'

Luc leaned back and smiled at her kindly. An unexpected flash of anger overcame her embarrassment: here was another man dictating her life, dressing up his offer as the perfect solution for her when in reality it was the perfect solution for *him*.

'No! I will not marry you! Last night…we must forget last night. It was a mistake. And there is certainly no need for you to marry me because of it. I do not wish to remarry, not now, not ever.'

'But you must marry.' Luc leaned forward, fixing her with his blue gaze. 'You are young, and beautiful and eligible. You must want children—' He broke off as she went white. 'I am sorry if what I am saying is painful, Marissa, but life moves on. Charles will never leave you, you will never forget what you shared together, but it will become part of your memories as you live your new life.'

Marissa gave a choked sob and jumped up, knocking over her cup. 'No! No, you are wrong!' How could he tell her that she would never forget when her whole happiness depended on her being able to forget Charles, push those awful years into a locked cupboard in her mind so she could start living afresh?

Luc stood, but did not approach her. 'I am sorry, it is obviously too soon to speak of these things. But why will you not come to London? You are overwrought. You need a change of scene and you would enjoy the balls, the theatre, the shops. You have been confined in the country too long and need diversion.' Luc picked up his cup and saucer and strolled to the window, looking out over the rolling parkland. He added lightly, 'And besides, Nicci needs you as her chaperon.'

'Miss Venables would enjoy the role, and perform it far better than I,' Marissa said stubbornly. She wanted so much to go to London, but she did not want to be with Luc. Close to him, under the same roof, how could she disguise the fact that her feelings for him were growing?

The underlying unhappiness in her voice reached him, and he put down the cup, crossing the room to put one arm around her shoulders, drawing her against his warmth and strength. 'Marissa, do not be so obdurate!' he chided softly. 'Let us not fall out over this. Can't you see—you are cutting off your nose to spite your face? I want you to come to London; Nicci wants you to come to London... Damn it, *you* want to come to London!'

Marissa had let her body relax against his for one self-indulgent moment, then common sense reasserted itself. She pushed hard at his chest and wriggled free. 'Take your hands off me! How dare you touch me...? And after what passed between us last night! Sir, you are no gentleman!'

Luc could not resist it. Confronted by a beautiful, angry woman, with the recollection of the silk of her skin and the taste of her lips still fresh in his mind, he could not ignore the provocation. 'But you, Marissa, judging by your responses on the beach, are all woman.'

She lifted her hand to slap him hard, but he caught her wrist in one hand and pulled her against his chest. His other hand cupped her chin and he bent to kiss her mouth.

Marissa set her lips tight and twisted her face

away, fighting the temptation to yield to him, cover him in kisses.

At the sound of the double doors opening slowly and of raised voices outside, Luc dropped Marissa's hand and took a step backwards. Marissa sank onto the window seat and remarked coolly, 'The park is looking quite lovely in the sunshine, my lord, do you not think so?'

Jackson, with Nicci hard on his heels, entered. There was colour in the butler's cheeks and Nicci had an unmistakable air of triumph about her. 'Jackson said you were busy and were not to be disturbed, but I told him that was nonsense, you were only having breakfast, and even if you were grumpy I need to talk to you... Oh, good morning, Marissa, I had not realised you were here! Honestly, Jackson, you are impossible—I would have come down directly if I had known Marissa was here.'

Jackson cast Luc a look of resignation and departed. Nicci was chattering on. 'Well, I am really glad you have come; I need to talk to you about jewellery. Luc is being incredibly stuffy about it; he will only let me take pearls and not Mama's diamonds or the emerald set...'

'He is quite correct, Nicci,' Marissa replied steadily, controlling her agitated breathing. She was relieved that the girl seemed not to have noticed anything amiss. 'You must not be disappointed, but gemstones are not considered suitable for a young lady in her first Season. Pearls will be lovely, and there is no reason why you cannot wear amber or rose quartz beads.'

'Oh, if you are going to be stuffy too, there is no point in arguing, I suppose. I am so excited—is it

really only two days until we set off? Are you
packed and ready? I am sure I will never be.'

Marissa paused, then explained awkwardly, 'I was
just saying to your brother that I am not coming with
you to London. But I am sure Miss Venables will
be a splendid companion for you…'

With a wail of disappointment and dismay Nicci
ran across the room and threw herself down on the
seat next to Marissa. 'Marissa, this cannot be true!
Why, why can you not come to London?'

Marissa struggled to find an acceptable answer,
unconscious that her gaze had strayed to Luc's sar-
donic face.

Nicci caught the look and swivelled round immediately. 'So that is it! It is Luc's fault, as usual—
I suppose he has upset you in some way, Marissa
dear, and now he is going to ruin my come-out!'

'No, no, Nicci—please do not blame your brother.
It is entirely my decision. I just felt, er, it was too
much. It is too soon. I mean…' Marissa's words
fizzled out in a trail of lameness. She had not even
convinced herself, let alone Nicci.

'Now, Marissa,' Luc interjected smoothly. 'You
are being unfair on yourself. Tell my sister the *real*
reason why you do not wish to accompany us to
London.'

Marissa stared at him in horror. Surely he would
not even hint at what had passed between them last
night, or what had been said this morning? Her
mouth opened; she sought for the right words but
nothing emerged.

'Very well, I see I shall have to be brutally honest.
Nicci, I am afraid that Marissa feels that you will
be too much of a handful for her. Now, I know she

wanted to spare your feelings, but you will have to accept that she is going to sacrifice her own pleasure on the altar of your wilfulness,' Luc said solemnly.

Nicci promptly burst into tears. Marissa, with one harassed glance at the girl, left her and marched over to where Luc was standing, one booted foot on the fender, arms crossed—and obviously thoroughly enjoying himself. 'Luc! How could you say anything so untrue and unkind to your sister? See how you have upset her.'

He smiled down into her furious face. 'Yes, I realise it is not very...gentlemanly of me, but it had to be said for her own good.' If he had hoped to goad her by flinging her accusation that he had not behaved as a gentleman back in her face, he had succeeded.

With a frustrated stamp of her foot Marissa turned back to Nicci, who was drooping miserably on the window seat, sniffing into a lawn handkerchief. 'It is not true, Nicci dearest. Luc is teasing you—and me. I simply said...that I was feeling very tired. I think the arrangements, and the hot weather, have sapped my energy. But do not mind it. I will be better directly: of course I will go to London with you!'

'Well, if you are sure. A change of scenery and occupation will soon chase away these megrims,' Luc said smoothly. 'Although I am certain you will miss the invigorating sea breezes.' He smiled wolfishly, his teeth very white in the lean, tanned face.

'I know what you are about, Luc,' Nicci accused suddenly. 'You are teasing Marissa about something and it is very unfair of you!' She stood, mustering her dignity, and extended her hand to her cousin.

'Come along, Marissa, we shall go upstairs and leave him to his beastly breakfast! I need you to tell me if any of my hats are fit to be seen in London.'

Despite her conviction that she would need an entirely new wardrobe for London, Miss Southwood still managed to pack enough valises to almost fill a travelling coach, and Luc was forced to add two more to the train of carriages that set forth from Southwood Hall on a brilliantly sunny day.

The journey was smooth and uneventful, but none the less Marissa was pleased to see Matthews's smiling face as he stood at the head of the staff gathered to welcome them to the Grosvenor Square house. She had been afraid that he would resent Jackson's arrival to usurp his position, but it soon became clear that the inexperienced young man welcomed direction in managing the Town house now the family were in residence.

The hall was soon full of servants and luggage and Marissa slipped away to the little morning room which overlooked the garden at the rear of the house. She stood by the windows, reflecting how different their arrival had used to be when she was married to Charles. He had hated commotion and disorder, and for that reason the luggage had always been sent well ahead, so that everything would be in its place by the time the Earl and Countess drew up at the front door.

The Grosvenor Square house was still decorated to Charles's exacting taste, yet although it was as cold and impersonal as Southwood Hall the memories it held were not as painful. Marissa had known that whenever they went up to London she would hardly see her husband from one day to the other. Charles had left her to her own devices, in fact had hardly spoken to her. He'd had his own circle, his own interests, and had spent much of his time at his clubs. After his initial courtship he had rarely accompanied her to Almack's or the numerous soirées to which they received invitations, leaving his wife to seek the escort of friends.

Marissa had spent many lonely days in London, but at least she had been free of Charles's dominating presence. And, curiously, here she had never been summoned to his bedchamber as she had in Norfolk.

Matthews's discreet cough behind her recalled her to the present. 'My lady, I was not certain which chamber you would wish to occupy.'

'Her ladyship will, naturally, have her usual suite of rooms,' Luc's voice responded before she could reply.

'No, surely Miss Southwood should occupy those rooms,' she protested, turning to find them both in the doorway.

'I insist. Matthews, see her ladyship's luggage is taken up before any of the rest.'

'Yes, my lord.'

'Oh, and Matthews, order some tea to be sent up: her ladyship is fatigued.'

When the door closed behind the under-butler Marissa snapped, 'Thank you so much for your concern, my lord, but I am quite capable of ordering my own tea.'

'You are as pale as linen, Marissa. I am sorry. I appreciate this must be painful for you.' Luc came and took her hand, leading her to a chair and gently pressing her into it. 'I should have realised you would have an attachment to this house and will find it difficult to see it occupied by others.'

'No, not really.' Marissa was startled into honesty. 'I never cared much for this house. It is not that I dislike it, simply that it has no character, no warmth. My lord ordered it decorated in the Classical taste, but I cannot but feel that it is not so successful in a house of this scale as it is at Southwood Hall.'

'How true,' Luc agreed drily, casting a critical eye around the morning room. The walls were ice-blue with white mouldings. The curtains, again in chilly blue, were draped with almost rigid perfection around the long casements and two marble nymphs flanked the empty grate. 'I have it in mind to redecorate throughout, but I would not want to do anything you would dislike.'

Marissa looked up with an animated face. 'Oh, yes! That is a splendid idea. I have always felt that this could be made into a real family home. The house has beautiful proportions, but it is not served well by my lord's taste.'

Luc's eyebrows rose. 'So, my impeccable late cousin had at least one failing, then?'

The animation drained from her and Marissa cast down her eyes to where her hands had tightened in her lap. 'As have we all, my lord.'

Luc dropped to one knee beside her chair and covered her taut hands with one of his. 'Marissa…'

She glanced up and found he was looking at her with such compassion that her heart knotted within her. If he would only take her in his arms now, hold her, tell her that her marriage had been a bad dream, that it would not be like that with him…

'Your chamber is prepared, my lady, and I have had the tea tray sent up.' Having delivered this message, Matthews withdrew as silently as he had appeared, but the spell was broken.

Marissa withdrew her hands from under Luc's fingers. 'Excuse me, my lord, I will go up now.' Luc rose silently from his knees, offering her his hand. Marissa stood gracefully, releasing his light grasp the moment she was on her feet. The moment of intimacy had passed, yet the pressure of his fingers still remained as though imprinted on her skin.

Her chamber, although tidy, seemed very full. Mary was shaking out and hanging up her gowns, a pile of trunks was stacked in the corner and Nicci, obviously too excited to sit, was pacing the room, chattering non-stop to the stoical maid.

'Marissa! There you are! Oh, do not bother with tea—can't we go out to the shops now, or for a drive in the park? Surely it is the fashionable hour to be seen.'

'Nicci, please sit down. You are badly in poor Mary's way, and I declare you are positively giving me a headache with your pacing. Sit down and have a cup of tea, then we must finish our unpacking, have a rest and a quiet family dinner. Tomorrow we shall go shopping, I promise you.'

'But I need so much—I cannot be seen in these clothes. And there is a pile of invitations and cards downstairs already! If I do not have the right gowns I will miss all the parties…'

Marissa regarded her over the rim of her cup. 'This is the start of the Season: there will be time—

and parties enough for you to go to. You know your brother will deny you nothing in the way of gowns.' Nicci was looking mutinous, so she added cunningly, 'You would not wish to appear to be a provincial by scrambling to attend every event you are invited to. We will be selective: you must not appear over-eager.'

'Very well. I expect you are right as usual, Marissa dear. Tell me about your come-out. Was it very wonderful? Did you have lots of lovely gowns and admirers?' She took her cup and sank down in a flurry of muslin skirts, ready for a good gossip.

Marissa looked at the girl's eager face and chose her words carefully. 'My lord proposed to me within a month of my come-out. And of course thereafter I always attended functions with him. But, yes, I had many lovely gowns.' And indeed she had. Her father, who had ignored her as an inconvenient expense throughout her childhood, had proved unexpectedly generous when it had come to her first Season. He had gambled away most of her late mother's jewels, but from somewhere he had found the resources to dress her in the very latest and most flattering fashions when she had made her debut.

Almost paralysed with nerves at her first dance, Marissa had not realised she was under the scrutiny of the eligible, uncatchable Earl of Radwinter until he had asked for a dance. He had appeared to admire her for her stately beauty, for the dignity of her demeanour so unusual in a girl of just eighteen years. She had rapidly discovered, although her nervousness had diminished and she had soon felt at ease in Society, that her lord preferred her to retain an air of control and distance.

Innocent and sheltered, Marissa had not realised until much later how unusual Charles Southwood's courtship had been. He had never expressed affection, or even partiality. He had never touched her, except to take her hand in the dance or to assist her from the carriage. He had appeared to admire her, but almost as though she were an object, to be selected and purchased, not a woman with feelings and emotions to be engaged.

And if she had been taken aback by her father's urgency that she accept this very first proposal and that the marriage should swiftly follow, then her puzzlement had been swept aside in the hectic preparations for marriage.

'Marissa?' Nicci's voice broke through the memories.

Marissa smiled at her. 'I am sorry, Nicci. I was just reflecting that I am quite jealous of your freedom. I was engaged within weeks of my come-out, so I never really had the opportunity to enjoy myself as a single girl for long.' She leaned across and took Nicci's hand, looking urgently into the girl's blue eyes. 'Nicci…take your time. Do not feel you have to hasten into marriage. Enjoy yourself while you can.'

The girl's expression was first puzzled, then she laughed. 'You sound like Miss Venables! Do not worry, Marissa, I do not intend to find myself entangled.'

'Especially as your heart has still not recovered from Mr Ashforde,' Marissa replied slyly.

Chapter Nine

After dinner the ladies left Luc to his brandy and repaired to the drawing room, where the conversation soon turned to plans for the next day. Nicci demanded to know the names of all the most fashionable *modistes* and insisted that Marissa and Miss Venables accompany her to all of them as early as possible the next morning.

'No, no, dear,' Jane Venables protested. 'It will never do to patronise a *modiste* at random. We must consider who will best enhance your style and make gowns suitable for a debutante.'

'I have heard well of Madame Franchot,' Nicci said excitedly. 'Diane—our dear friend Madame de Rostan, who lived near us in Jamaica—patronises her when she comes to England, and Diane always wears the most stunning gowns.'

Marissa, a slight flush on her cheeks, said nothing. Miss Venables marked this and stored it away to puzzle over later. 'No, dear, that would not be a suitable choice. Madame Franchot does not specialise in gowns for debutantes; you will be able to shop at her establishment when you are married. But far-

ther down Bruton Street there is an establishment
owned by a dressmaker who previously worked for
Madame Lavall, and I hear she produces the most
charming, fresh gowns that will be quite your style.'

'Oh, yes! And then I will need shoes, and bonnets,
and reticules and stockings…' The girl prattled on
happily.

Miss Venables glanced at Marissa and was reassured to see she had regained her customary composure. She was laughing at Nicci's ambitious pro-
gramme. 'We will need to plan our days like a
military campaign, Nicci, if we are to get through it
all!'

A floorboard creaked and Jane looked across to
see Luc standing in the doorway, watching Marissa's laughing profile. Now *that* would be a suitable match, she thought. Entirely appropriate for her
dear Marissa, and who knows? Perhaps his lordship
could lift the mysterious shadow from her heart.
However close, however intimate she grew with Marissa, Jane Venables had never been able to pinpoint
the source of this deep and secret sadness in her
cousin.

The Earl walked into the drawing room, a wicked
smile on his lips, his tall figure immaculate in evening dress. 'Nicci, I am sorry to disappoint you, but
Marissa is coming shopping with me tomorrow.'

Marissa looked up, startled, then sent him a reproving frown for teasing his sister.

'Luc, don't be a beast,' Nicci protested. 'And Marissa can't go shopping with you. It would not be
proper for her to go to tailors and bootmakers! Even
I know that.'

'Oh, I was not intending to buy clothes, sister

dear. No, we have something far more important to engage us. Marissa is going to assist me in redecorating this house.'

Nicci was immediately diverted. 'How wonderful—I knew Marissa could not really like this chilly place, although naturally I would not say so! Now, for my room I want a pink silk tented ceiling and gauze bed curtains, and a shell-shaped bath in my dressing room...'

'Tell me, little sister, how have you managed to imagine a room better suited to a class of lady I devoutly hope you will never encounter?'

'My lord,' Miss Venables cautioned, but Nicci simply pouted at her brother.

'Stuffy man! I saw it illustrated in the *Lady's Intelligencer* last month. It was *beautiful*.'

'Well, I have no intention of redecorating your room, whatever your journals say. It will soon be buried under piles of shopping in any case. No, we will begin with the hall and the Salon. Marissa, at what hour tomorrow would it be convenient for you to accompany me to Schomberg House? Harding, Howell and Company are reputed to have the latest styles in furniture.'

The thought of spending an intimate day in Luc's company choosing furnishings like a married couple was dangerously attractive. Marissa dropped her eyes demurely and replied, 'I regret that I will be unable to give any attention to furnishings until we have ordered our gowns, my lord. Surely you would not have the house redecorated but none of us fit to entertain in it?'

Luc crossed one leg over another and looked at

her steadily. 'Come, Marissa, you are reneging on our agreement.'

'Not at all. I am more than willing to assist you,' she replied with spirit. 'But all in good time: I had not realised that you were in quite such a hurry, my lord.'

'I know what it is,' Nicci teased. 'Luc is going to catch a wife and he wants the house to be in the mode to impress the ladies! Is that not so, brother? Deny it if you dare!'

There was a silence before Luc replied, 'Of course. And I must be sure that the house will reflect the taste of the lady I would marry.'

'Aha!' Nicci said triumphantly. 'Hoist by your own petard! You cannot be in a hurry, for how can you redecorate until you have found the lady and discovered her taste?'

Luc laughed. '*Touché*, little sister. Very well, I release Marissa for your orgy of shopping, but I reserve the right to claim her later.'

Marissa's eyes flew to his face and her heart thudded. What a thing to say. What a wonderful thought! It appeared he was still bent on marrying her, but she would not, could not fall in with his plans for her to be the new Countess of Radwinter. The realities of marriage would be far worse this time, for she loved Luc; she knew that now. She could not bear to have that love destroyed by marriage, when he would realise she could never be a true wife to him.

Miss Venables's sharp eyes moved from one face to another. What was going on—and why did Marissa seem so discomfited? She spoke firmly to break the mood. 'If we are to make an early start tomorrow we should retire. Nicci, if you do not go to bed this instant, I can promise that you will have black circles under your eyes! Come along now, say goodnight to your brother and Marissa.'

Left alone, neither Marissa nor Luc spoke. She because she could not, he because he seemed quite at his ease simply sitting and regarding the flames of the small fire flickering in the grate.

At last the silence became so oppressive, and the tension of waiting for him to speak so great, that Marissa blurted out, 'May I take the barouche...?'

Luc spoke at the same moment. 'Would you like to take the barouche tomorrow morning?' He laughed as their words collided. 'We appear to think as one.'

'On that matter, sir, yes,' she responded, as repressively as she could. 'I would be grateful for the carriage, and if I may I will take James: I suspect that the groom will find the number of packages too many for him to manage alone.'

'Take all the footmen; you will probably need them if my little sister has her way. I think I had better go and speak to my banker tomorrow: I will likely have to sell out of Government stocks to pay for this come-out!'

Marissa looked anxious. 'Perhaps you should let me know what limit you would set on Nicci's expenditure and then I can ensure she remains within it.'

'No, let her have what you feel is suitable. There is nobody whose taste and judgement I trust more than yours, Marissa. But do not let her monopolise all your time—you have your own plans, I know.

And,' he added, his eyes warm on her face, 'I look forward to seeing you out of mourning.'

Marissa flushed at both compliments and rose. Luc got to his feet in response. 'Jane is quite right, as usual. I will retire,' she said. 'We have all had a fatiguing day, with the prospect of another tomorrow. Goodnight, Luc.'

She smiled and turned to leave, but he came and took her hand in his, brushing his lips lightly over her knuckles in a formal salute. 'Goodnight, Marissa.'

He continued to stand after she had left, gazing thoughtfully at where she had sat. Marissa was an enigma to him, behind the perfect façade of control and elegance was a laughing, passionate, instinctive young woman. And yet the passion seemed to go only so far and was strangely innocent, at variance with her previously married state. It was almost as if it was curbed by something. He searched his mind for the word, but only 'fear' came to mind. That was too preposterous. He shook his head in denial and went to pour himself another brandy from the decanter. What in the world could Marissa have to be afraid of?

'Oh, Marissa, may I really have the figured silk?' Nicci breathed. 'It is so lovely.' She twisted and turned in front of the cheval glass, holding her hands away from the white fabric as though afraid to touch it.

'Yes, I think it will be perfect as your best ball-gown. But, *madame,* it must be cut a little higher in the bodice, and I am not certain about the silver floss at the hem. Jane, what do you think?'

Miss Venables turned from her scrutiny of several bolts of muslin and considered the gown. 'I agree, dear. It is too fussy for Miss Southwood: I always believe that understatement is better on a young girl.'

'Might I suggest a pearl beading, as we have on this gown?' Madame Lefevre crooked a finger and an assistant scurried forward with a sample.

'Yes, very pretty, and if that could be repeated on the puff sleeves along the line of the lace…'

'But, yes!' the *modiste* exclaimed. 'Your ladyship has impeccable taste. May I show Miss Southwood any other gowns?'

The little assistant, who seemed scarcely older than Nicole, brought the ladies glasses of orgeat and almond wafer biscuits and they reviewed their purchases.

'Now, we have the white silk ballgown for best, the pale green for less formal parties, the fawn walking dress with the chocolate-brown pelisse…' Miss Venables ticked off on her fingers. 'Your riding habit we will have tailored—your country one will do for the meantime. What you are lacking are simple day dresses. I suggest we visit some of the linen drapers and select some dress lengths for Mary to make up for you.'

Nicci clapped her hands with sheer pleasure. 'More dresses! Oh, yes please!'

They arranged for the delivery of the new gowns as soon as possible and made their way out to the waiting barouche. Nicci's dread of being seen in an open carriage in a dress of less than fashionable cut had been forgotten in the excitement of driving behind her brother's newly acquired matched bays with a liveried coachman on the box and two foot-men standing behind.

'Shoes next, I think,' Marissa remarked, consult-ing her notebook. 'Then Grafton House for dress lengths, and we will end at Dickens and Smith for stockings and trimmings. Bond Street, please, Henry,' she ordered the coachman. 'Seymour's shoe shop.'

The shoe shop was more a boudoir than a shop. Its curtains were of silk, the patrons were seated upon divans arranged tastefully around the room, and despite the sunshine outside the interior was lit by discreet lamps of fashionable design.

There was one other customer already seated, an assistant kneeling at her feet gently slipping a daring scarlet kid slipper onto her foot. She looked up and cried out in pleasure when she saw who had entered.

'My dear Lady Southwood! How well you look, and what a pleasure it is to see you back in Society again.'

'Lady Valentine,' Marissa responded, moving for-ward to take the other woman's proffered hand. 'May I make known to you my companion, Miss Venables, and my cousin, Miss Southwood? Jane, Nicole: Lady Valentine.'

The older woman cast an openly appraising glance over Nicole. 'So, you are the new Earl's sis-ter from the West Indies, are you not?'

'Yes, ma'am,' Nicci said, bobbing a curtsey but looking from under her lashes at the young man in uniform who was lounging negligently against the wall, apparently waiting for her ladyship.

Lady Valentine caught the look and waved the young man forward. 'I had quite forgot you were there, Andrew. Lady Southwood, ladies, may I make known to you Captain Andrew Cross of the Seventh Light Dragoons. Andrew: Lady Southwood, Miss Southwood, Miss Venables.'

The Captain swept the ladies a bow, his cropped dark hair gleaming in the subdued light. Nicci batted her eyelashes, admiring his red jacket, gold braid and highly polished boots.

'Sit here beside me, all of you,' Lady Valentine suggested, patting the seat. 'Are you all here to buy shoes?'

'For Miss Southwood only this morning,' Marissa said coolly, nodding to the assistant who was hovering in the background. The young woman hastened forward and listened attentively as Marissa outlined the types of shoes they were looking for.

Lady Valentine extended one foot, drawing up the hem of her jade-green walking dress to expose an elegant ankle and turning her foot in one direction then the other. 'Andrew, what do you think of these? Will they do?'

Miss Venables drew in her breath sharply at the impropriety, and glared at Nicole, who was openly staring at the older woman.

'Very nice, Susan,' Captain Cross drawled, his eyes lingering on the blatantly exposed ankle.

Fortunately at that moment the assistant returned with some walking shoes and Nicci was distracted. Unable to resist it, Marissa enquired sweetly, 'And how is Sir Michael, and your three dear little boys?'

'Oh, well enough, I suppose. I am sure Sir Michael would write if anything were amiss. They are still at home in Bedfordshire. Sir Michael finds

Town such a bore: I always tell him not to disturb himself, coming up on my account.'

Marissa repressed a smile at Miss Venables's snort of disapproval and added maliciously, 'But your dear sons, how could you bear to leave them?'

'Oh, the country air is better for them,' Lady Valentine responded, with a toss of her head which sent her luxuriant dark curls bouncing. 'Besides, there is very little for them to do in Town.'

Captain Cross had wandered off, scarcely bothering to conceal his boredom at this talk of domestic circumstances, but now he reappeared, a dashing half-boot in his hand. 'Try this, Susan.' He dropped to one knee and eased the scarlet slipper from her foot, his finger lingering at her ankle. Marissa became aware of Nicci's dropped jaw and astounded expression and jabbed her briskly in the ribs.

'Pay attention, Nicole, does the shoe chafe your toes? The colour is perfect for your new walking dress, do you not agree, Miss Venables?'

But even Miss Venables was distracted by the outrageous behaviour of Lady Valentine and her male companion. He was buttoning the half-boot with fingers which strayed frequently to the skin above.

'Andrew, behave,' Lady Valentine admonished indulgently, bending down to pat away his questing fingers. 'Yes, I will take those too.' She gestured for the assistant and while her purchases were being packed enquired of Marissa, 'Do you make a long stay in Town?'

'We are here for the Season; Miss Southwood is making her come-out.'

'I shall see you again, then.' As she passed Lady

Valentine touched Nicci's cheek. 'Charming, so fresh. Andrew, stop staring and come along. Good afternoon!'

It was as much as Marissa could do to keep Nicci quiet until they reached their carriage. 'Well,' the girl burst out. 'Showing so much ankle—and letting Captain Cross put her shoe on like that! How very fast she was! The Captain is extremely handsome, but surely quite a bit younger than she is? And does her husband not mind?'

Miss Venables twitched her pelisse straight and fixed Nicci with a gimlet eye. 'That is what happens when a lady allows herself to behave in a fast and indecorous manner. Let that be a lesson to you, my girl.'

'You mean I would attract handsome army captains and wear beautiful scarlet shoes?' Nicole asked, wide-eyed.

'Do not be pert, Nicole, this conversation is at an end. I think we have had quite a surfeit of shopping today and I am in need of a cup of tea. Marissa, shall we return to Grosvenor Square?'

Chastened, Nicole refrained from sulking, and the three ladies were soon wearily ascending the front steps where Matthews held the door wide.

Their energies returned the next day, however, and a prolonged expedition saw Nicci's muslins, stockings, ribbons and laces purchased. An early start enabled them to scour the shops before the crowds grew too great, and Marissa then indulged herself with a lengthy consultation at Madame Lavall's. Miss Venables displayed an unexpected interest in evening gowns herself, and it was three very tired, but very excited ladies who finally returned home for tea.

'Is my brother at home, Matthews?' Nicci enquired as the under-butler held the door open for the laden footmen to stagger in under their burden of hat boxes, packages and parcels.

'I believe he has just gone out, Miss Southwood. Shall I have tea sent to the Blue Salon?'

'No, to my room, please. Marissa, Miss Venables—let us take tea upstairs and unpack all our purchases. I have quite forgotten what I have bought, we visited so many shops!'

The ladies spent a very agreeable and thoroughly frivolous hour re-examining every item, spreading the muslins out for Mary to see and thoroughly confusing the maid by disagreeing over which pattern in the *Mirror of Fashion* she should use for which fabric.

Miss Venables had invested in a pair of long buttoned kid evening gloves with silver embroidery. Now she was having second thoughts. 'Are they a little much, my dear?' she asked Marissa anxiously. 'I normally wear much plainer gloves, but these are such beautiful work I could not resist.'

'They are very fine, Jane. I agree you have nothing suitable to wear with them, but just think of that lovely cream silk shot through with silver we saw in Debenham's. You could have that made up in a simple, elegant style for evening and that would quite set off the gloves.'

'I do declare, Marissa, you are too extravagant. To buy gloves and then have a gown made to match is quite the wrong way round—I do not know what has come over me!'

Marissa jumped up. 'I know, the gauze scarf I brought with me would be perfect with such an ensemble. Let me fetch it and we will try it out with the gloves.'

She darted out of the door, leaving it ajar, and ran lightly down the corridor. Behind her she heard Jane call, 'Marissa, come back. This is really too frivolous for me!'

She spun round and called back, laughing, 'Nonsense, Jane, it will be just the thing, you will see!' Turning back, she stumbled and found herself colliding with a strong, warm male body. 'Oh! Oh, Luc— I thought you had gone out.'

'Did you?' he asked gently. 'What have you been up to?' He looked down into her flushed, laughing face, noting the sparkle in her eyes. 'Mischief, by the look of you. I like that gown.' His words were warm, his gaze appreciative as he took in her dress of jonquil twill, which moulded the soft curve of her breast and emphasised her slender waist.

Marissa's heart beat like a captive bird inside her ribcage, her breathing constricted by a strange excitement and an overwhelming desire to press herself against him, drink him in in a kiss that would bind him to her in the passion they had shared on the beach.

Something of her desire must have reached him, for he went very still, his blue gaze intent on her hot face as the laughter faded, leaving her staring up at him, wide-eyed and beseeching.

'No...not mischief. Shopping with my minx of a sister,' he said softly, the look in his eyes at odds with the light words. 'I like you like this. I wish I too could make you laugh.' His fingertip traced the curve of her cheek, down the fine line of her jaw, then up to her lips. He let it rest there on the full softness until Marissa let them part. Slowly, almost of its own volition, the tip of her tongue crept out to touch the pad of his fingertip.

A sharp intake of breath was his first response, but then he swept his arms around her, pulled her to his body and bent to kiss her. Behind them the sound of footsteps ascending the staircase made them both freeze, then Luc stooped, swept Marissa up into his arms and shouldered open her bedroom door.

She surrendered to his strong clasp, trying to believe that it would be different this time, that she could give herself to him completely. And then she could accept his offer of marriage...even if he did not love her it would be enough if she could give him everything...

Luc kicked the door shut behind him and made for the bed. For one giddy moment the passion swept her along, then, despite her desire for him, instinct froze her, made her limbs rigid, the breath catch in her throat. Luc stopped and looked down at her questioningly before turning to the chaise and sitting down, holding her on his lap.

To her great surprise he did not kiss her, instead he held her against his chest, stroked her hair and waited until she relaxed a little.

'Now, what was that about?'

'What do you mean?' she asked, her voice shaking.

'Just now you wanted me to kiss you, you would have met and answered my embraces, yet you froze in my arms. And on the beach you were the same. Tell me what is wrong, Marissa.'

In that instant she wanted to pour out everything to him. How she loved him, how she wanted him. He had shown her it was possible for a man to give pleasure to a woman, but that was only before the act itself. But two years with Charles had destroyed her ability to give herself, even to a man she loved. If Luc took her to his bed she would either freeze again or break down—and no man, however understanding, would tolerate that from his wife.

Luc waited patiently as she struggled for the words to describe to him something so intimate she could hardly even allude to it to a female companion, never mind a man! His fingers lifted the soft curls at the nape of her neck and stroked the sensitive skin beneath with mesmeric slowness.

No, it was impossible. She could find no way to explain to him that she could never respond to his lovemaking, that the very act was so abhorrent to her that, even loving Luc as she did, it would solve nothing. The words, when she finally spoke them, were true, but not the whole truth.

'Charles…you look so like Charles it is a constant reminder…' She struggled, but failed, to speak aloud the words in her head. *He treated me so coldly, used me so badly, that I can never give myself to you as I crave to.*

Luc became very still, his fingers arrested on her skin. When he spoke his voice was dry. 'I understand. You are trying to tell me that you are still in love with your husband. I am sorry that my attentions give you so much pain. I am afraid I can do nothing to alter my outward appearance, but believe me, I shall no longer press my attentions upon you.'

Marissa gave a little sob, burying her face against the lapels of his coat. Luc gritted his teeth and resisted the temptation to kiss away her tears. Of all the damnable luck: no wonder she responded at first to his lovemaking! She had fallen into his arms seeking the husband she had lost. Well, that was a salutary lesson to his pride—he was a poor substitute for Charles, and if he had not looked so like his cousin Marissa would not have given him a second glance, let alone let him glimpse the passion that burned within her.

'Marissa! Marissa, dear, where are you?' There was a tap on the door and without waiting Miss Venables bustled in. 'Have you lost that scarf? I thought I saw it—' She broke off, her face scarlet with embarrassment.

Marissa scrambled to her feet, equally flushed. 'Jane…er, his lordship was just…'

'Quite…er, that is…I will go back to Nicci. Oh, dear…' Miss Venables could be heard retreating along the landing, muttering, 'Oh, dear…oh, dear…' in very agitated tones.

It broke the tension between them. Luc caught Marissa's eye and broke out laughing. 'Poor Miss Venables! Will she ever recover?'

'It is no laughing matter, my lord,' Marissa reproved, but she too could see the humour in the scene. 'She will think me quite beyond redemption. I will tell her that we… Oh, dear, I cannot think of anything to tell her that is not thoroughly improper!'

Luc got easily to his feet, the laughter dying out of his face to be replaced with a rueful gentleness.

'Forgive me, Marissa, I would not have embarrassed you for the world. Tell Miss Venables what you will. I promise I will stand any amount of lecturing from her on the subject of my morals!' He smiled at her and left.

As she entered Nicci's room, carefully avoiding Jane's eye, Marissa thought, I do *like* Luc: he is so very kind, and he does make me laugh. It had never occurred to her that she could have that sort of friendship with a man, least of all one she was in love with. Perhaps she could learn to accept that friendship and keep her other thoughts, her love for him, secret always.

'Marissa, you have forgotten the scarf,' Nicci observed. 'And what have you been doing? You are quite pink in the face and your hair is disarrayed.'

'Oh, is it? Well, I thought the scarf might have dropped down behind the clothes press so I leaned over to look. I expect that made the blood rush to my face.'

Miss Venables cleared her throat reprovingly and stared out of the window. Much as she liked Luc, and considered him a highly eligible candidate for Marissa's hand, she was shocked to the core to have found them in such a compromising situation. And for Marissa to add an untruth to immoral behaviour...well, she would have to speak to her later, when they were alone.

Marissa, however, was unconscious of her companion's disapproving thoughts, her mind still on Luc, her hand touching her nape where his fingers had rested, her memory storing away each word, each gesture.

A discreet tap at the door, answered by Nicci,

revealed Jackson, a broad smile on his face. 'Miss
Nicci, Madame Diane has arrived.'

'Diane—here in London?' Nicci jumped up in a
shower of paper patterns, her eyes sparkling. 'But
we did not look to see her for several weeks, I
thought.'

'The winds from Jamaica were good, I understand,' the butler responded, still grinning.

'But where is she staying? Has she opened up the
London house?' Nicci demanded. 'She must come
to dinner...'

'You can ask her yourself, Miss Nicci—she is below in the hall. I must find his lordship—have you
seen him recently?'

Miss Venables cleared her throat again, and Marissa said hastily, 'No. Perhaps he is in his study,
Jackson.'

Led by Nicci, the ladies crossed the landing to
where the sweep of banisters gave a view of the hall
below and the lady who waited there. From above
Marissa gained the impression of extreme elegance,
of superbly coiffed honey-blonde hair just visible
under the brim of a hat in the very latest mode, and
of a woman no longer in her first youth but with a
mature beauty that was still dazzling.

Then Luc's footsteps sounded on the marble floor
and the woman swung round, threw her arms wide,
sending furs and parasol flying across the hall, and
was swept up into the bear-hug of Luc's embrace.
Marissa stood stunned as he kissed Madame de Rostan full on the lips without restraint. And the embrace he received in return was just as uninhibited
and generous. So Nicci had been right: this woman
had been—still was—Luc's mistress.

'*Chéri,* I have missed you so much!' Diane cried when, after what seemed like minutes, they broke the kiss. 'You look so handsome, Luc—I thought you would have become all pale and uninteresting after a few months in this soggy country!' She ran a proprietorial hand down his lapels and across his chest.

Luc caught her hand in his, laughing down into her face. 'Behave, Diane, we are not alone,' he said huskily. The low-voiced words, caught by the acoustics of the hall, seemed to stab Marissa in the heart. Thank goodness she had not succumbed to the desire to tell him everything, especially how much she loved him.

Nicci, never one for subtleties, ran down the stairs, crying, 'Diane! Diane!' and threw herself into the Frenchwoman's arms. 'I have missed you so much! Are you well? Was the voyage dreadful? But you look *beautiful*, so you cannot have been seasick…'

Diane patted Nicci's flushed cheek with one gloved hand. 'You are prettier than ever, *ma petite*, but I regret to see that your manners have not improved one jot! You must introduce me to these ladies.'

Marissa reached the bottom of the stairs and found herself caught in the warmth of the Frenchwoman's personality. Smiling, deep blue eyes regarded her from a face lightly coloured by the sun but virtually unlined, even after reaching the age of thirty-nine in a tropical climate.

Luc stepped forward, a trace of colour on his cheekbones. 'Lady Southwood, may I make known to you Madame Diane de Rostan of Jamaica, an old friend of the family? Diane—the Dowager Countess of Radwinter, my cousin, who has graciously consented to act as hostess for me and help bring Nicci out this Season. Miss Venables—Madame de Rostan; Diane—Miss Venables, Lady Southwood's companion.'

The ladies exchanged polite bows and the entire party moved into the drawing room, followed by Jackson and a footman with a tray of refreshments. Luc conducted Diane to the sofa and waited while the other ladies settled themselves before moving to stand, one foot on the fender, his arm resting lightly on the mantelshelf.

Marissa studied Diane while the footman handed out glasses of ratafia and almond biscuits. Madame de Rostan was tall, almost willowy, but with a full and voluptuous bosom which the high-waisted fashionable afternoon dress showed off to perfection. The fine wool cloth was a soft, deep blue, the colour of periwinkles, in the highest kick of fashion and unmistakably French-cut. The overall effect was to make Marissa feel washed-out and almost provincial in the jonquil twill which had pleased her so much that morning when she had donned it.

For a tall woman Diane had delicate hands, sheathed in fine kid gloves just a shade paler than the blue of her gown. Below the braided hem of her gown peeped fine blue kid slippers. Sipping her ratafia and maintaining a polite flow of conversation, Marissa struggled with the unworthy feeling that she disliked this woman on sight.

Nicci was chattering on, demanding news of mutual friends and of old servants. Marissa let her attention wander until she suddenly realised that from across the room Luc was watching her intently. Bringing her eyes up, she met the look with one of bland but polite indifference.

Madame de Rostan broke off from a description of someone's new plantation house to say, 'But, Nicci, you must stop asking me about Jamaica. We are discussing matters and people that are of no interest to Lady Southwood and Miss Venables.' Nicci instantly obeyed, apologising prettily to Miss Venables and Marissa.

Marissa was piqued by this instant obedience from Nicci, so much in contrast to her wilful behaviour when in Marissa's charge. She felt her brows drawing together into a frown and hastily rearranged her expression, feeling ashamed of herself. She was jealous of Diane de Rostan, jealous not only because she was Luc's mistress but also because she was so beautiful and Nicci held her in such affection.

It was a thoroughly unworthy emotion, Marissa chided herself, but she could not shake from her memory the passion with which Luc and Diane had clung together in the hall, the history of past passion that had shown in that embrace.

Marissa suddenly felt a great weariness, as if all her vitality had drained away. So much for her hope that she and Luc could be friends, that she could still be part of his life even if she could not marry him. Now he had Diane, who would doubtless take a discreet step back when he found a wife, but for now seemed more than ready to resume her former role as his mistress. With her and with his sister for female companionship Luc would not need Marissa and her tiresome emotions.

Suddenly she could not bear to sit there any longer.

'Madame, I do hope you will join us for dinner this evening? If you will all excuse me I must leave you: I had promised I would call on Lady Valentine this afternoon. I look forward to seeing you later.'

As she left she heard Nicci remark with her usual tactlessness, 'That is strange, I was not aware that Marissa had an engagement this afternoon, were you, Jane?'

The door closed behind her, leaving Jane to catch up the thread of the conversation and cover her gauche behaviour. Madame de Rostan glanced down into her ratafia glass. *Alors!* London was going to prove more interesting than she had thought.

Chapter Ten

Marissa came down to breakfast at eight, expecting to have the room to herself. Normally Miss Venables would have partaken of a slice of bread and butter and a cup of tea early and gone out for her daily constitutional in the gardens in the centre of the Square. Nicci never rose before ten and habitually took breakfast in her room. Luc, who had still not shaken the habit of rising early in order to take advantage of the cool of the morning in Jamaica, would have breakfasted by half past seven and be dealing with the day's business in his study.

To her surprise, however, they were all three at the table, deep in animated conversation. They broke off politely as she entered. Luc rose, but the moment she was seated and they had exchanged good mornings they carried on their conversation around her. After last night's dinner, where Diane had been very much the centre of attention, Marissa was feeling in need of reassurance. Diane had been stylish and effortlessly charming, the room illuminated by her personality. To Marissa it had seemed that the Frenchwoman had broken into the circle of friendship and intimacy which had begun in Norfolk and had flourished in the family atmosphere of the Grosvenor Square house.

Diane had been charming to her, and had been at pains to include Marissa in all the dialogue over dinner, but none the less she had felt excluded and lonely, as though she were no longer the hostess. Miss Venables had revealed a fascination for the flora of the West Indies and had been delighted to discover that Madame de Rostan was a passionate gardener who had designed a large garden on the island. With Jane constantly asking questions, everyone except Marissa had been drawn into the discussion of the great houses and estates of Jamaica.

'Would you pass the chocolate, Jane, please?' Marissa prompted as her companion, deep in conversation with Luc, had failed to notice she was waiting for it. 'What shall we do today?' she asked, with a brightness she did not feel, once she had their attention.

'I am going shopping with Diane,' Nicci enthused. 'She has promised to take me to her glovemaker and to buy me a pair to go with my evening dress. My very first pair of long kid gloves!'

'But I thought we had agreed that we would buy your gloves at Schomberg House,' Marissa said, surprised.

'But *anyone* can buy gloves at Schomberg House,' Nicci protested. 'Diane knows a French glove-maker—very exclusive.'

Marissa waited for an invitation to join the shopping party, but it did not come and she did not care to invite herself. The lid of the chocolate pot rattled slightly as she put it down on the table. 'Well, that sounds very nice, Nicci: do not forget to take a sample of the dress fabric with you. Jane—shall we go to Hatchard's this morning? I believe they have a recent book by the author of *Waverley*—it is called *Guy Mannering*. I recall you saying how much you enjoyed *Waverley* when it came out three years ago.'

'Oh, did I not say last night, dear? Madame de Rostan has offered me an introduction to an old friend of hers who is an expert on the flora of the West Indies and has the most wonderful collection of native species in his conservatory here in London. Madame de Rostan promised to drop me off to visit Sir Frederick Collier and his sister this morning, on her way to the shops with Nicci.'

'I see,' Marissa said shortly, stung that everyone appeared to have their morning well planned without any thought of her. She turned to Luc and said, with a forced smile, 'Well, it seems there is absolutely no call on my time this morning. Shall we venture forth to those furniture warehouses you were speaking of and look for suitable items for the dining room and salon?'

There was a silence, broken only by the clink of cutlery as Luc's long fingers played with his knife and fork on his now empty plate. 'Please, do not be troubled with that: I was being very selfish asking you to give up your time in that way when you must have so much to do and so many friends to visit. Besides,' he added fatally, 'Diane has already offered to assist me.'

'She has wonderful taste,' Nicci enthused tactlessly. 'She chose all the draperies for our house at White Horse Cay.'

I am sure she did, Marissa thought acidly, unreasonable anger burning within her. Diane had been so pleasant to her, yet she found herself disliking her more and more. And the knowledge that this was entirely unworthy and due to jealousy did nothing to improve her mood.

She retreated to her chamber before Madame de Rostan arrived to collect Jane and Nicci, but she could not resist watching from behind the drapes as the stylish barouche drew up. The sun was shining from a vivid blue sky, gleaming on the railings around the formal central gardens and causing ladies on foot to raise their parasols like so many bobbing flowers. From above all she could see of Diane de Rostan was a dashing plumed hat in chip straw worn with a costume of eau-de-nil. Marissa craned to see details but could make none out, and withdrew hastily when Nicci and Jane came down the steps and were handed into the carriage by the attentive groom.

Marissa paced restlessly. There were many things she *could* do on such a lovely morning: she could walk to Hyde Park, order her carriage to take her for a drive in Green Park or to visit Hatchard's to buy *Guy Mannering*. She could call on Lady Valentine, but her languid manner and the presence of ever-attentive Captain Cross would only irk her in her present mood.

And it was all very well for Luc to suggest she visit friends when all she had was casual acquaintances. Her father had never brought her up to London before her come-out, she had been educated by a governess so had no schoolfriends, and after her swift marriage to Charles her husband had made it plain that close companions were unacceptable to him. 'After all,' he had said, 'you have your duties as my wife. What more should you require?'

But at least Charles had left her financially well-provided-for. Marissa knew it was shallow, and showed a weakness in character, but the only occupation that appealed to her that morning was to go shopping—and as extravagantly as possible. Diane had succeeded in a very short space of time in making her feel colourless and provincial. She rang the bell for Mary. 'Please arrange for Mr Hall to call tomorrow to give me a new crop,' she instructed. 'I really cannot be seen with this mass of hair; it is quite unfashionable.'

Mary looked shocked. 'Oh, but, ma'am, you have such lovely hair, so thick and curly. It's a crime to cut it off!'

'Nonsense! Now, get ready to accompany me, and order the carriage for half-past. I am going shopping.'

Marissa was just drawing on her gloves when the knocker sounded and she heard masculine tones in the hall. Matthews entered. 'Sir George Kempe, my lady.'

'My father! But, Matthews, I am not at ho—' But it was too late. Her father was striding into the room on the under- butler's heels.

'Not at home! Nonsense, you cannot deny your own father! Come, kiss me, child.'

Marissa stepped forward and kissed him on the cheek with as much self-assurance as she could muster. She sat, pulling off her gloves, and said coolly, 'Please sit, Papa. May I offer you refreshment? Matthews—the decanters, if you please.'

It was three years since she had seen her father and she was shocked by the change in him. Sir George was tall, heavily built, and when she had last seen him his tight crop of curls had still been black. Now it was iron-grey, his face lined and reddened with pouches and broken veins. His figure had thickened to corpulence, making his fashionable trousers strain across the tops of his thighs. His eyes, despite his show of bonhomie, were cold and assessing beneath the shaggy grey brows, and Marissa could detect no sign of pleasure at seeing his only child again after so long.

'You are well, Papa?' she enquired dutifully and to break the silence. 'It is a long time since I have seen you.'

'Hah!' He barked. 'And whose fault was that? Denied the right to see my own daughter by that cold fish of a husband of yours! Much good it did him, all those high and mighty airs—in his grave at forty-five!'

'You did not come to the funeral,' she said quietly.

'What would have been the point of that? All the expense of posting up from Hampshire and not a chance the tight cove would have left me so much as a guinea in his will.'

'The hope of gain should not be the motive for attending the funeral of your son-in-law!' Marissa retorted stiffly.

'Spare me the moralising. You are as bad as your mother ever was.' Sir George removed his snuffbox with some difficulty from his waistcoat pocket and helped himself to a large pinch. 'He showed me no respect as his father-in-law, why should I pretend any for him?'

Marissa fought down the revulsion that came flooding back at the memory of the awful scenes between her father and her husband. In the end Charles had thrown Sir George off the estate with the threat that he would cut off even the small allowance he had agreed to pay his father-in-law if he showed his face again in either Norfolk or Grosvenor Square.

'He paid you an allowance; you had no cause for complaint.' It was hard for Marissa to keep calm, not to crumble in the face of this blustering man who had neglected her all her young life then thrust her into marriage with unseemly haste.

Matthews came in with the decanters, pouring a large brandy to Sir George's instructions. The baronet tossed it back as if it were water and thrust out the glass again. Expressionless, the butler replenished it. 'Will there be anything else, my lady?' he enquired pointedly, his eyes anxious on her face. It seemed to him that he had made a mistake in admitting her ladyship's father without asking first: he did not like the look of the man and her ladyship seemed none too pleased to see him.

'Thank you, Matthews, that will be all.' He bowed, and was closing the door behind him when he heard her say, 'Why are you here, Father?' Well, that did it—he was going to have a word with Mr Jackson. He would know what to do.

'Why do you think, you ungrateful child? Why have I heard nothing about my allowance being increased and the man's been dead over a year? I always thought that lawyer of yours was a slow dog.'

'Why should you expect to hear anything?' Marissa raised a haughty brow. Even a year ago her father would have browbeaten her; now, a year of independence had stiffened her resolve and given her the confidence to withstand his bullying manner. 'The allowance continues as before.'

'But does not increase?' he blustered. 'Now that arrogant husband of yours is gone, I expect a dutiful daughter to consider what a man needs to live on.'

All her life her father had been in debt, spending on racing, gambling and loose women. The colour rose in her cheeks. 'If you did not spend it on drinking and cards and paid attention to the estate you would have a very fine income, Father.'

'What do you know about affairs?' He heaved himself to his feet and poured another brandy, the neck of the decanter rattling against his glass. The blood vessels in his neck were beginning to swell and Marissa, inwardly trembling, recognised the signs of one of his frequent rages developing. He tossed back the brandy and began to pace the carpet in front of the fire. 'I haven't come here for a sermon; I have come here for you to tell that lawyer of yours to increase my allowance.'

Marissa gripped her hands together in her lap, the knuckles showing white, but she kept her voice steady. 'Charles would not have wished that.'

'*Charles would not have wished,*' he mocked, coming to a halt in front of her. 'Very dutiful, I'm sure, for a silly little ninny who was bought for five thousand guineas!'

'Bought? What can you mean?' Her hands moved to clutch the sides of her chair as the room tilted.

'The damn fool wanted you so much that he was

prepared to pay off my gambling debts and forgo a dowry to get his hands on you.'

Shocked though she was, Marissa felt a sudden stab of amazement: Charles must have truly loved her at the beginning after all—what had gone wrong?

Her father saw the play of emotion on her face and pounced. 'Oh, don't think he was in love with you,' he sneered. 'He was quite frank with me: he wanted a well-bred girl who was young enough to be moulded to his…ways. And you happened to be the youngest and the prettiest that was available. I wanted to hold out for more, but I'll give him his due: he was a cunning bastard. Told me that if I did not sell you to him he would make damn sure your reputation was sullied and you would marry no one.'

'I do not believe you. You are lying,' she stammered, the blood draining from her face.

'Did he ever say he loved you? Did he ever show you any sign of affection? I would doubt it, knowing his reputation!'

'Reputation?' Could it be that Charles's cruelty and coolness were more widely known than she had realised? 'How could you do that to me, if you knew what kind of man he was?' she cried, starting to her feet, her hands clenched by her sides, wanting to hit out at that smirking red face.

'You are my daughter. Mine to dispose of as I saw fit. Girls are no good for anything else but marriage.'

'You are despicable. I hate you,' she choked out. 'You will not get another farthing from me. I shall stop your allowance today—'

He snatched at her wrist, pulling her towards him

with some force. They were so close she could smell
the brandy on his breath, see the broken veins in his
cheeks. 'Tread very carefully, Marissa. There are
things I could make known about your *esteemed* late
husband that would ruin you and create a scandal
that would blight the Southwood name.'

Behind them neither heard the door open until
Luc spoke. 'Good morning.'

Sir George spun round, his fingers still clamped
round Marissa's wrist, fury etching his features.
'Who the hell are you?'

'Lucian Southwood. Would you do me the favour
of unhanding Lady Southwood?' It was not a re-
quest.

The baronet's face darkened to a damson-red, but
he did not relinquish his grasp. 'What's it got to do
with you? I am talking to my daughter.'

'You are hurting your daughter.' The words were
quiet, but full of menace. 'I shall not tell you again.'
Luc stalked forward, his eyes cold and narrowed on
the other man's face.

Sir George released Marissa's wrist. Luc took it,
his thumb gently massaging the white marks on the
fragile skin, his eyes still locked with the baronet's.
'Get out of my house, and do not come back unless
her ladyship asks for you.'

Marissa realised that her father was more likely
to raise a fist to Luc than to obey. 'Papa, go now,
please, and I will say nothing more about the matter
of the allowance.' She realised that Jackson had
joined them and was standing, just inside the doors,
his muscular arms folded across his broad chest.

'Jackson—see this…person off the premises. He
is not to be re-admitted except with her ladyship's

express permission.' Luc turned his back contemptuously on the older man.

It was Jackson who saw Sir George lunge forward, Jackson who grabbed him before the blow could fall. But it took both men to wrestle the enraged baronet down the stairs and out of the front door.

Marissa stood in the middle of the room, frozen with shock, her fingers rubbing her bruised wrist. The front door slammed and then the knocker was pounded furiously for several seconds. Finally, with a great roar of anger, her father gave up and there was silence.

She heard Luc and Jackson clattering back up the stairs, their voices animated. They entered together, both men flushed and triumphant, somehow larger than life, Jackson massaging his knuckles. They stopped abruptly at the sight of Marissa's pale face and shivering form.

'Shall I call your maid, my lady?' Jackson was immediately the perfect butler once again.

'No…no, thank you, Jackson.'

Luc poured a glass of brandy and pressed it into her hand before leading her to the sofa. 'Drink this; it will help to calm your nerves. Jackson, send for Dr Lavery: her ladyship's wrist is badly bruised.'

'No, please do not! How could we explain how it occurred?' Marissa exclaimed. 'Witch hazel will soothe it; please do not concern yourselves.' She took a sip of the brandy and coughed as it burned its way down her throat. She tried to hand the glass back to Luc, but he urged her to take another sip.

As the door shut behind Jackson, Marissa raised her face to Luc. 'I am so sorry, Luc. I apologise for my father's disgraceful behaviour. I would not have admitted him, but Matthews was unaware of my lord's orders forbidding Sir George the house, and by the time I had realised it was he it was too late. Goodness knows what the neighbours will make of the hubbub in the street.'

Luc suppressed the urge to gather her into his arms and kiss her until the pain and humiliation had disappeared from her hazel eyes. 'Then this incontinent behaviour is not a new phenomenon?'

'I wish I could say yes, but sadly I have never known him be anything but domineering and given to frequent rages when crossed. I believe that strong drink aggravates his natural choler. My lord tolerated him until we were wed, but his constant demands for money and his drunkenness so disgusted Charles that he forbade him the house. He made him a small allowance, which of course I have continued.'

It was so humiliating to have to recount her father's weaknesses of character in front of a man she loved and respected. What must he think of her now that he had seen her parent at his very worst?

Luc got to his feet and stood at the window looking out across the Square. 'You should not have to deal with him. I will speak to Mr Hope and have him offer your father a single—final—payment in return for the ending of his pension and on condition that he never troubles you again.'

'No!' The syllable rang out across the room.

'But why not? Better to get rid of him now than to have him constantly dogging your footsteps.'

Marissa stared at him, white-faced, her mind able to comprehend nothing but the fact that Charles had paid five thousand guineas for her hand—no, for her body. The thought of Luc following in her husband's footsteps, however unwittingly, to buy off her father for a second time was too abhorrent to contemplate.

It was on the tip of Luc's tongue to ask if her father was attempting to blackmail Marissa. He had heard the tail-end of Sir George's menacing threat to 'create a scandal that would blight the Southwood name.' He knew that Marissa's loyalty and pride would force her to do whatever lay in her power to prevent such a disclosure—whatever it was. Yet if she would not confide in him, how could he ask? He felt the same frustration he had felt so often before with Marissa: the feeling that at the core of her was another, secret woman he could not reach.

'You do not know him like I do,' she was explaining. Luc jerked his attention back to the present. 'My father would spend whatever you gave him in a matter of months—gamble it away, drink it away, spend it on...' she hesitated, biting her lip '...loose women. And he would still come back for more. The only hope is to continue to pay his pension, for he would be reluctant to lose that.'

'Then *I* will pay it so he will have no excuse to approach you in the future.'

'No! He is my father; it is my responsibility.'

'But *you* are my responsibility now, Marissa,' he said quietly. Luc came over to her, took her chin gently in his warm palm and tipped up her troubled face. For a long moment each gazed into the other's eyes, then Luc said, 'You are my cousin, after all,' and dropped a chaste and cousinly kiss on her flushed cheek.

'Oh!' Marissa did not know what to say, or do. She was overwhelmed by his closeness, by the warmth of his body, by the scent of his cologne. Whatever else she wanted to be, it was not his cousin. With an effort she banished her thoughts from her face and said calmly, 'Thank you, Luc. I would be glad to be rid of the responsibility, I must admit. I am happy to abide by whatever you and Mr Hope decide is for the best. Now, if you will forgive me, I think I will go and lie down.'

In her room Marissa found Mary tidying drawers, and sent the concerned maid off for witch hazel and lint to bind her bruised wrist. The girl wanted to make a soothing tisane and help her mistress into bed, but, despite her excuse to Luc, Marissa was determined not to give in to her nerves. Fresh air and sunshine were what she needed, not moping inside letting her mind run endlessly over her father's cruel words, the realisation that her husband had effectively bought her.

A new primrose-yellow pelisse with wide cuffs hid the bandage around her wrist, and a deep-brimmed cottager bonnet shaded her pale face from scrutiny. Marissa picked up her gloves and reticule and descended to the carriage waiting at the front door. The under-footman swung up behind, jammed his cocked hat down firmly on his curled wig, and hung on as the coachman took the corner into Grosvenor Street at a stylish clip.

Luc had sent down his matched Cleveland bays for the barouche, and Marissa was human enough to be well pleased with the fine picture the equipage presented. Once into the street the coachman was forced to rein back the spirited team, but the slower pace gave Marissa the opportunity to bow to acquaintances as the open carriage passed others out for jaunts or on shopping expeditions in the warm sunshine.

Marissa found, despite her recent shock, that the expedition was raising her spirits. It would be hard to remain indifferent to the colour and bustle of the streets as they drove through them, occasionally coming to a complete halt as a heavy wagon loaded with coal manoeuvred around a corner or a hackney carriage plying for trade created a temporary jam outside a fashionable establishment.

Street traders cried their wares: 'Pots mended... Chairs caned, chairs caned... Fresh milk, straight from the cow... Ribbons and laces, French laces... Knives sharpened. Bring me your knives... Latest broadsheets! Read about the hanging of Black Jack the Highwayman...!'

New Bond Street gave way to Old Bond Street and they turned left into Piccadilly, past the front of Burlington House. Marissa had dutifully accompanied her husband to view the Elgin Marbles when they had been exhibited there, but had not admired their cool beauty. The Earl of Radwinter, on the other hand, had been deeply impressed and, Marissa had suspected, not a little put out that Lord Elgin and not himself had acquired them.

The memory of Charles was uncomfortable, and Marissa metaphorically shook herself as they approached Hatchard's. The coachman skilfully pulled into a space right outside the double windows of the bookshop and the footman jumped down to lower the steps and open the door of the carriage. Marissa took his arm and stepped lightly down, making her way past the bench where footmen in livery chatted and gossiped while their masters and mistresses browsed inside.

Mr Hatchard himself hastened forward to attend personally to such a distinguished customer, and led her to a table where the anonymous writer's latest *oeuvre* was set out. 'The set in half-calf, my lady, or the blue tooled leather? A very handsome set in that binding, but perhaps a little masculine…?'

Ashamed of her mood at breakfast time, Marissa purchased the half-calf edition of *Guy Mannering* for Miss Venables, and then browsed happily. It was pleasant buying gifts: Marissa found some thoroughly frivolous love poems for Nicci, and Southey's stirring *Life of Nelson* for Luc.

Finally reseated in the barouche, with her parcels piled on the seat beside her, Marissa ordered the coachman to return to Grosvenor Square through Hyde Park. The sunshine was so bright that she raised her sunshade, a new acquisition in amber silk that cast a flattering glow over her pale complexion. The Park was green and verdant and, despite the fact that it was early for the truly fashionable promenade hour, many members of London Society were taking the air on horseback, in open carriages or on foot. The coachman was called upon to pull up several times, for Marissa to exchange greetings with acquaintances or simply because the press of phaetons, curricles and barouches slowed the traffic to walking pace.

After half an hour their circle through the Park had brought them almost to Grosvenor Gate Lodge and their exit into the top of King Street. The footman leaned over and said, 'Excuse me, my lady, but

I do believe that is Madame de Rostan waving to you.'

'Pull up, please, Morton,' Marissa ordered, firmly quelling a desire to pretend she had not seen the other woman. To her surprise, Diane was alone and on foot and there was no sign of Nicci. 'Good morning, *madame*,' Marissa greeted her politely. 'Has Nicci returned to Grosvenor Square already?'

'Indeed, no,' the older woman laughed. 'She met the Misses Richardson in the linen drapers and they invited her to luncheon. I let them take my carriage—and of course my maid is with them and will ensure Nicci comes directly home afterwards. I do hope you have no objection?'

'Indeed, no. How could I?' Marissa rejoined rather coolly. 'Nicci is not my ward, nor do I have power to control her doings. I am sure her brother would have no objection to any decision such an old friend as yourself might make.'

As soon as she said it Marissa regretted the words and the cool tone. A slight shadow crossed the Frenchwoman's beautiful face, but she smiled and said merely, 'Would you join me in a short stroll, Lady Southwood? The shade under the limes is very pleasant.'

Marissa descended and they strolled in silence for a few minutes, the footman bringing up the rear, discreetly out of earshot. After a while Madame de Rostan broke the slightly prickly silence. 'I think you may underestimate the influence you have over young Nicole, Lady Southwood. She holds you in high regard and affection.'

'She is a very charming child,' Marissa replied neutrally.

'And I must say that a year in your company has greatly improved her demeanour. She always was a sweet child, but a sad romp, and our easy ways in Jamaica are not appropriate for London Society.'

'You are kind enough to say so, *madame,* but I must deny any influence. Any improvement in Nicci's behaviour must be put firmly at the door of Miss Venables, who has much experience as the preceptress of young people.'

Another silence ensued. Madame de Rostan unfurled her own parasol and under cover of that slight diversion sought for another conversational gambit. Despite her best efforts Diane was well aware that she had singularly failed to charm Marissa. In fact, it was not just that the younger woman appeared indifferent to her overtures of friendship, but that she seemed positively to dislike her. And Diane de Rostan was not used to being disliked by men or women. She suspected that she knew where the problem lay, but it was hardly a matter she could broach openly, even with a woman who had been married before.

'It is strange to see Nicci—and Luc, of course—away from Jamaica. Do you not find it odd when one encounters people out of the *milieu* one is accustomed to seeing them in?'

'I really could not say,' Marissa replied indifferently.

Diane gritted her teeth, but continued to smile as she tried again. 'I have known them both for such a long time...'

'So I believe.'

Yes, she was correct in her guess, Diane thought. There was undeniable frost in the young woman's tone now. She persevered. 'Of course in any relationship things change over the years. Feelings alter and mature, passions mute into friendships... I always think it is a wonderful thing when friendship survives when other, more intimate emotions wane.'

Marissa stopped abruptly and turned a surprised, yet candid look on the Frenchwoman, who smiled at her. 'You understand what I am saying to you?'

'I do—you are telling me that you are no longer Luc's mistress.' She could feel the colour stain her cheek at the frankness of her own words, but she continued, 'But I do not understand *why* you should tell me that.'

'Do you not?' The blue eyes sparkled quizzically. 'Well, perhaps this is not the time or place to say more. Let us just leave it that I thought things would be clearer between us—more comfortable, shall we say?'

Marissa blushed furiously. Were her feelings for Luc so transparent that in such a short space of time this woman—even though she had never set eyes on her before—should realise that she needed to be reassured? And if Diane, not knowing her, could see it, was it blindingly obvious to Nicci, to Jane—to Luc himself?

Diane smiled and patted her burning cheek. 'Do not upset yourself *chérie*. You are afraid you are being obvious, *non?* But you are not. Sometimes perhaps it takes an outsider to see what those who are close to us cannot.'

'You think I am in love with him!' Marissa protested hotly.

'Well?' The Frenchwoman raised an eyebrow. 'You are, are you not?'

'Certainly not! I am, after all, in mourning for the late Earl.' Marissa's fingers twisted the reticule in her agitation.

'Mourning?' Diane's eyes ran up and down the stylish primrose-yellow outfit, the frivolous bonnet and the jaunty parasol.

'Well, just out of mourning. And Luc is my late husband's cousin...'

'And that makes him no relation to you,' Diane interposed smoothly.

'I like him very well. He has been kind to me during a very difficult period in my life.'

'Kind?' Diane seemed to be considering the word. 'So that is how he strikes you? Well, if I have misinterpreted the situation, please accept my apologies, Lady Southwood.'

Marissa turned and began to walk back to the barouche. When they had passed the waiting footman and were safely out of earshot again she said, 'Indeed, you have misinterpreted my feelings. I do hope I can rely on your discretion to say nothing of this conversation to the Earl of Radwinter?'

They reached the carriage and Diane waited until the door was closed and Marissa seated. 'I would never gossip to Luc.' She smiled. 'Goodbye, Lady Southwood. I have enjoyed our little chat.'

As the carriage drove out of the Park and into King Street Marissa reflected uncomfortably that Diane's parting words had hardly been the reassurance she had requested.

Chapter Eleven

By the time she reached Grosvenor Square Marissa's unease had turned into a strong suspicion that Diane had been laughing at her for being naive. The entire conversation had been shocking and improper: Diane was obviously fast, Marissa concluded, and must have taken delight in scandalising someone she saw as a prim and proper dowager.

Sweeping across the hall, untying the ribbons of her bonnet as she went, she had one foot on the bottom stair when she heard the study door open and Luc demand, 'Where have you been? I thought you were resting in your room.' Marissa spun round, her already warm cheeks flaming in embarrassment at seeing him so soon after Diane's improper references to him. 'Look at you!' he exclaimed, seeing her heightened colour and bright eyes. 'Are you sure you are not running a fever?'

Luc took a hasty step towards her and Marissa's temper snapped. 'No, my lord, I am not running a fever! And I was not aware that I had to seek your permission before going out. I am, naturally, extremely grateful for your assistance this morning, but that does *not* give you the right to order my comings and goings!' Jackson, who, hearing voices, had emerged through the green baize door, hastily withdrew again. 'I am not your sister, my lord!'

'For heaven's sake, Marissa, come into the study—the whole household can hear you!' Luc took her hand to lead her into the room and inadvertently touched her bandaged wrist.

'Ouch! There is no need to manhandle me, my lord!'

Gently, but firmly, Luc propelled her through the study door and closed it behind them. 'What is the matter with you, Marissa? And, please—' as she opened her mouth '—will you stop calling me "my lord" every second sentence?'

Marissa paced agitatedly across the Turkey rug before Luc's desk. She could hardly tell him that the source of her irritation was a conversation she had newly had with his mistress—or, if Madame de Rostan was to be believed, his ex-mistress. 'Oh, I do not know! It has been a horrid day. No one wants my company; you all have something better to do. And then my father arrives, and now you are shouting at me! I think I will go home to Norfolk,' she almost wailed, managing to sound just as young and silly as Nicci in one of her tantrums.

The next moment she was in Luc's arms. He was laughing down into her face, amused by her outburst, his blue eyes sparkling like the sun on the waves.

'You are laughing at me!' she said indignantly. If she had had any space to do so she would have stamped her foot, but he was so close, holding her so tightly, that she could not. 'Luc, that is not fair.

I feel so miserable…' And she gave up struggling and buried her face in the fine wool of his jacket. It was so very comforting, being held against his chest: warm and reassuring, yet with a hard strength that excited her strangely.

He had stopped laughing, and his breath stirred the fine hair at her temple. 'Poor Marissa. Poor darling.' Her heart leapt at the endearment. 'You are having a miserable time, are you not?'

'I am all right,' she said faintly. 'I am just being silly…'

'No, I keep forgetting that you must feel so alone. You have been used to being protected and cherished by Charles.' She was so close that the words seemed to echo in his chest. Was she imagining it, the constraint in his voice as he spoke of her late husband? If only he knew the truth. But she could never tell him.

Marissa put her hands on Luc's chest and pushed him away slightly. 'That part of my life is gone. I must put it behind me, stop dwelling on it. I was being foolish just now. I am tired and my father upset me. You were right; I should not have gone out.'

Luc looked down at her bowed head. If she meant it, if she really thought she could put her feelings for his cousin behind her, perhaps she would consider a proposal of marriage from him now. There had been a long enough interval between the offer he had made in the wake of their passionate encounter on the beach: she had had time to put the confusion and embarrassment of that tumultuous meeting behind her. And, despite his scruples about her love for the late Earl, perhaps it was his duty to make the offer again. She needed protecting, looking after.

'Marissa, look at me.' She did as she was bid, lifting shadowed eyes obediently. 'Marissa, if you mean it, if you can put the past behind you, will you make a future with me? Marry me, Marissa.'

For one long moment she looked at him, unable to speak, overwhelmed by the rush of love for him, by the sensation of joy that he too might love her. But, no, she could not do it, could not promise herself in marriage when she could not be a proper wife to him.

The doubt chased across her face and Luc, seeing it, hastened to reassure her. 'It would be an entirely suitable match—you are young, beautiful, educated. You are already the perfect chatelaine for Southwood Hall; you have proved that. My cousin made a wise choice!' Marissa threw up one hand as if to ward off the words. 'No, wait, Marissa, do not dismiss the suggestion too hastily! There are great benefits for both of us in this suggestion.'

'You do me great honour, my lord, but I cannot agree to marry you—as I told you once before. Thank you for your flattering offer, but let us speak no more of it.' Marissa turned from him in agitation and took a hasty step towards the door, fighting down the impulse to throw herself into his arms and tell him how much she loved him and wanted to be his wife. But it was because she loved him that she could not assent, and blight his life by tying him to a woman who could not share his bed or bear his children.

If she thought her words would rebuff him she was wrong. 'Wait, Marissa—I will not take no for an answer unless you will tell me why. Surely we are good enough friends, you and I, for you to give me an explanation?'

Marissa turned, cornered. How could she explain, even if she could find the words for the fear and the pain she had always encountered whenever Charles demanded that she do her wifely duty? Marissa bit her lip, avoiding Luc's searching gaze as he stood patiently but implacably waiting. She could not give him a reason for saying no, so finally, bluntly she said, 'Yes, very well, if you insist. I will marry you, Luc.'

The coldness of her words seemed to take him aback and she saw the animation in his face freeze into formality. He took her hand and brushed his lips across her knuckles. 'Thank you, Marissa. I am honoured by your acceptance. I shall do everything in my power to make you happy. I know our friends will be delighted for us.'

'Oh, please, no, Luc, do not tell anyone, not yet. Can we not keep it our secret for a little while, at least until I have become more accustomed to the idea?'

'Of course, Marissa, if that is your wish. I am yours to command, as always. Now, will you not go and rest?' He made no move to touch her, let alone kiss her as she had both hoped and dreaded.

Without another word Marissa slipped out the door and hastened upstairs.

The next week was Derby week, and in the flurry of activity as the household prepared to move down to Epsom for the races Marissa managed to avoid being alone with Luc. She swung wildly between elation at the thought of marrying the man she loved and utter despair when she realised that she could not go through with it.

Unable to sleep, she paced her room into the small hours, frantically seeking for a way out. How could she have been so stupid to allow herself to be cornered into saying yes? Now she could think of a dozen reasons for turning him down: unfortunately all had eluded her at that critical moment when he had pressed her to be his wife. And whereas they were all perfectly acceptable reasons for turning him down in the first place, none of them were convincing excuses for going back on her word after the passage of several days. And the longer it went on, the more impossible it became.

Whenever she caught Luc's eye she saw a question in it, but would only smile and shake her head slightly. Heaven knows what he thought her reasons for wanting to keep their betrothal a secret were, but she made sure they were never alone for him to press the point. Her appetite waned until even Nicci, usually so preoccupied with her own concerns, noticed that she had lost weight. Pressed by Miss Venables to eat more, Marissa murmured vaguely about the heat and the noise of London, assuring her friend that all would be well in the peace of the countryside.

Luc had taken a lodge within five miles of Epsom racecourse for a week and they set out, Nicci in a high state of excitement, on the Wednesday morning. They intended to attend the Derby on the Thursday then spend the rest of the time rusticating before another flurry of balls and parties.

The grooms had gone ahead with the riding

horses, the barouche and most of the luggage. The ladies would follow in the travelling carriage and Luc intended to drive himself down. He refused point-blank his sister's pleas, demands and cajoling to be allowed to ride in the curricle with him and take the reins once they were out of London.

'No, Nicci,' he said firmly for the fourth time as he handed the three ladies into the travelling carriage. 'And I do not care if any of your acquaintances are allowed to drive on the public highway—you are not. And that is an end to the subject.' He regarded his sister's mutinous countenance and added, 'And do not sulk and make Miss Venables and Lady Southwood regret that we did not leave you at home!'

'Now then, Nicci,' Miss Venables said firmly. 'Surely you do not wish to drive all that way on dusty roads, ruining your complexion? Why, you would end up sadly freckled, like Miss Richardson, and that would never do.'

The thought of the unfortunate Miss Richardson's complexion seemed to mollify the girl somewhat. She settled willingly enough in the seat opposite Miss Venables and began to prattle about hats, wondering aloud if she would have the prettiest bonnet at the races or whether a last-minute shopping trip to the Epsom milliners would be necessary in the morning.

Luc took the opportunity to exchange a few words with Marissa, catching her hand to restrain her as she began to step up into the carriage. 'We have much to speak of, Marissa. We must find time to be alone at the Lodge.'

'Yes, indeed,' Marissa replied in a colourless

tone, before settling in her seat and tucking her reticule safely beside her. Mary, her dresser, was waiting patiently to take her place beside Nicci, with their back to the horses, so Luc was forced to step aside and make no further attempt at conversation. Mary was almost beside herself with self-importance and excitement as she sat, straight-backed, her mistress's jewel case held tightly on her knees.

The journey was uneventful, if rather stuffy, as Nicci repeatedly pointed out. The latter half of May had been exceedingly warm and dry but the countryside was still green and burgeoning except where the chalk dust from the highway cloaked the leaves.

'Diane is taking her barouche down,' Nicci complained. 'And she will be able to have half the roof down and not be so stuffy. Why could we not have taken the barouche today, Marissa? This is such an unfashionable coach and I have the headache.'

'Then take some *sal volatile*,' Marissa said quite sharply. She did not want to discuss Diane de Rostan, whom she had not met since that encounter in Hyde Park, nor did she want to be reminded that the other woman was staying with friends in Epsom and was sure to be much in evidence at the races. Luc's low-voiced comments about discussing their future filled her with unease. Sooner or later matters would come to a head, and she would either have to tell him the truth—which was impossible—or find a convincing excuse to cry off. To go through with the marriage was impossible.

The Lodge turned out to be a charming small house of only ten bedrooms, secluded from the road behind high beech hedges and with a delightful view of the Downs. The air was fresh, the house well aired, the servants installed, and everyone soon felt at home. The small party dined early, fatigued by their journey and in readiness for an early start on Derby Day.

After the ladies left Luc to his port, Marissa slipped out into the garden and began to wander along the grass paths. The garden, sloping away from the terrace which skirted the house, had been laid out with beds of fragrant roses underplanted with lavender. Now, in the very last days of May, they were in full bloom, their scent almost drugging in the still evening air.

As she strolled, twisting a rosebud between her fingers, Marissa felt soothed and calm. Away from London things seemed simpler: she must tell Luc that she had made a mistake and that she had decided to stay single for the rest of her days. There was no need to give him an explanation for that decision. It would be best to speak now, and, after all, only his pride, not his feelings would be hurt. He had never pretended to be in love with her, and it had formed no part of his declaration. Thank goodness she had not let him announce the engagement!

It cost her heartache to come to this conclusion, but Marissa knew, deep down, that any hope of happiness with Luc was doomed.

It all seemed perfectly clear and simple, if painful—until she came round one corner of the lawn and saw him leaning on the balustrade of the terrace, an unlit cigarillo between his fingers, his gaze fixed on the darkening Downs over the trees. The late sun glinted on his blond head, the dark blue superfine coat of his evening dress sat perfectly across his

broad shoulders and his face was thoughtful and relaxed.

Marissa's heart leapt with love for him, and his
name escaped her lips before she could step back
behind the sheltering rose bushes.

His face lit up with pleasure when he saw her,
and he tossed aside the cigarillo, vaulted the balustrade and with two strides was by her side. She was
wearing the periwinkle-blue that suited her dark colouring so well. Her slender figure was set off by the
high-waisted gown and the elegant sweep of her silver shawl caught up over her elbows. He stood for
a moment, drinking in the picture she made, before
gathering her in his arms and kissing her.

Every sensible resolution that Marissa had
reached evaporated at the first touch of his lips. She
melted into him, her nightly dreams becoming reality as she returned his kiss with ardour. If only,
she thought hazily as his tongue parted her lips and
teased the tip of her own, if only this was all there
was to marriage. If it only stopped here, on this tide
of sensation and pleasure, and went no further...if
the only invasion was that of his tongue, the only
violence the strength of his arms holding her to him.

It was Luc who finally broke the kiss. He spoke
huskily into her hair, his hand running caressingly
over her nape exposed by the low-cut gown. 'Thank
heavens you are still of the same mind. I had thought
you had changed your mind, grown cold towards me
this past week. But that, my darling Marissa, was
not cold...'

She shivered against him as he bent and began to
feather soft kisses down the slope of her shoulder,
his progress impeded only by the cap of her sleeve.

His right hand slipped from her other shoulder and grazed subtly down the curve of her breast to stroke her peaked nipple through the silk of her gown. Marissa gasped and arched towards him. Encouraged, his fingers explored further under the fabric, both the silk and the fine cambric of her shift beneath.

'You are so beautiful,' he said against her neck. 'Ever since that night by the sea I have been haunted by the memory of your perfect white body in the moonlight, of the way you opened to me on the beach.' His voice was not quite steady, his breathing ragged. 'I cannot wait until our wedding night, when all of you will be mine…'

Marissa's ecstasy was chilled by the thought of that wedding night, of the pain and recrimination that would surely follow…

'Marissa!' It was Miss Venables's voice, approaching rapidly from the direction of the drawing room. 'Marissa, my dear, are you out here? You will catch your death of cold.'

Luc seized Marissa's hand, and, pushing through the door of the gazebo which stood at the end of the terrace, closed it swiftly behind them. They stood entwined in the wood-scented gloom until they saw Miss Venables pass by the leaded window and vanish around the corner of the house.

'Now, where were we?' Luc murmured, bending once more, catching her around the waist and imprisoning her in his embrace.

'No, Luc, stop…' Marissa protested shakily. 'I must go in—Jane will be worried about me. And we should not be doing this.'

'Why not?' he said, his voice smothered as he nibbled delicately at her earlobe. 'I fully intend doing this—and more—all the time when you are my wife.'

'Oh, yes…I mean, no, *stop it*. You make it so difficult,' she added weakly, pushing him away.

'You are right. The wooden floor of a gazebo is hardly the right place for the first time—any more than a sandy beach was.' He opened the door for her to slip through, adding, as she turned to run along the terrace, 'But do not make me wait too long for you, Marissa.'

Those words sounded almost threatening in her ears as she slowed to a sedate walk and re-entered the Salon through the long windows which opened down to the ground. Fortunately Nicci had retired, but Jane Venables was waiting anxiously for her.

'There you are, dear! I have been to look for you. I was worried you might get chilled—the evening air is so treacherous. Did you not hear me call?'

Remembering the circumstances under which she had heard Jane, Marissa blushed rosily. Miss Venables, after a searching look at Marissa's heightened colour and escaping hair, said sharply, 'Marissa! Have you been alone again with his lordship? Is there anything you wish to say to me?'

'Er…no.' Marissa felt like a naughty schoolroom miss caught kissing the music master. 'I just happened to meet Luc in the garden. The roses are most delightful; we must pick some for the breakfast table.'

Miss Venables had not been a governess for over ten years without being able to detect prevarication when she heard it. 'Really, Marissa, do you think I was born yesterday?' she demanded robustly. 'I am not lecturing you. Heaven knows I am not responsible for your morals. After all, you have been a married woman and are old enough to conduct your own affairs. But do consider the proprieties! I will say no more. I will retire and say goodnight.'

May 30th dawned clear and bright, and the ladies breakfasted in their rooms to hasten the business of getting ready. At ten o'clock Miss Venables, magnificent in bronze twill with an almost jaunty bonnet of moss silk and feathers, popped her head around Marissa's bedchamber door.

'Are you almost ready, my dear? Oh, now, that *is* nice!' she said approvingly. 'I knew you were right to choose that simple fern-green jacconet cloth—it sets off the lines of your new pelisse to perfection. Understatement is the very essence of elegance, especially when one has the height and figure to carry it off, as you do.'

Marissa smiled her thanks at the compliment as she took her seat at the dressing table to allow Mary to set the dashing O'Neil hat, with its high crown and curving brim, on her head. She had heeded Luc's plea not to have her hair cropped, and the maid had piled up the luxuriant mass on her crown and allowed only the little curls around her hairline to peep out from under the arc of the brim.

'How very fashionable, dearest!' Miss Venables exclaimed. 'When did you buy that?'

'Last season, in Norwich. I could not resist it, even though I knew I could not wear it for some time. Is Nicci ready?'

'She was so excited last night I doubt she has been to bed, so she had better be! Her brother warned her that if she were not down by ten he would leave her behind—and I fear he was not speaking in jest.'

Marissa had pushed thoughts of Luc firmly to the back of her mind, determined that nothing should spoil her day at the races. She would face up to breaking her betrothal later that week. The fact that the evening before she had quite made up her mind on her course of action and it had only taken a second in his arms for her resolution to crumble utterly she conveniently ignored.

The clock struck ten and both ladies picked up their reticules and sunshades and stepped out onto the landing as Nicci's door opened.

For a moment both were speechless, then Miss Venables's cry of dismay echoed clearly round the landing. '*Nicole!* You cannot go out attired like that. Go and change immediately! Where did you get that hat?'

'It is a lovely hat and I am not going to get changed and I think this will be the most striking outfit on the course.' Nicci stamped her foot and refused to move.

Marissa's thunderstruck gaze travelled from deep purple pumps, up the length of what had begun as a simple white cambric gown but which was now transformed by an abundance of dark ribbons and braid, to Nicci's crowning glory, a bonnet of midnight-purple curled silk, edged, trimmed and lined in white satin, high in the crown with an abundance of white bows.

She finally found her voice. 'You bought that in London when Madame de Rostan left you with the Misses Richardson, did you not, Nicci? How you could have thought for a moment that this would be suitable for a young girl, a debutante…'

'What is going on?' Luc ran up the stairs. 'The carriage has been at the front door these last fifteen minutes and I do not care to keep my horses waiting… Good God, Nicci, you look like a magpie! Marissa, whatever possessed you to allow her to rig herself up like that?' Despite his words he sounded more amused than annoyed.

'My lord, I believe you may lay this unique outfit at the door of your friend Madame de Rostan: I can claim no credit for it. Nor do I intend to make any further comment—doubtless you can prevail upon your sister to change into something more suitable: it seems that neither Miss Venables nor I have that sort of influence any longer.'

Marissa swept downstairs with a faintly clucking Jane on her heels. She had surprised herself at the sudden wave of anger that had swept through her. In the carriage, listening to the raised voices issuing through the front door, she examined her mood. Annoyance with Nicci, of course, but also, maddeningly, annoyance with herself, that Luc's attention had been entirely on his sister's outrageous outfit and diverted from her own appearance. She had wanted to look good on his arm, to do him credit, to be seen and admired with him on this one day before she broke off the betrothal. And to be blamed for the effects of Diane de Rostan's influence was the very last straw.

Five minutes later Nicci swept triumphantly out of the door, her outfit intact. Luc, on her heels, caught Marissa's eye and shrugged resignedly. She returned the look frostily and averted her face.

Miss Venables was still protesting as the doors of the barouche were shut behind him and he took his seat. 'But, my lord, you cannot possibly permit Miss Southwood to appear in public in such an unsuitable outfit!'

'Why not?' he enquired laconically. 'Do you fear some gamekeeper will mistake her for a magpie and shoot her? Quite frankly, Miss Venables, I am just thankful that she is decently covered. And when people laugh at her she will soon learn her lesson.'

'Ha! Much you know about it,' his sister riposted. 'All eyes will be upon me.'

'Precisely,' Luc said drily, and looked out at the passing countryside.

Derby Day was one of the highlights of the Season and the *ton* was out in force. The racecourse was already a sea of colour from the fashionable gowns and parasols, the uniforms of many officers, the silks of the jockeys and the gay bunting on the pavilions. The barouche drew up alongside many other elegant conveyances and Miss Venables exclaimed with pleasure at the sight of many acquaintances.

Nicci was bouncing in her seat with excitement. 'Come on, come on, we are missing everything! Let us promenade.'

'Calm down, Nicole,' Miss Venables chided as the footman helped them to descend. 'Too much excitement is so unsophisticated—surely you do not wish to appear gauche?'

Effectively quelled, Nicci fell in beside the others and began to stroll meekly along, casting looks from under her bonnet-brim to see what effect her outfit was having.

Luc shepherded them through the entrance into the Royal Enclosure and found a place by the rail where they could assess the horses being led around the ring. He had acquired race cards for them all, and now described the runners and riders.

'There were fifty-one entries, but only eleven are running: that is not unusual,' he explained, as Marissa tried to separate what seemed at first sight to be an indistinguishable crowd of horses. 'The favourite is Nectar, owned by Lord Cavendish—see, over there, the bay colt. He looks very well, does he not? And he has already won the Two Thousand Guineas.'

'It does look a very fine horse,' Miss Venables observed. 'What are the odds, my lord?'

'Ten to six: hardly worth putting money on at this stage, I would have thought. Let us choose horses with longer odds—it will be more exciting. How about Lord Stawell's chestnut, Pandour? It is from the same sire as the favourite, but it is at sixteen to one.'

Both Miss Venables and Nicci agreed to place a guinea each on Pandour, but Marissa was feeling perverse and was in no mood to take any advice from Luc that morning. 'Which is that?' she asked, pointing a gloved hand at a large bay as it passed them close by the rail.

Luc checked the colours against the race card. 'That is Prince Leopold. It is running in the colours of Mr Lake, the Duke of York's Master of Horse, but I believe it is owned by His Royal Highness himself. First time out, and the odds are long— twenty to one. With no form to go on, I would not hazard your guinea on him, Marissa.'

'A guinea? Why, nothing so paltry,' she declared with a toss of her head. 'I shall place ten guineas on Prince Leopold. Here.' She felt in her reticule and handed him ten coins. 'Will you place the bet for me, please, my lord?'

Luc looked down into her eyes, noting once again how green they sparkled when she was excited or emotional. In all the furore over Nicci's outfit he had not had the opportunity to tell her how beautiful she looked, and in that moment he wished the crowds a thousand miles away so he could take her in his arms and make love to her. 'You are an inveterate gambler, Lady Southwood! I had not suspected it.'

He collected the bets from the others and went to find a bookmaker while the ladies continued to view the parade of horses. Miss Venables now held the race card and pointed out the Duke of Grafton's horse, Alien, and Mr Blake's John of Paris. 'What a magnificent appellation,' Jane declared. 'Perhaps I should have put my guinea on him after all.'

'Good day, ladies.' They were greeted by Lady Valentine, who joined them at the rail. She was dashingly attired in fawn twill, her new scarlet half-boots peeping from under the hem. On her head she sported an outrageous toque of Ionian cork, cut like mosaic and adorned with scarlet tassels and plumes. Nicci's jaw dropped until she was jabbed sharply in the ribs by Miss Venables. 'My dear Lady Southwood. You do look...well,' she remarked, leaving everyone in no doubt that she considered Marissa's tasteful outfit to be dull. She merely raised an eyebrow at the sight of Nicci's magpie magnificence, commenting only that she thought her hat to be 'So droll.'

'Oh, I am forgetting myself. Let me make Mr Templeton known to you. Captain Cross you know already, of course.'

Mr Templeton bowed to the ladies as they were introduced, but his attention was obviously all for Lady Valentine, who hung onto his arm possessively. He was a remarkably well-set-up young man, with broad shoulders, muscular thighs and a handsome profile under dark brows. Captain Cross gave the distinct impression of a man whose nose had been put out of joint, and he lost no time in making eyes at Nicci from behind the backs of her chaperons.

Lady Valentine's party took up position on the rails a few yards farther along and Nicci almost imperceptibly drifted along until she was in a position to chat with Captain Cross. Miss Venables, who would normally have spotted such a manoeuvre, had been diverted by the arrival of her new friend Sir Frederick Collier, with whom she had been visiting museums and galleries ever since Diane de Rostan had introduced them. The distinguished banker bowed gallantly over her hand and Marissa thought she had never seen Miss Venables look so handsome. Skilfully he drew her off to one side and Marissa found herself alone, fondly thinking that dear Jane might have found a little romance of her own in her middle years.

Marissa was smiling to herself when her mood was shattered by the sight of her father, pushing his way aggressively through the crowd towards her. Her heart sank, then rose as she saw Luc, Diane de

Rostan on his arm, cross her father's path. There was a brief conversation of which she heard nothing, but she saw Sir George's florid features darken and he turned abruptly and stomped off.

Luc uttered a few words, obviously explaining the uncouth stranger to the Frenchwoman. To Marissa's relief Diane released Luc's arm, patted his cheek and made her own way off towards the pavilion.

'Well, here is your betting slip,' he greeted Marissa as he joined her at the rail. 'Put it safely in your reticule, although I doubt you will need it—the more I look at that horse of yours, the less I like it.'

Tension was growing as the horses lined up at the start. The starter dropped his flag and they were off. Nectar took the lead and stayed there, running strongly, the rest of the field bunched behind. Luc groaned at the performance of his choice, then gave a great yell as, a furlong and a half out, Pandour and Prince Leopold took up the challenge.

'Come on, come on, Prince Leopold!' Marissa screamed, her unladylike behaviour lost in the sea of noise all around them.

'Pandour!' Luc urged, but Nectar was holding them. Marissa found she was jumping up and down on the spot, her hand gripped tightly onto Luc's sleeve. Suddenly, with the winning post only five lengths away, Prince Leopold sprang forward, straining under his jockey's whip. They ran neck and neck for a few seconds, then, as they flashed past the post, Prince Leopold was seen to have taken the lead by half a length.

'He has won, he has won!' Marissa shrieked, and threw her arms round Luc, kissing him on the cheek. In response, hidden by the milling crowd of excited racegoers, all intent on the track, he bent his head and kissed her full on the lips. Instinctively she kissed him back, and suddenly it was as if they were alone in the garden again.

'God, I want you,' he groaned.

The thrill of winning after the tension of the race had left Marissa dizzy with reaction. All she knew was that she loved him and she wanted him too. Mutely she nodded.

Luc looked around, spotted Sir Frederick with Miss Venables, and, leaving Marissa by the rail, crossed to speak with them. 'Sir Frederick, may I beg a favour of you? Lady Southwood is quite overcome by the crowds and I must take her back to the Lodge. Could I ask you to escort Miss Southwood and Miss Venables for the rest of the day? Lady Southwood would be so distressed to think she had destroyed their pleasure.'

The baronet willingly agreed, took charge of the winning betting slip with a word of congratulation and could be heard soothing Miss Venables. 'No need to worry, my dear Miss Venables. Your friend is in the best of hands and would not wish to mar your day. Now, a little luncheon, some champagne, perhaps…'

Marissa felt dazed as Luc swept her out of the Enclosure into the press of other racegoers. 'How extraordinary… No, I must be mistaken. I thought I saw my father with Madame de Rostan,' she exclaimed.

Luc soon had her seated in the barouche. With a short word of explanation to the groom and coachman the carriage was soon wending its way slowly against the press of vehicles still flooding onto the course.

'Luc,' Marissa whispered. 'We should not be doing this…'

'Yes, we should,' he murmured back. 'I am going to make you mine—and then we will name the day.'

Chapter Twelve

The journey back to the Lodge seemed interminable to Luc, but frighteningly short to Marissa. She loved him, she wanted him—far too much to even think about impropriety. Yet she dreaded the moment he discovered that she could not respond to him as a lover, as his wife should do. But for the moment it was enough to be with him, and one corner of her mind told her that it was better he discovered the truth now rather than when they were married.

They sat close together, outwardly totally proper in the open carriage, the footman standing behind. But through the fabric of her skirts Marissa could feel the heat of his hard thigh pressed against hers. Her mouth still burned with the intensity of that last kiss, of the sweet invasion of his tongue. Despite her apprehensions she was tingling with anticipation and longing.

As the footman let down the folding steps Luc said, 'Take the rest of the day off, both of you.'

'But, my lord, all the servants are at the races—

only the watchman left in the gate cottage. Who will wait upon you?'

'Do not concern yourself; we will wait upon ourselves. Today is a festival—go and enjoy it.' He slipped a gold coin into each grateful hand and watched them take the barouche round to the stable.

'Now, my lady,' he said as he bent and effortlessly lifted her up into his arms, shouldering open the door and kicking it closed behind him. Marissa was conscious of the strength of him as he carried her up the stairs and into the master bedroom. She could hardly breathe as he laid her on the bed, hat, parasol and all. Crossing to the windows, he threw them open, then tugged the billowing white drapes closed, filtering the hot sunlight across the polished boards.

Shrugging off his jacket and tugging loose his neckcloth, he stood looking down at her. For a long moment neither moved, then he tossed her reticule and parasol to one side and eased off her hat, releasing her hair to tumble down across the snowy white pillows. Marissa lay still and watched the man she loved gently unbutton, then push off her pelisse. His hands found the ribbons tying her kid pumps and his fingertips tickled her ankles as he untied each one and tossed the shoes off the bed.

Her heart was thudding so hard she could hardly breathe: she wanted him to hurry, and yet for every moment to last for ever. Now he raised her in his arms so he could reach the row of little buttons securing her gown, and with surprising skill he removed it, and the petticoats under it, to join the rest of her clothing on the floor. Left naked except for her stockings, tied by their ribbon garters above the knee, Marissa was swept by self-consciousness and tried to pull over the sheet to cover herself.

'No,' he said with gentle insistence, removing the sheet from her nerveless fingers. 'You have a beautiful body. Every night I have dreamed of seeing it in daylight.'

Obedient under his gaze, Marissa lay watching as he shrugged off his shirt impatiently. Then he joined her on the big bed and, bending over her, traced hot kisses from her mouth to the tip of her aching nipples, catching them between his lips and teasing, tantalising the swollen peaks.

She moaned, catching his head in her hands, pressing his mouth against her soft flesh. Her fingers tangled in his blond hair, tasting it with her fingertips, alive to every texture of his body.

Luc released her nipple, shifting against her to reach her mouth, kissing her slowly, deeply, marvellously. When she thought she would surely drown in sensation he broke the kiss to look down into her face. 'You taste of wine and strawberries— even better than the salt.'

The reference to their moonlight encounter brought the delicate colour flooding up under her skin. She buried her face in his shoulder, licking his satiny skin with the tip of her tongue, letting her fingertips trace the muscles under the smoothness of his back until they encountered the waistband of his trousers.

In response to her impatient fingers he groaned, rolling over on his back to release the fastening and discard the final garment. Marissa gasped at the sight of him, naked and aroused, and shut her eyes as his weight came over her and the heat of him burned her aroused skin. His lips sought hers blindly, and he kissed her again, the invasive pressure of his tongue echoing the urging of his body. It was the moment she was dreading, and despite Luc's skilful lovemaking, his attention to her pleasure, she felt the paralysis creeping through her limbs, the fear rising in her breast.

It was enough to give him pause. 'Marissa? You do want this, do you not?'

Her eyes were very wide and green in the subdued light, and he experienced the uncanny feeling that it was not he that she saw. 'Don't hurt me. Please don't hurt me...'

He ran the back of his hand gently down the soft curve of her cheek. 'Hurt you? I would never hurt you, Marissa darling.'

The endearment gave her the courage to wrap her arms around his neck, pull his head down to hers and kiss him as she had never kissed him before. He groaned and entered her, too goaded by her enticement to realise until it was too late that the yielding, passionate woman had turned to stone in his arms.

When it was over he gathered her tenderly into his arms and stroked her quivering body until she stilled. He kissed her damp forehead and then her eyelids and realised that it was not passion that had made her quiver, but soft sobs.

'Marissa? Marissa—do not cry. You must tell me what is wrong. What have I done?' He sounded deeply troubled and her heart contracted with love for him. She hastened to reassure him.

'It is only that it has been such a long time, and I was shy... I am quite all right, Luc, believe me.'

But he could not. Luc Southwood had never taken an unwilling woman, nor would he ever. But although she had hidden it so much better than she had on the beach, hidden it to the point that he had, for the moment, been totally deceived, Marissa had been afraid at the moment he had taken her.

They lay together quietly, Luc nuzzling her hair, stroking the white slope of her shoulder until Marissa dozed. When he was sure she was settled he gently eased his encircling arm from under her and pulled the sheet over her body. Then he lay back on the pillows, hands behind his head, gazing up at the ceiling as though the chaste classical moulding could furnish him with a clue.

She had wanted him, had responded to him with an ardour and passion he had never experienced before. And the thought came to him again, as it had done after the night on the beach, that her responses had an edge of innocence which did not square with her married state. If he had not known better he would have sworn she had never been kissed before.

He shook his head as if to clear his thoughts. It was not his lovemaking that had frightened her, but the act of possession itself. She had begged him not to hurt her, but it was not her heart she feared for, but her body. What sort of man had his cousin been, for heaven's sake, to frighten his beautiful young wife so? He felt uneasy, remembering the odd hint he had picked up in the clubs that the late Earl had had…unusual tastes. He recalled the chilly perfection and discipline of Southwood Hall, the reticence of the staff and estate workers to say anything about their late master, good or bad.

Luc shifted restlessly. Could he talk to Marissa

about this? He instantly dismissed the idea. If she was capable of speaking of it she would have done so—she had been so reluctant to allow him to make public their betrothal. No, he could not talk to Marissa, but he needed a woman's viewpoint. Miss Venables was obviously out of the question, but he could discuss anything with Diane. Friendship had always been more important to them than their physical affair.

He had just come to this conclusion when Marissa murmured and stirred. The she opened her eyes, and as soon as she saw Luc coloured and drew the sheet up to her chin. 'I must get dressed before the others get home and the servants return,' she stammered.

She was so obviously embarrassed he made no move to detain her, handing her his dressing gown and tactfully turning his back as she gathered up her scattered clothing and hastened quietly from the room.

It was a very thoughtful Earl of Radwinter who stood at the drawing room window as Sir Frederick's carriage brought Jane and Nicci home. He had heard Marissa moving around upstairs but had made no attempt to speak to her. The servants had returned an hour ago and were busy preparing the evening meal.

Luc went out onto the steps to greet the returning party, offering his hand to Miss Venables to assist her to alight. She thanked him frostily, turning to bow to Sir Frederick and thank him in a shaking voice for his kindness in conducting them back to the Lodge. Nicci, her face flushed under her ridiculous hat, bobbed a schoolgirl curtsey before scuttling into the house, her hot face averted from her brother's puzzled gaze.

Sir Frederick was still standing in the open carriage as Luc came down the steps to offer the baronet his thanks. 'Will you not come in and take a glass of wine? I am most obliged to you for escorting Miss Venables and my sister.'

'No trouble, old chap, a pleasure,' the banker replied with a twinkle. 'But I will not accept your kind offer—I rather think you will be glad to have no strangers in the house this evening.' And on that enigmatic note he sat down, resumed his hat and called out, 'Drive on, John!'

Luc was barely in the hall when the storm broke. Nicci was halfway up the stairs, Miss Venables at the foot. 'Come down here immediately, Nicole, and tell your brother how you have disgraced yourself.'

'No, I shan't!' Nicci sobbed, sitting down on the stair and putting her head in her hands.

'Oh, Lord!' Luc muttered under his breath, before stepping up to Miss Venables. 'Nicci, come down here. Marissa is not feeling well and I do not want her disturbed by you making a hullabaloo out here. Miss Venables, let us go into the drawing room and you can tell me what has occurred.'

Nicci, descending reluctantly, stood sniffing while Miss Venables recounted how she had discovered her young charge. 'I can hardly bring myself to use the word, my lord, but there is no other way of putting it—she was in the embrace of a…man! An officer, and behind the pavilion! Anyone could have seen her! My lord, I am so sorry that I have failed in my duty as a chaperon…'

Luc cut across the anguished apology. 'But *did*
anyone else see them?'

'Only Sir Frederick, and on his discretion I believe we may rely absolutely. As soon as I realised
she was missing, during the second race, he accompanied me in search of her. Oh, I would never have
believed she could behave so...' Miss Venables
rummaged in her reticule until she found her smell-
ing bottle and waved it wildly under her nose.

'Who was the man?' Luc enquired with dangerous calm. Damn Nicci, now he supposed he would
have to come the heavy brother. Thank heavens
Miss Venables had interrupted them, or he would
have found himself calling the man out on top of all
the other things he had to concern himself with at
the moment! 'Nicci, stop snivelling, take that blasted
hat off and answer me: who was it?' He had never
spoken to her like that before, and his sister
wrenched off the bonnet and cast it aside.

'Captain Cross,' she wailed.

'And who the devil is he? Don't tell me you just
picked up some uniformed whippersnapper on the
racecourse,' he roared, incensed at the thought of
his sister in the arms of a complete stranger.

'A friend of Lady Valentine's,' Miss Venables
said grimly, as if that summed it all up.

'That trollop!' For once, Miss Venables did not
wince at the word—she was inclined to agree.

'I fear,' she ventured, 'that Miss Southwood's attire may have misled the Captain into thinking she
was older and more worldly-wise than she is.'

Luc regarded both ladies with a smouldering eye.
'And I suppose you are going to say it was all my

fault for letting her out dressed like that?' He gestured furiously at Nicci's crumpled outfit.

Wisely Miss Venables did not respond to this question. She got to her feet and took Nicci's arm. 'Come along, Nicole, I think you had better take supper in your room tonight.'

Luc waited until the ladies had disappeared around the curve of the stairs before tugging the bell-pull to summon Jackson. 'My compliments to Lady Southwood, and I shall not be dining at home this evening.'

'Very good, my lord. Shall I say where you are going?'

'No. But should you have need of me I shall be at Madame de Rostan's.'

Minutes later Luc was cantering down the drive, gravel spurting from under his horse's hooves. Half an hour later he was entering the busy streets of Epsom, thronged with racegoers either flush with their winnings or drinking away their sorrows. Reining back to a trot, he entered the quiet street where Diane had borrowed a friend's house for the week.

Although he was not expected, he was swiftly admitted and was shown into the Salon. Despite having no guests for dinner, the Frenchwoman was as beautifully attired as ever in a simple cream silk gown, her hair in artfully arranged ringlets, her family diamonds gleaming at her throat.

'*Chéri!* What a surprise, but always a pleasure to see you.' She rose gracefully from the chaise and offered her cheek for his kiss. 'I must confess I had not looked to see you tonight. You will dine, of course?' She pulled the bell before resuming her seat.

Luc dropped into a chair, his long booted legs stretched out in front of him. He knew Diane so well that every nuance of her words was plain to him. 'Why so surprised to see me tonight? And, yes, if you will excuse my informal attire, I would like to dine here.'

The butler appeared, received his mistress's instructions and vanished discreetly after pouring his lordship a glass of Madeira.

Diane waited until the door closed behind him before replying, with a wicked curve of her lips, 'You forget, I saw you leave the racecourse this afternoon with Lady Southwood.'

'And?' Luc raised an eyebrow, not liking the implication that his intentions had been so transparent.

Diane laughed at him affectionately. 'My darling Luc, it is only I who would have realised the significance of you taking Marissa home in the early afternoon.' Again her lips curved, this time in remembrance. 'She really is a very charming young woman: I must congratulate you.'

'I am glad I have your blessing,' Luc said drily, sipping his dry wine. 'However, I fear it may be a little premature.'

'But if you have been making love to her you really must marry her, you know,' Diane teased, then, seeing his face darken, was suddenly serious. '*Chéri*, what is the matter?'

'I only wish I knew,' he confessed. 'Yes, we did make love...but there is something wrong. Diane, she responds to me with passion and fire, and yet...there is a part of her that remains untouched, for all the intensity of our lovemaking. It is almost as though she were afraid.' His blue eyes were puzzled as he looked at his former lover.

'But she was married—for two years, was it not?' Diane broke off as the butler entered.

'Dinner is served, *madame.*'

Both the butler and a footman were standing attentively by the high buffet, but Diane waved them away. 'Thank you, Henry, Monsieur le Comte will carve; we will serve ourselves.' As soon as they were alone she said, 'A little salmon, please, Luc, and if you will pass the dish of peas… Thank you, darling. Now, where were we?'

'You were asking how long Marissa had been married. It was just over two years, I believe; she wed very young. And yet… I find this difficult to believe, Diane, but I could swear she had never been kissed until I kissed her.'

'Perhaps it is simply that she has not yet fully recovered from the loss of her husband? Would you pour me a glass of the Sancerre?'

Luc complied, absently passing her the glass. 'She can hardly bear to speak of him. I found her in tears in front of his portrait and she is always very formal when she speaks of him, as though she wants to keep me at a distance from the marriage. And, of course, my likeness to him is a constant reminder of what she has lost. Do you know, she fainted dead away the first time she saw me? She must have loved him very much.'

'Loved him…or hated him. They are two sides of the same coin, Luc.'

He put down his wine glass with great deliberation, his eyes fixed on her intelligent, concerned face. 'Hated him… But, Diane, that would explain a great deal. One day, soon after the funeral, I found her in the family chapel. She was standing by the mausoleum, and when she saw me she was terrified, as if I were his ghost. And her words… They struck me as strange at the time, but I put it down to the shock of her loss.'

'What did she say, Luc?' Diane's food lay untouched on her plate.

'She said, *"He has really gone, has he not? He will not be coming back?"* Naturally I assumed that her words were spoken in grief.'

'Oh, no.' Diane shook her head, making the ringlets fall over her shoulder. 'Oh, no, she wanted to make sure he was really dead. That is why she needed to see the tomb, to make certain he was in it.' She forked up a piece of salmon and chewed thoughtfully. 'Did you see me speaking to her father? *Mon Dieu,* but that man is a pig. How one such as he could have sired Marissa, I cannot imagine! All the time he was talking to me he was undressing me with his eyes, leering at my bosom. Urgh!' She shivered and sipped her wine, as if to wash away the thought of Sir George's lecherous behaviour.

'It is not like you to tolerate such a type: why did you remain with him?'

'I was curious to know more of Marissa. The first time I met her I could tell she was not happy, that she was hiding something. And I tell you, that man would sell his soul to the Devil, never mind his daughter, if the money was right. That first marriage was all wrong. Yet I can tell she is in love with you.' She met his arrested gaze with a smile. 'Yes, she is in love with you, you fool! How could you doubt it?'

Luc pushed his chair back and stalked over to the buffet. But then he stopped, the carving knife and fork in his hands, staring at the roast capon with unseeing eyes. 'But if she loves me why was she so reluctant to agree to marry me, and, when she finally did agree, why did she insist we keep it a secret?' He hacked at the chicken, producing a ragged lump of breast meat.

'And?' Diane prompted gently, knowing that something else was eating at him.

'And when I made love to her this afternoon, she wept.'

'Because she was happy?'

'No,' Luc said bleakly. 'Because she had forced herself to go through with it.'

'She was unwilling?' Diane asked incredulously.

Luc abandoned the capon and paced away, to stare down into the dark street below. 'Not at first. For God's sake, Diane, you know I would never force myself on a woman!'

'I know, *chéri*,' she said soothingly, recognising what all this was costing him.

'Then I thought she was shy—and, after all, it is over a year since her husband died…'

'But there is more,' the Frenchwoman stated.

'Yes. It is fear, Diane. I know fear when I see it, and she was afraid. How can that be?'

'Has it occurred to you that your highly respectable late cousin was not all he seemed? That perhaps he had tastes which, how shall we say, were unusual, that made his young bride afraid?'

Luc stared at her, aghast. *'What?'*

'Oh, for heaven's sake, Luc, you are a man of the world. You know there are other men who take pleasure in inflicting fear. She was a very young woman, a virgin, when she came—was sold—to the Earl. How was she to know it could be any other way?'

'And every time I made love to her...' He dropped into his chair and held his head in his hands. 'I would remind her of him every time she looked at me. She was waiting for me to be cruel to her as he had always been.' A vivid image of her reaction on the beach, when the moonlight must have increased the likeness even more, stabbed through him.

Eventually he raised troubled blue eyes to Diane's. 'But how can I confront her with this? How can I ask her to resurrect the humiliation of her marriage? Yet if I do not we could never be happy together; it will be doomed from the beginning.'

'But knowing you love her, she will come to trust you,' Diane said gently, then saw his face. 'You have told her, have you not?' None of the pain this conversation was causing her showed on her lovely face, yet inside it was as though she was being pierced by a thousand needles. She had loved Luc ever since she had known him, had allowed their *affaire* to dwindle into friendship because she knew that she was not the right woman for him. She was ten years older than he, and she had known from the beginning it could never last, but that did not make it any less painful.

'No: how could I speak of love when I thought she was still in love with Charles?'

Diane uttered a particularly unladylike word in French, jerking Luc out of his thoughts. 'Why are men so *stupide?*' she demanded. 'Tell her you love her, tell her you know that Charles was a beast and that you are not. Make love to her until she forgets he ever existed. And do not,' she added with a wicked twinkle, 'tell me you cannot do that!'

He smiled back warmly, sharing the memories for a moment. He stretched across the table and took her hands in his. 'Then I can only attribute it to my excellent teacher. Thank you, Diane, for all your love and warmth.'

'Foolish man!' She caressed his cheek affectionately. 'Now go. Do not waste time here. Go to your Marissa and tell her you love her.'

'Bless you.' He dropped a kiss on her cheek and was gone.

As the sound of the street door closing reached her, she whispered, 'But do not forget your loving friend.' Two fat tears trickled unheeded down her smooth cheeks and fell onto her plate.

The moon was high as Luc sent the bay gelding flying back along the road towards the Lodge. The air was warm and balmy, clouds of gnats danced above the thick hedgerows, and amongst the tangled banks of dog roses nightingales pierced the silence with their bubbling song.

All Luc could think about as the hooves thudded beneath him was that Marissa loved him and that they could be happy together.

His mind was so full of her that he was not surprised when he opened the door, stepped into the hall and she ran headlong down the stairs and cast herself into his arms. For a moment he was so overwhelmed to find himself holding her warm, urgent form, clad only in her nightgown and peignoir, that he held her close, his mouth in her hair, drinking in the scent of her.

Then he looked up into the reddened eyes of Miss Venables, at Jackson standing behind her, looking grave and concerned. Luc cast round and realised the hall was full of people—both footmen, a weeping lady's maid and even Cook, tangling her hands in her apron.

Gently he released Marissa's grip on his body and, keeping one arm protectively around her shoulders, asked Jackson, 'What the Devil is going on?'

'If you would take the ladies into the drawing room, my lord,' the butler said repressively, 'I will join you directly. Thomson, take the rest of the staff back below stairs. Cook, please send up tea.'

Luc, baffled, conducted Marissa into the drawing room while Jackson helped a weeping Miss Venables to an armchair. When the door had closed Luc demanded, 'Now, will someone please tell me what is amiss?'

'Oh, Luc,' Marissa began. 'I am so thankful...'

'No, let me tell him; it is all my fault,' Miss Venables wailed, but then could get no further, tears overcoming her again.

It was this, the sight of the redoubtable Jane Venables sobbing into her handkerchief, that convinced Luc that this was more than the usual domestic upset.

'Perhaps, my lord, I could be permitted to explain,' Jackson said stolidly as Marissa slipped out of the room, closing the door behind her.

'I wish you would,' Luc replied grimly. 'Sit down, man.'

The big man dropped into an armchair opposite

his master, and it was as if the crisis had transported them back to their old, informal relationship in the West Indies. 'It's Miss Nicci, Luc. She's gone—off with that Captain Cross, if I read her letter aright. I was about to take the curricle out after her when you came back.'

'Bloody hell!' Luc swore, getting to his feet, raking his fingers through his wind-disordered hair. 'Stupid little fool!' He paced the carpet, then turned to face his old friend. 'You're sure she's with Cross? There can be no doubt?'

In reply, Jackson handed Luc a sheet of writing paper, crumpled and tear-stained.

I have gone to Andrew, because you are all so beastly to me. And he says I would make a wonderful army wife and would enjoy all the balls and parties that the Regiment holds. I shall marry him and then you will be sorry you were so unkind. Do not follow me, for I shall never return willingly.

'Stupid child! Even that milksop curate would have been better than this! Jackson—do we know where this Captain Cross lodges?'

'No, Luc.' Jackson shook his head. 'From what Lady Southwood remembers of his uniform, the regiment is one of those based down in Brighton: he obviously came up for the races this week.'

Miss Venables blew her nose and peered over the handkerchief, red-eyed, but finally in control of herself. 'My lord, I think I may be able to throw some light on this. While I was with Sir Frederick Collier this afternoon we encountered an old friend of his,

Colonel Seymour. He is the officer in command of
Captain Cross's regiment, for he mentioned that he
and several of his officers had taken lodgings in Epsom for the races.'

'Do you know where?'

'No, but Sir Frederick will, for they dined together last night.'

Ten minutes later the curricle was at the front
door, Jackson already in the seat. As Luc gathered
up the reins Marissa appeared on the doorstep, fully
dressed, a cloak around her shoulders. 'Luc!' she
cried. 'What are you going to do?'

'Call on Sir Frederick, find the Colonel, get Captain Cross's direction—and kill him,' he replied
grimly.

'Take me with you! She is going to be in such
distress, and if we are seen my presence may help
reduce any scandal.'

'It makes sense, Luc,' Jackson murmured, swinging out of his seat to sit on the Tiger's perch behind.

'Very well, then.' Luc stretched down a hand and
almost pulled Marissa up beside him. 'Hold tight,'
he warned, laying the whip across the bays with a
snap.

If Sir Frederick Collier was surprised to be interrupted as he sat reading in his study, he was too
well mannered to show it. He urged Marissa and Luc
into the room and listened gravely to Luc's frank
explanation of why they were there. He crossed to
his desk and wrote an address on a slip of paper.
'Here, this is Colonel Seymour's direction. You may
rely on my total discretion. Now, hurry.'

The Colonel, fetched from a game of cards by his
batman, was less phlegmatic. His florid complexion

darkened dangerously, but he checked the oath that
rose to his lips in deference to Marissa. None the
less Luc had the distinct impression that the Colonel
would be exacting his own price for the Captain's
behaviour. 'I will come with you, my lord. Ma'am,
perhaps you would be more comfortable here: I will
ask my wife to come down to wait with you.'

'Thank you, no. The fewer people involved the
better, I feel, and Lady Southwood may be able to
lend some countenance to my sister if she is seen
leaving this man's lodgings.'

The Captain's lodgings, ten minutes away on the
edge of town, were in darkness save for lights on
the first floor. Luc, thankful that the house seemed
a respectable one, tugged at the bell-pull impatiently, and when a manservant answered shouldered
past him. Jackson followed, his hand on Marissa's
elbow.

'Stand aside, my man, and do not raise a noise if
you know what's good for you. Better wait down
here, my lady,' he added, as the sound of Luc ham-
mering at an upstairs door echoed through the house.

'No! Who is to say what will happen if I am not
there? Come on, Jackson.' She hurried in his wake
up the stairs, her heart in her mouth. From the moment the note had been found her thoughts had all
been for Nicci: how she would ruin her life for this
single moment of childish defiance. For she doubted
that Nicci understood the enormity of what she was
doing, or the danger she had placed herself in.

But when Luc had returned her joy and relief at
seeing him had turned to cold fear that either he
would kill the Captain, and have to flee the country,

or that he himself would be injured in the duel that he would surely force.

The scene that confronted them as they entered the room close on Luc's heels would have been comic if it had not been so serious. Nicci, whose riding habit at least explained how she had arrived there, sat by the fire, her pretty face a picture of indignation. The gallant Captain seemed determined to put as much distance between them as he could, for he was backed into a corner, a hunted look on his face.

'Thank God you have come, my lord!' the young man exclaimed at the sight of the Earl of Radwinter.

It gave Luc pause and he stopped, his eyes narrowed as he looked from one to the other.

'I did not ask her to come here, believe me, my lord,' the Captain said with feeling. 'I have never been so glad to see anyone in my life as I am to see you.'

'Andrew! How could you?' Nicci cried, her cheeks burning with humiliation. 'After all the things you said to me...'

'What things, Captain?' Luc enquired dangerously.

Marissa pushed past the men and gathered Nicci in her arms. 'Oh, do be quiet, both of you! There, there, Nicci. We have come to take you home. You are quite safe now.'

'She was quite safe before, let me assure you!' the Captain interjected indignantly. 'Kiss a girl at the races, and the next thing you know she turns up on the doorstep without a handkerchief to her name!'

Luc looked hard at the defiant young officer, a

sneaking sympathy growing on him, although he allowed no hint of it to show on his stern face. 'Well, Captain Cross, this is a pretty pass: when *are* you intending to marry my sister? I am sure we can obtain a special licence: I believe I saw the Bishop of Chichester at the races yesterday. He will doubtless be happy to expedite matters.'

'Marry her!' the unfortunate Captain squawked. He was appalled, and it showed on his handsome face, sending Nicci into fresh sobs. 'Damn it, my lord, I never intended to marry her!' He saw the darkening look on Luc's face and hastened into speech again. 'I did not ask her to come here—I admit I was flirting, stole a kiss, but that is all, I swear it.' He was now becoming desperate, beads of sweat standing on his forehead.

Luc was beginning to enjoy himself. He felt the tension uncoiling from his muscles. He was certain that Captain Cross was as innocent of any attempt at seduction as he claimed, and that any blame could be laid firmly at the door of his silly, impetuous sister.

Marissa watched with her heart in her mouth as Luc strolled across the room to stand in front of the quaking Captain. 'You have had a very narrow escape, my friend,' he drawled, the Caribbean lilt suddenly strong in his voice.

'You...you aren't going to call me out?'

'No, although that was not what I meant. You have had a very narrow escape from finding yourself yoked to probably the silliest girl in England. She would have led you a merry dance, and you would have soon found that kisses come very expensive.'

Marissa, her arm around Nicci, let out her breath

in a shuddering sigh of relief. Luc was not going to challenge him; the man she loved was not going to hazard his life in a pointless duel.

Leaving the Captain wilting visibly, Luc ushered them downstairs, leaving Jackson to locate Nicci's horse and ride it back to the Lodge. The journey was silent, broken only by Nicci's hiccuping sobs of mingled relief, humiliation and fury at her brother and Marissa's murmured words of comfort.

A relieved and furious Jane Venables swept Nicci up to bed, leaving Marissa and Luc alone. 'Oh, Luc, I have never been so glad to see anyone as I was to see you when you came home this evening!'

Luc looked across at her pale face, her eyes huge with worry and tiredness. 'Marissa, darling, there is something I must tell you,' he began, walking towards her, meaning to take her in his arms and tell her how much he loved her.

But Marissa was still too wrapped up in the events of the evening to take in his words. 'Where were you?' she continued. 'Jackson said you were not dining at home, but he was so vague…'

Without thinking, intent only on the declaration of love he was about to make, Luc said, 'I was with Diane.'

Marissa froze, her face becoming set. So, unable to find satisfaction in her arms, he had sought it in the bed of his mistress. Had he told Diane how cold she was, how unresponsive? Had the other woman smiled secretly to herself at the thought of Marissa's failings?

'Marissa,' he persisted, 'there is something I must tell you…'

'I do not want to hear it, my lord. But here is something *I* must tell *you:* you may consider our betrothal at an end.' And she turned on her heel and swept up the stairs.

Chapter Thirteen

It was a silent and subdued party which arrived back in Town, three days ahead of schedule. Miss Venables, still inclined to blame herself for Nicci's appalling behaviour, found that she was missing the congenial company of Sir Frederick Collier. He had sent round to her a warm note in response to her own message apologising for missing their planned picnic on the Downs and thanking him for his help and discretion.

Luc, brooding darkly over Marissa, spent most of the journey back fixing his sister with a look of such glacial indifference that Nicci was firmly convinced he was planning to send her back to Southwood Hall in disgrace.

For her part Marissa was in a state of despair. She had believed that when he made love to her she had disguised her fears: but she must have failed—again—if he could not wait to go straight from her arms to those of his charming and practised mistress. Why, she thought, plunging herself even further into gloom, should a man like Luc want to marry her when he could have a wife who would return him passion for passion?

And, indeed, there was no reason why any other woman would not respond to him, for her instincts had been correct. Luc might bear an uncanny resemblance to his cousin Charles, but there the similarity ended. It seemed, after all, that not all men were as her late husband—cold, cruel, controlling.

The next morning Marissa was breakfasting in her own chamber when she heard the sound of the door-knocker and, looking out, saw Sir Frederick Collier's carriage at the kerb. Hastily she dabbed her lips with a napkin and hurried downstairs.

Jackson was standing in the hall, in the act of placing Sir Frederick's hat and cane on the mahogany chest. 'Good morning, my lady.'

'Good morning, Jackson. Which room have you shown Sir Frederick to?'

'The Blue Salon, my lady. But,' he added as she turned towards the door, 'Miss Venables is already there.'

'Yes?' Marissa raised a dark brow, puzzled at his tone.

'I believe, my lady, that Sir Frederick was desirous of seeing Miss Venables alone.'

Marissa stared at the butler in wild surmise. 'You mean he…? My goodness Jackson, why have I not noticed? She is my dearest friend…'

'You have had one or two other things on your mind, my lady,' Jackson supplied drily, his eyes lifting in the direction of Nicci's chamber above.

Marissa entered the morning room to wait for the suitor to emerge. She sat down, picked up a book, then tossed it onto the sofa and wandered over to a small table to fiddle with the flower arrangement on it. Having effectively wrecked Jackson's floral scheme, she fidgeted over to the window and was rewarded by the sight of Luc descending the steps and striding away across the Square in the direction of Ryder Street and his club.

She stood watching his broad shoulders in the dark blue jacket, the long line of his legs as he strode down the street in the warm sunshine. At the corner he paused, doffing his hat to a passing lady, and Marissa caught a glimpse of his face, paler than of late and, she thought, thinner.

Her heart turned over with love for him: the worry over Nicci must be taking its toll on him, and Madame de Rostan was not yet back in Town for him to seek solace with.

Marissa's fingers tightened heedlessly, crushing the pale primrose drapes. Oh, what a mess they had got themselves into! She loved him, and he at least wished to marry her, but how could she when her failure to be a true wife to him would always send him back to the arms of Diane and whoever succeeded her? Looking back now, Marissa realised that the one saving grace in her marriage to Charles had been that she had not loved him, and therefore his capacity to hurt her had been that much reduced.

Sounds in the hallway distracted her. The front door opened and Sir Frederick stepped out, his face alight. He turned as he was about to get into his carriage and waved, and Marissa realised that Jane must be in the doorway.

Thank goodness her dear Jane had found happiness! Marissa told herself she must have been blind not to have seen the growing affection between the retired banker and her friend. Before she could go out to her the door opened and Jane almost flew in. Her normally sallow complexion was rosy with colour, her eyes sparkled and she looked almost pretty.

'My dear! I am so happy for you.' There could be no doubting Jane's good news. Marissa embraced her cousin warmly, feeling the tears running down her cheeks in mingled happiness for Jane and regret at her own circumstances.

Fortunately Jane was too happy to notice any ambiguity in Marissa's response, and for a long moment the two women hugged each other wordlessly.

At last Jane broke free and sank onto the sofa as though her legs would no longer support her. 'Marissa, I was never so surprised as when he declared himself! I had believed at my age I was past all such hopes of happiness.'

'But you have so much in common, so many shared interests, and he is a truly kind man.' And he loves you, she thought wistfully, remembering Sir Frederick's face as he turned to wave. 'And when will you be married?'

Jane's face creased with a sudden worry. 'I told Frederick that I could not think of it at the moment because of Nicole. She needs close supervision.'

'I will take care of Nicci,' Marissa said firmly. 'You must place your own happiness first, Jane—for once in your life!' And after all, Marissa thought, what else is there for me to do with my time?

'Oh, dear, look at the time!' Jane jumped to her feet. 'Cook had asked me to look at the week's menus—she is in such a taking with us arriving back early that I really must spend some time with her or we will be eating cold cuts all week.' Jane bustled out, leaving Marissa feeling breathless.

The square outside was bustling with activity as the Quality took advantage of the lovely weather to drive and ride out. Marissa, suddenly decisive, got to her feet. She would not sit moping; it would change nothing. She would order the barouche with the top down and go and buy Jane a present. She had so admired a beautiful ivory silk shawl they had seen whilst shopping in the Burlington Arcade, but had dismissed it out of hand as too expensive and quite unsuited to her lifestyle.

As the wife of a distinguished public figure dear Jane would find many opportunities to wear it, and Marissa was pleased with her inspiration as she called for Matthews.

The under-butler sent orders for the carriage, then apologised for the absence of footmen to accompany his mistress. 'I am sorry, my lady, but they are all out on errands: will it be acceptable if I accompany you instead?'

'Yes, of course, Matthews. Thank you. Tell the coachman I wish to go to the Burlington Arcade, if you please.'

Marissa strolled through the Arcade, Matthews behind her, already carrying an awkward collection of parcels which, in addition to Jane's scarf, included a pink-lined parasol, some rose water, a pair of embroidered slippers and a length of linen for a chair-cover Marissa had decided to embroider.

The beadle, on duty to curb the excesses of any unruly children and to uphold the rules of the Arcade, touched his hat as she passed and re-emerged into a sunlit Piccadilly. 'I will just stroll over to

Fortnum's and see if they have that blend of tea in that his lordship particularly likes, and then I will go into Hatchard's. Please have the barouche wait, Matthews.'

Luc meanwhile was still in his club. He had chosen a quiet corner in Brooks's to sit and think through the coil he found himself in. Despite what his sister thought, she did not feature in his musings at all. He knew her too well to think that she would repeat her escapade; equally he knew something— or someone—else would happen to take her mind off Captain Cross. Sooner or later his little sister would grow up and the right man would come along…

No, it was Marissa who filled his thoughts. Thanks to his conversation with Diane, he now realised that whatever Charles had done had scarred Marissa deeply: she had not been mourning for her husband; she had been having nightmares about him.

Luc had gone from being jealous of the man he had believed she still loved to wishing the man was not already dead so he could strangle him himself. How could he ever overturn the legacy of that marriage? Convince Marissa that with him she could forget two years of hell? How could he convince a woman who had been badly hurt that he would never hurt her?

His dark, brooding face convinced many acquaintances who saw him across the room that he had either had a heavy night on the tiles and was suffering as a result or had had major losses at the races. It did not, however, deter Sir Frederick Collier.

The baronet, full of the joys of spring, had come

directly to his club from his successful meeting with Jane Venables, soon to be Lady Collier. His spinster sister would be delighted at the news, but she would fuss too, and he needed time to contemplate and reflect on his happiness alone in this male preserve.

The clubs of St James's—Boodles, Brooks's, White's and many other lesser sanctuaries—provided havens for the gentlemen of the *ton,* for no lady could cross the threshold, nor even be seen driving down St James's itself.

Shaking his head at an invitation to join an early game of whist, and deflecting a suggestion that he dine that night with a group set on finishing the evening at a cocking pit, Sir Frederick strolled through to the library.

He thought himself alone, then saw in the farthest window embrasure the long-legged figure of the Earl of Radwinter. Luc was sitting, legs outstretched, hands thrust deep into his pockets, chin dropped on his chest in thought.

Usually a sensitive man, Sir Frederick was too buoyed up with happiness to notice the mood of the other man, and strode over to greet him. 'My lord! I am so glad to have seen you. May I share with you, in confidence, my happy news?'

Luc looked up and said drily, 'I would appreciate happy news.' After all, he could see that Sir Frederick was going to tell him anyway.

Sir Frederick pulled up another leather wing chair and said, 'It will be announced next week, but I am delighted to tell you that Miss Venables has done me the honour of agreeing to become my wife.'

'Good God!' Luc was startled out of good manners. 'My dear fellow, I do apologise, but this is a shock to me—I have obviously been most unobservant. You have my heartiest congratulations: Miss Venables is an admirable woman, and will make you very happy. My sister Nicole will miss her very much.'

Sir Frederick tugged the bell-pull and when the footman appeared, ordered Madeira. 'And my dear Jane will miss Miss Southwood greatly: it is something which concerns her, and is frankly making her reluctant to set the date.'

'I am surprised, after my little sister's last escapade, that Miss Venables does not seize with delight on the prospect of being free of her!' He looked at the other man wryly and sipped his wine. 'And I must thank you again for your help and discretion in the matter...'

The men fell silent for a moment, then Sir Frederick ventured, 'I do hope that Lady Southwood was not too distressed by that evening's events. I thought at the races that she looked happier than I had ever seen her: I would be sorry to think that her new-found freedom should be marred by any anxiety.'

'Freedom?' Luc queried sharply.

'Ah.' Sir Frederick winced. 'Forgive me, my lord, for speaking out of turn. Please, ignore my tactlessness.'

'No, please, you interest me. I know little of Lady Southwood's history. You must know this is not something I would normally speak of, but I have a specific reason to ask and I know I can trust your discretion.'

The baronet got to his feet and checked that the other window bays in the quiet room were empty before resuming his seat. 'Indeed you may. What is it that you wish to know? I had forgotten that you have been living abroad.'

'Tell me about my cousin Charles,' Luc asked quietly. 'What manner of man was he?'

'I assume you do not need me to tell you that he was a patron of the arts, a man of highly refined artistic taste and the most rigorous standards?'

'No, you assume correctly. I need to know what manner of man, what manner of...husband he was.'

'My lord, what I am about to tell you is well known in certain circles, but never spoken of. The late Earl had certain very discreet tastes. You will have observed the strict discipline of his household affairs: I believe he took a similar approach to his amatory affairs. Not every woman is prepared to tolerate such demands: a very young, very innocent wife may be cowed into it. And, of course, if you know where to purchase them, these pleasures may always be bought.'

'The bastard,' hissed Luc. He had gone white and his fingers clenched tightly on the stem of his wine glass. He had expected to hear that Charles was unkind, uncaring, demanding the highest standards in his self-centred existence, but not this.

'Indeed,' the baronet concurred.

Suddenly Luc needed to know more, to understand the full depths of his cousin's character. 'And can you put a name to an establishment he patronised?'

Sir Frederick picked a sheet of notepaper from a rack by his side and dipped the quill pen in the standish. He scratched a few lines, dusted it with sand and folded the note. 'Here.' He passed it over. 'If you really have the stomach for it.'

Luc glanced at it, then tucked it into his pocket-book. 'Thank you. If you, and others, knew of this, how could it be that her father did not?'

Sir Frederick got to his feet. 'Oh, he knew all right. But Sir George would never let a detail like that worry him if he saw the chance to sell his daughter and finance his own dissolute life.'

Luc walked slowly into the hall and waited while the doorman found his hat and cane. He did not want to visit Madam Hall's establishment, but he had to; he urgently needed to understand exactly what the woman he loved had endured. Only then could he seek to heal her. Only then could he teach her to trust again.

Ignoring the passing hackney carriages, he struck off on foot along King Street and across St James's Square, into Charles Street towards the Haymarket, and thence Panton Street.

As he entered the Haymarket Marissa was climbing into the barouche outside Hatchard's. 'Matthews, can you recall where that art gallery was that Lady Smithson recommended when she called the other day? I think you were in the room serving tea when we were discussing it. I must think of a wedding present for Miss Venables, and Lady Smithson said they had some interesting Italian Renaissance canvases which might appeal.'

'Oxendon Street, I believe, my lady. It is just off the Haymarket. Shall I direct the coachman to take you now?'

'Yes, please.' Marissa settled back against the silk upholstery and let her thoughts stray as they made their way along the crowded thoroughfare. As usual, they strayed to Luc, and a little smile curved her lips as she thought of him. The warmth of the sunshine soothed her, the bustle of the street surrounded her with life and vitality, and her spirits rose. Could there be some way for them to be happy together? She could not deny her love for him, her response when he kissed her. And he desired her, liked to be in her company, was a friend to her...

Without any plan, without any clear idea of what she could do to get out of this coil, still Marissa felt suddenly optimistic, almost happy. He was a good man, a kind man...there must be a way for them...

As she thought it the carriage turned into Panton Street and there he was in front of her, on the right-hand pavement, just turning to ascend the short flight of steps to a glossily painted front door. 'Matthews! There is his lordship! Coachman, pull up!'

'Drive on!' Matthews commanded with uncharacteristic sharpness, and the startled coachman flicked his whip over the bays' rumps. The horses broke into a canter and the barouche was past the house before Luc's hand dropped from the knocker.

'Matthews!' Marissa twisted round in her seat to glare at the under-butler, perched up behind on the footman's seat. 'How dare you? I had expressly asked the coachman to pull up!'

'I am sorry, my lady,' the man stammered, red to his hairline. 'I think you were mistaken and that was not his lordship... I wished to save any embarrassment caused by you greeting a perfect stranger.'

It *had* been Luc, and Matthews was so obviously lying that Marissa was momentarily speechless. When she recovered herself she realised she could hardly pursue the subject in an open carriage. The

be thinking… What hell is she going through if she thinks I am like him?'

'You can't talk to her, Luc, she's gone. Two hours since.'

'Where?' he demanded, raking his hand through his already disordered hair.

'Back to the Hall. One of the footmen overheard her orders to the coachman.'

'No, she would never go back there. But she will go back to the Dower House: it is the only place where she has no memories of him.' Luc stopped, thinking. 'Pack a saddlebag and send to the stables for the new bay stallion: it is fresh enough to get me a good distance before I have to change.'

'Yes, Luc, but I'm coming with you.' Jackson tugged the bell-pull with such force that three footmen arrived simultaneously and were sent off at the run to obey his orders.

It was dark when Luc and Jackson, stiff, tired and travel-stained, trotted into Newmarket and reined in in the yard of the Three Crowns. 'Look, Luc.' Jackson pointed to the travelling carriage, standing, its empty shafts on the cobbles.

'Thank goodness. This is a respectable house; she will be all right here tonight.'

'But aren't you going in to talk to her?' Jackson furrowed his brow in perplexity as Luc dug his heels in and trotted out of the yard.

'Not here, man! This is hardly the place for the sort of conversation we are going to be having! Here is the King's Head; let's hope they have beds for the night.'

The following morning Luc played a waiting game, eating his breakfast by the window of the inn until he saw the travelling coach, with his own coat of arms on the door, clatter past over the cobbles. He and Jackson followed at a discreet distance, letting the coach go out of sight in case they were seen and the driver thought he was being followed by highwaymen.

It was a long day, but Marissa insisted that her coachman keep going, changing horses whenever he saw fit, but she refused his pleas to stop and rest for the night. Even though it was June the sun had set before the Hall came in sight. Marissa averted her gaze and waited, with sudden impatience, for the Dower House to appear.

For the long journey she had sat silent, frozen and almost immobile, responding automatically to Mary's worried attempts at conversation until the girl had finally given up and fallen silent. She supposed she had had something to eat the night before, but could not remember what. Nor could she remember sleeping, although there seemed to have been moments of unconsciousness.

Lights were twinkling as though in welcome in the windows of the old house. At the sound of carriage wheels on gravel Whiting threw open the front door, and at the sight of his familiar, kind face Marissa felt the ice that had been covering her break. Life, and with it pain, flowed back into her limbs and mind. Seconds later Mrs Whiting appeared at her husband's side, exclaiming with mixed worry and delight at the sight of her mistress.

Marissa half tumbled from the carriage into the housekeeper's arms, hugging her convulsively, determined not to cry.

'It is all right,' she was explaining. 'I have not

been very well—London is so hot and noisy. I just need to be back in the country for a while.'

The Whitings broke off from their worried greetings as the sound of hooves travelled clearly on the still night air.

'Who can that be at this time?' Whiting asked, then his jaw dropped at the sight of the two riders.

'Marissa!' Luc's voice reached her clearly through the twilight.

She took to her heels and ran, through the hall, up the stairs and into her chamber, slamming the door and locking it behind her.

Chapter Fourteen

Marissa twisted the key in the lock and leaned back against the panels, her bosom rising and falling with her panting breaths.

What was Luc doing here? How had he managed to follow her so closely—and what did he want with her? She braced herself for the sound of pursuing footsteps, expecting at any moment that he would pound on the door, demand that she come out.

It was not that she feared him: even after yesterday's awful revelation that he was visiting the same house of ill repute as her husband had she knew in her heart that Luc would never raise a finger to her. A sob rose in her throat and Marissa stumbled away from the door to throw herself across the four-poster bed. If only she could make any sense of it! Luc had always been so kind, so patient, so considerate to her. In his dealings with his sister he was loving and indulgent, and even after her worse excesses in Epsom he had not punished her in any way.

All this, and her instinctive love for him, was totally at odds with the sort of man who frequented *that* sort of place. Marissa stiffened as the sound of muted voices reached her through the heavy door, then there was the scrape of moving furniture. Puzzled, she sat up, scrubbing her hand across her wet eyes, but all was once more silent.

How long she lay curled up on the bed, fully dressed, before she fell asleep she did not know, but she was woken by the chorus of dawn birdsong and fitful sunshine through the undraped east window.

Marissa swung her legs off the bed and stood up stiffly. What time was it? She rubbed her eyes and looked around the room, all the while listening for sounds that the servants were up and about their business.

All was still, but on the washstand stood a jug of cold water, and soaps and towels were laid out ready. Pulling off her travel-stained clothing, Marissa washed swiftly, wincing at the chilly caress of the water, but grateful to feel clean and fresh once more. She pulled the remaining pins out of her tangled hair and brushed it hard until the dust was gone and it clouded out from her head in a dark mass.

All her clothes were still in the travelling cases, presumably in the hall. Marissa pulled open drawers in the dresser and found a nightgown and peignoir of pale biscuit-coloured lawn. Clean and clothed, she climbed back into bed and prepared to wait patiently until the servants were up and about.

There was no chance she would fall asleep again: her head, now she was properly awake, was spinning with thoughts of Luc. Where was he? Presumably he had gone back to the Hall to spend the night, but she had no doubt that he would be back at the Dower House soon after breakfast to demand an explanation for her precipitate flight. And what could she possibly say to him? *I love you, but I know you patronise a house where...* No, she could not even think the words, let alone say them.

If she had not seen Luc with her own eyes she would never have believed he could share any of her late husband's tastes, for Charles had been a cold, cruel man in thought as well as deed. But Luc...Luc was warm, loving... She shivered pleasurably at the recollection of his lovemaking, of his eagerness to pleasure her before himself. No, that did not sit with the picture of a man who indulged in secret vices, closet cruelties.

A realisation that she might have been too hasty in her conclusion was dawning on Marissa. She caught her breath, sitting up, her heart racing with sudden hope. Could there be another explanation for his presence on that doorstep on Panton Street? And, that being the case, did she not owe it to the man she loved to ask him what it could be?

Seized with hope and optimism, Marissa felt her stomach growl, and for the first time in what seemed like days giggled. How ridiculous, after all this heartbreak and drama, to feel something as mundane as hunger. But she was starving. The sound of the hall clock striking five came faintly through the panels: it was no good sitting here waiting for another hour. She decided to make a foray to the kitchen to see what the larder held.

Marissa climbed out of bed and padded silently to the door. She did not want either Mary or Mrs Whiting fussing over her, or feeling that they should get up and attend to her needs. Using both hands, she eased the key round in the lock, starting as it clicked. Then she opened the door and stepped out onto the shadowed landing, her eyes fixed on the corridor to her left where the servants' wing lay.

All was still and silent so she turned towards the stairs—and almost cried out in alarm. A heavy carved armchair had been pulled up and blocked her way. It was occupied by the sprawled, sleeping figure of Luc. Jacket off, cravat loose at his neck, boots discarded by his side, he slept deeply.

Marissa found her hands had flown instinctively to her chest, to still her thudding heart, but he did not wake. She gazed down at him, at the relaxed, stubble-shaded face, the thick dark eyelashes fanning his cheekbones, at the firm mouth now faintly smiling, perhaps at some dream. Instead of spending the night in his own comfortable bed he had been here all the time, sleeping across her threshold as if guarding her.

A wave of love swept through Marissa and her hand crept, as if of its own volition, to stroke his tanned face. But before she could touch him his eyes opened, wide and blue, and he smiled at her. 'I was dreaming about you,' was all he said as he stood to sweep her into his arms.

Kicking open the bedroom door, Luc strode to the bed and laid Marissa down against the pillows. For a long moment he stood looking down at her, as if deciding something, then to Marissa's surprise he crossed to shut the door, twisting the key in the lock. Carrying the key across, he dropped it on the bedside cabinet by her hand then went to sit on the window seat.

Marissa met the steady, grave look he fixed on her face. 'You spent all night out there on the landing?' she asked, almost in disbelief. 'Why?'

'I was worried about you,' he replied simply. 'You ran away from me.'

She flushed, biting her lip, and for a moment could not meet his eyes. But Luc did not help her out. Marissa realised that this was the turning point: she could be honest, trust him, tell him what she knew and had feared, or she could prevaricate and send him away. If she trusted her instincts and she was wrong about him, then they had no future together—but if she did not grasp this nettle they had no future anyway, and she wanted a future with Luc.

'I saw you going into a house. One that Matthews told me Charles used to visit...'

'Yes.' The single syllable was like a blow: one part of her mind had been clinging to the hope that Matthews had been wrong, or that it had not been the right house.

'You don't deny it?' she almost whispered, her hands creeping to her throat.

'No, I don't deny it—but why do you think I went there?' His voice was even, but she could see the pulse beating in his throat and his body was tense.

'At first I was shocked. I thought you were going there for the same reason as Charles had always done. I was devastated that I could have been so wrong about you. That was why I ran, because I could not bear to be close to you if that was the truth.'

'At first?' he queried. 'What do you think now, Marissa? What do you believe?'

'I believe I was wrong.' Her eyes were huge in the early-morning light and he could see how much it was costing her to speak so frankly.

'Lov…knowing you as I do, once the shock wore off, I knew there had to be another explanation.'

Luc stood and walked slowly to the foot of the bed, his eyes fixed on her face. 'There is another explanation. You have been very discreet about Charles, very loyal—but I knew he had hurt you very badly, had frightened you to the point where I feared you could never love me.' Marissa caught her breath: did it matter, then, that she loved him? He smiled at her and carried on speaking gently. 'I had heard something of my late cousin's tastes…I decided to seek out the truth for myself.'

'But why? Why does it matter to you? He is dead.'

'But his shadow still lies over you, and, loving you as I do, I want you to be free.'

'You love me?' Marissa breathed, afraid to believe her own ears.

Luc came and sat beside her, gathering her hands in his, a rueful smile on his lips. 'It has taken me a long time to say it, but I think I must have loved you from the moment I saw you. For a long time I believed you were grieving for Charles, that you could never love anyone else, especially someone who reminded you so painfully of what you had lost.'

'*Lost!* I lost only fear and cruelty. You taught me that not all men are like that, that I could love, and trust a man not to hurt me…'

Marissa's voice broke and she shut her eyes against the tears that threatened to fall. She found herself gathered in Luc's arms, held so tightly against his chest she could hardly breathe. 'The bas-

tard!' he ground out, before covering her face in
kisses.

When she emerged, breathless, she saw he was
searching her face, a touch of doubt in his eyes.
'You do love me, Marissa? When we made love I
could sense your reserve.'

'Yes, I do love you. I knew I loved you when you
went back to Jamaica and I ached for you, lived for
your letters to Nicci.'

'Then why would you not marry me?' His hands
were straying down her shoulders, stroking through
the lace, tangling as his fingers sought the ribbons
tying her peignoir.

'I believed I could never be a true wife to you,
that Charles had so affected me that I could never
give you everything. And I believed that you would
turn to Diane for comfort. Loving you as I do, I
could not bear to share you.'

'Diane? It has been all over between us for a long
time…before I left Jamaica to come to London just
before Charles's accident. She has been a true friend
to me, and,' he added in gentle admonishment, 'to
you too. It was she who made me see that there must
be a reason why you could not surrender to me completely.'

His fingers had now found their way beneath the
fine cotton lawn and were stroking the swell of her
breasts. It made it difficult to think, to speak, to do
anything but give in. 'But, Luc, I do not know if I
can,' she said in a despairing tone. 'I do not know
if I will ever be able to love you as I want to.'

To her shock he stopped caressing her and sat
back, watching her with smiling eyes. 'Then now is

the time to find out. Make love to me, Marissa: you take control; you do what you want.'

He was shrugging off his shirt and breeches as he spoke. Marissa's eyes were wide with shock. 'But…I don't know…I mean, I've never…Luc, what do you want me to do?'

Luc threw himself on the bed beside her and with a deft twist of his arm caught her up, stripping off the peignoir and nightdress and throwing them across the room. 'Right.' He lay back against the pillows, pulling her on top of his aroused body. 'Now, Marissa, you are in charge.'

Suddenly liberated, fearless, Marissa took his face in his hands and kissed him deeply, exploring the taste of him with her tongue before pulling back to look down into his face. Something in the quality of the light—or was it his obvious delight and love for her?—made him look only like Luc, not in the slightest like his cousin.

She nibbled his earlobe and he gasped as her lips moved relentlessly down the hard planes of his chest, teasing his nipple before, daringly, exploring further. His skin was satiny, hot with his desire for her, yet she could sense his restraint as he let her set the pace.

It served only to incite her. Impatient with his patience, she twisted round, pulling his glorious weight on top of her, opening her body to him. 'Luc,' she managed to say, 'I cannot wait any longer. Make love to me, *please.*''

And he did, gently at first, but he too was beyond restraint, swept along with the passion of her surrender which when it came shocked and delighted them both.

It seemed hours before they stirred, then Marissa opened her eyes to find him looking into hers with such love that she was almost unable to say, 'Is that how it is meant to be, my love?'

Luc's voice was shaky as he replied. 'I have no idea. I have never experienced anything like it. But...' he smoothed her damp hair back from her forehead '...I suggest we spend the rest of our lives finding out.'

Half an hour later Mrs Whiting with a tea tray and Mary with a ewer of hot water met outside the bedchamber door. Their eyes fell on the empty carved chair, then the firmly closed door. Without a word they turned and made their way downstairs.

* * * * *

MILLS & BOON®

Makes any time special™

Mills & Boon publish 29 new titles every month. Select from...

Modern Romance™ Tender Romance™

Sensual Romance™

Medical Romance™ Historical Romance™

MAT2

FREE

2 BOOKS
AND A SURPRISE GIFT!

We would like to take this opportunity to thank you for reading this Mills & Boon® book by offering you the chance to take TWO more specially selected titles from the Historical Romance™ series absolutely FREE! We're also making this offer to introduce you to the benefits of the Reader Service™—

- ★ FREE home delivery
- ★ FREE monthly Newsletter
- ★ FREE gifts and competitions
- ★ Exclusive Reader Service discounts
- ★ Books available before they're in the shops

Accepting these FREE books and gift places you under no obligation to buy; you may cancel at any time, even after receiving your free shipment. Simply complete your details below and return the entire page to the address below. *You don't even need a stamp!*

YES! Please send me 2 free Historical Romance books and a surprise gift. I understand that unless you hear from me, I will receive 4 superb new titles every month for just £2.99 each, postage and packing free. I am under no obligation to purchase any books and may cancel my subscription at any time. The free books and gift will be mine to keep in any case.

HOZEC

Ms/Mrs/Miss/Mr ....Initials ....

BLOCK CAPITALS PLEASE

Surname ....

Address ....

....

....Postcode ....

Send this whole page to:
UK: FREEPOST CN81, Croydon, CR9 3WZ
EIRE: PO Box 4546, Kilcock, County Kildare (stamp required)

Offer valid in UK and Eire only and not available to current Reader Service subscribers to this series. We reserve the right to refuse an application and applicants must be aged 18 years or over. Only one application per household. Terms and prices subject to change without notice. Offer expires 31st March 2001. As a result of this application, you may receive further offers from Harlequin Mills & Boon Limited and other carefully selected companies. If you would prefer not to share in this opportunity please write to The Data Manager at the address above.

Mills & Boon® is a registered trademark owned by Harlequin Mills & Boon Limited.
Historical Romance™ is being used as a trademark.